In Her Own Right

A Novel of Lady Mary Tudor

AMANDA SCHIAVO

Black Rose Writing | Texas

ISBN: 978-1-68513-235-4
PUBLISHED BY BLACK ROSE WRITING
www.blackrosewriting.com

Printed in the United States of America
Suggested Retail Price (SRP) $20.95

In Her Own Right is printed in Georgia

*As a planet-friendly publisher, Black Rose Writing does its best to eliminate unnecessary waste to reduce paper usage and energy costs, while never compromising the reading experience. As a result, the final word count vs. page count may not meet common expectations.

For my brilliant and loving mother, Carolyn, who awakened my passion for history. Thank you doesn't begin to cover it.

&

For my best friend William, a genuinely remarkable soul who was taken from us far too soon. You are always in my heart.

In Her Own Right

CHAPTER 1

1518

Princess Mary stood before the envoys from France looking elegant beyond her few years in a dress of cloth of gold and a black velvet cap. Cardinal Wolsey, her father's chief minister, placed a small diamond ring on her tiny finger to symbolize her engagement.

The visiting ambassadors evaluated the doll-like girl who would one day be their queen. They were at her father's court to discuss a treaty between the two nations, which would be sealed with Mary's betrothal to the dauphin.

"Are you the Dauphin of France?" Mary asked in her small but regal voice. Even at the tender age of two, Mary had all the grace and charm of a queen consort in waiting. From the moment she was born her parents and caretakers had been drilling into her a strong sense of duty. A rigorous education in languages, religion, and the responsibilities of being a king's daughter took precedence over the carefree nature of childhood. Mary's aptitude for learning made her tutors' job much easier than it would have been with any other pupil her age.

"No, Mademoiselle," the ambassador said. "But I represent the interests of King Francis and his son, the dauphin, who is most excited at the thought of marrying such a beautiful and sweet princess."

Mary smiled and told the ambassador she had a gift she would like presented to the dauphin. At her signal, the ambassador knelt beside her, and she placed a delicate kiss on his cheek.

"Please give this to the dauphin," Mary said when she pulled away. The ambassador beamed, and the court erupted in a mix of amused applause and joyous laughter. Mary turned to look at her parents seated on their thrones behind her. Her father, England's mighty King Henry VIII, was smiling proudly, while her mother could hardly contain her unhappiness.

Queen Katherine, Princess of Spain and the daughter of the magnificent Queen Isabella, did not like her daughter being given away in marriage to France, her native country's long-time enemy. The whole court—Mary included—knew of the queen's unhappiness.

Just the previous day, while her governess, Lady Margaret Pole, escorted Mary to her parents, they were stopped cold by the ugly sounds of a heated argument. The uncomfortable expression on the guard's face standing outside the door told them the fight had been raging for a while.

"How could you *think* to give *my* daughter away to France, the enemy of my people, without even consulting me?" Queen Katherine shouted in her heavily accented English, her voice quivering at the betrayal. The King and Queen were oblivious to the presence of Mary and her governess outside the door, who were hearing every word.

"Mary belongs to England, and England belongs to me! She is mine to do with as I see fit," King Henry hollered back. "You have been Queen of England these last nine years. It is time you accepted that England's enemies are your enemies and England's friends are your friends. And today that means France. We could be more selective in whom Mary takes as a husband were we to have a son of our own!"

Henry's last words were a sharp blow to the queen. Katherine knew Henry blamed her for not having a living son.

"Mary can rule after you, Henry, as my mother ruled Castile. We can teach her. She can be a great queen for England. Her reign will be a golden age."

"A woman will never rule England! She cannot! It is an unnatural thing," Henry screamed. "Much like marrying your brother's widow!"

Katherine was shaken by what her husband had said. The queen prayed daily for a son and heir. She knew the long-desired prince would reassure the English people and bring peace to her marriage. Yet, it seemed that no matter her prayers or how often the king and queen enjoyed the marriage bed—which was becoming less frequent—no son seemed to be coming.

Katherine was still grieving the loss of her last child, a daughter born the previous November. The baby was weak and did not live long enough to be christened.

Then there was Prince Henry, the baby boy born in 1511. He would have been seven years old now, but God had called the child away after only a few months on Earth.

Every day since she laid eyes on the lifeless little body of her son, Katherine yearned for him. She'd give almost anything to look into his crystal blue eyes again, feel his warm little body in her arms, listen to his soft cooing as he slept. She hadn't been with him when he died and spent years wondering if she would have been able to save her precious baby boy.

Prince Henry should be here now, she thought. He and Princess Mary should be two of a gaggle of Tudor children, but six pregnancies had produced only one surviving child—the daughter whose future was now being decided by the direction of the nation's political wind.

At age 33, Katherine feared further loss was on the horizon— that of her husband's love. She was devastated by the thought that she may not again have the chance to give the king a son.

• • •

Mary's eyes filled with tears at the sound of her parents' battle. Her sweet and kindly governess knelt beside her and offered comfort.

"Fret not, little one. All will be well, you'll see," she said, touching her forehead to Mary's. "No two people who love one another as your parents do can stay angry for long. The responsibilities of a crown can cause immeasurable stress on those who wear it. Sometimes that stress erupts in anger. But no matter how upset their majesties may be with each other, their love will win out in the end."

The child let out a sigh of relief, though much of what was told to her made little sense to her young ears. But Lady Pole had worked her special brand of magic. As dear as her own mother, Margaret Pole held a special place in Mary's heart.

"Please announce to the king and queen that her grace, Princess Mary, has arrived," Lady Pole told the guard. He looked as if he would rather empty a poor man's chamber pot than enter that room, but the stone cold look on Lady Pole's face told him he had no choice.

Lady Pole, while kind and intelligent, wore the burden of her royal blood on her face which had become lined with age. Though one could see underneath all this the pretty young woman she had once been.

Margaret told Mary once how they were related. Margaret was the daughter of a royal duke and niece to two Kings of England, the kind King Edward IV, Mary's great-grandfather, and the wicked King Richard III, Mary's great great-uncle. Mary had heard stories of King Richard, how he murdered the young sons of his dead brother, King Edward, then took the English throne for himself. But then Mary's grandfather, the first Henry Tudor, came to England and saved the people from King

Richard's tyranny. He married Edward IV's eldest daughter, the beautiful and virtuous Princess Elizabeth of York and established the Tudor dynasty. Lady Pole was the late Queen Elizabeth's cousin. Mary remembered the story so well because of the enthusiastic way her father would tell it.

"My father defeated that murderous traitor at the battle of Bosworth," Henry had told Mary one evening at supper. The girl was enraptured by the story of the battle, hardly touching her food as she pictured her grandfather riding on horseback across the field, his sword drawn as he advanced to find King Richard.

"My father slew the tyrant, and the whole of England rejoiced at his victory," Henry exclaimed, though that wasn't exactly the truth. But Henry wasn't about to tell his young daughter how unpopular Henry VII's kingship had been at the start. Nor how weak his father's claim to the throne had been—needing to marry Elizabeth of York to secure the crown.

Mary was curious about her paternal grandmother, who was said to be very gracious and beautiful. Reportedly, she and the dead king loved each other very much. But as much as Henry boasted about his own father, he was quiet about his mother. Mary's own mother, the queen, told her King Henry loved his mother so much that her unexpected death in childbirth caused him much grief, and many years later, the king still mourned.

When Mary entered the room, her father and mother were on opposite sides. She and Lady Pole bowed, and Henry bid them to rise. In what seemed like a single stride, Henry went to Mary from across the room. He swept her up into his arms and whirled her around in the air, her long, crimson colored silk skirts swooshed around her. The princess shrieked with delight, and the king kissed her lovingly on the cheek, his thick, red beard scratching her face.

Mary was in awe of her father. In her mind, he was everything a God-anointed king was supposed to be: tall, lean, athletic, with a passion for education and religion. His majestic blue eyes seemed to look deep into a person's soul. The princess thanked God nightly for such a father. She wrapped her arms around Henry's neck, hugging him tightly, basking in his love.

She could see her mother over his shoulder, standing off by a window, looking out at the palace's snow-covered gardens, avoiding the loving scene between her husband and child. She tried to hide the tears in her eyes, but Mary could see her mother's distress.

"How is my sweet princess?" King Henry asked as he held Mary out in front of him. "Are you ready to meet the French envoys tomorrow?"

"Oh, I am, sir," Mary said excitedly, forgetting for a moment the ugly scene between her parents. She was delighted by her father's love and attention. "I have been practicing my French with Lady Pole, and I pray that I will make you proud."

"Of that, I have no doubt," Henry said, smiling as he placed the girl back on the ground. "Tell me, how are you finding life away from the court?"

"Oh, it's wonderful, Papa," the child exclaimed as she and her parents settled down for a meal together. "The tutor you sent to me is quite brilliant. He isn't old and stuffy like my last instructor. Learning languages is my favorite part of the lesson."

Henry stood by, stunned and impressed by his daughter, who effortlessly switched from English, to Spanish, and then French as they conversed.

"But going out to ride is the best part of the day," Mary said happily, knowing how much her father enjoyed the pastime too. "But don't worry, Papa, I never neglect God or my prayers. I visit the chapel several times a day, staying to pray long after mass is over."

Katherine and Lady Pole had instilled in Mary a strong devotion to God, the pope in Rome, and her Catholic faith. Before she could speak in full sentences, Mary knew the names of many saints and was well acquainted with the story of the life and death of Jesus Christ. Her mother and governess also made sure she understood the Pope was a revered figure to be obeyed in all things as he was the successor to St. Peter, chosen to lead God's church and interpret His laws.

"I am so proud of you, sweetheart," Henry said as his daughter beamed at him. "We'll have to go out for a ride together, just you and me, so I can see if you are really as accomplished a horsewoman as you claim."

"Oh, I am, Papa, I am," Mary said, giggling.

"I have a gift for you, sweetheart," Henry said, and with a wave of his hand one of the grooms of his chamber brought over a green velvet pouch tied closed with gold string. When Mary opened it, she couldn't believe what she saw.

"Look at it," Mary exclaimed. "It's beautiful! Thank you so much, Your Majesty."

Beaming, Mary showed off her new necklace to her governess and her mother. It was an exquisite necklace with gold filigree and a large emerald surrounded by pearls in the center. "May I wear it for the ambassadors tomorrow?"

Her father nodded his agreement as he studied his daughter. He was thrilled at Mary's astuteness, her intelligence, and her effortless regal quality; she was so like him in many ways.

There was nothing Henry loved more than riding out for sport. He'd rather be doing that than tending to the business of his realm, which Cardinal Wolsey would often take care of while the king was at his pleasure. Wolsey was the mastermind behind Mary's French marriage, and the queen had nothing but contempt for the cleric for that reason — among many others. There were many at Henry's court who looked down on the cardinal for his low birth and the disproportionate influence he had on the king. Many at Henry's court saw Wolsey as the true power behind the throne.

Henry looked at Mary, who was now running her tiny slender fingers over the jewels in the necklace and could not help but think *if only she had been born a boy.* But for all his lamentations of not having a son, Henry adored the small, flame-haired child standing in front of him. "The pearl of my world," Henry would call his daughter, and Mary loved the adoration in her father's voice when he said it.

•   •   •

Henry made good on his promise to take his daughter out riding before she had to return to her country home. It was a rare and thrilling experience to have her father all to herself for an afternoon. Mary's poor little pony was no match for the king's large stallion, and after a while, Henry had Mary ride with him. Henry mounted his horse and scooped Mary up with the help of the footman, placing her in a side-saddle position in front of him. He wrapped one arm around his daughter, gathering the reins up in his free hand.

Mary squeezed her father tightly as he pushed his horse faster and faster until he and the exhausted creature finally needed a rest. So they could enjoy a meal together before returning to the palace, the attendants had set up a magnificent feast under the awning of a large tent.

Mary watched as her father joked with his servants, making even the lowest in his retinue feel like they were special to the king. His common touch was inspiring. Having the same relationship with the people of France when she eventually became queen burned within her, even though the idea of leaving England and her family still unsettled her.

"Your Majesty," Mary said, "when do I have to go to France?"

"Not for a few years, darling. First, you must learn how to be a good queen, and you must grow into a woman so you can provide the dauphin with sons and continue his family line."

"Like how mamma left Spain to marry you and be your queen?" Mary asked innocently.

Henry hesitated before responding, and when he did there was an edge in his voice. "Not exactly. You are my daughter, and I know *you* will not fail in your duty to your husband when the time comes."

Mary didn't understand what her father was saying. She couldn't comprehend how her mother may have failed him, but something told her not to ask that question.

"Will I like living in France?"

"I'm sure you will, Henry said. "But you have a duty to your king and your country, so you will have to make the best of the situation no matter how you feel."

Something about her father's answer left Mary feeling unsettled and threatened to wash away the joy she felt from earlier in the day. But before it could overtake her, her father asked if she was ready to return to the palace. They jumped back onto the king's horse and rode back home as fast as the animal could carry them.

•   •   •

Not long after Mary's departure, the queen found an opportunity to get away to visit her at the child's country home in Ludlow. It was rare for Queen Katherine to be away from the court and the king, and she regretted not being able to spend much time with her daughter. But Henry was busy with his French alliance, not to mention his newest mistress, and there was a calm taking hold over the realm.

Katherine determined it was the perfect time to take the days-long journey to visit her dear child. While Henry was happy enough to have Mary around and show her off as another pretty trinket, a bargaining chip in Europe's political schemes, Katherine devoted herself to her child, enjoying the privilege of being her mother. Still wounded by the fight with Henry about giving her daughter away to the French, Katherine—in her stoic manner—decided to make the best of the situation.

She would use the child's engagement as a way to see her daughter more often to prepare her for her role as the future Queen of France and instill in Mary the same education, sense of duty, and loyalty to God that her mother imparted to her. Traits she had needed when preparing for her new life in England.

When the queen arrived, Mary could hardly contain her excitement. She, too, wished she and her mother could spend more time together, alone. Fighting the urge to leap into her mother's arms, Mary formally welcomed the queen with lowered eyes and a deep but childishly wobbly bow.

"Welcome, My Lady Mother," Mary said. "I am pleased Your Majesty has come to visit me." Then she bowed again.

"Thank you, daughter," the Queen said, smiling lovingly at her child. "I have brought you a gift. Come with me."

Katherine took her daughter by the hand and led Mary outside. A servant in his green and white livery, the colors of the royal house of Tudor, stood holding the lead to a beautiful black horse, a standard palfrey, though the animal looked enormous to the child. "He is beautiful!" the girl cried, bounding over to her new gift.

"Gently, Your Grace," Lady Pole said, standing just behind the queen. "Don't spook the poor creature." Katherine looked back at her longtime friend, giving her a nod and an affectionate smile.

Mary slowed her stride and walked steadily over to the animal, who was more interested in finding the perfect blade of grass to consume and not above yanking the boy holding him here and there to find it. But Mary didn't mind, she loved horses for their grace and strength as well as their funny antics.

Riding was her favorite pastime. She enjoyed being out of doors far more than her lessons, although she was skillful in many subjects. Mary was a fine pupil, intelligent and eager to learn, excelling in languages including French, Latin and Greek, not to mention Spanish, which she and her mother conversed in regularly.

"Does he have a name?" Mary giggled as the animal abandoned his grass and began to nuzzle at her, knocking the pearl-lined gable hood off the child's head.

"Why don't you decide on a name, my darling," Katherine said.

Mary thought for only a moment. "His name is Geoffrey." Mary had begun reading stories by the famed English author Geoffrey Chaucer, and they were quickly becoming her favorites.

Once she was convinced to tear herself away from the horse, Mary joined her mother in the parlor where they could enjoy each other's company intimately. A roaring fire had been lit, and spiced wine and candied fruits were brought in as Mary peppered Katherine with questions about life in Spain, her awe-inspiring grandmother Queen Isabella, and what it was like to leave your homeland in the pursuit of a greater destiny. Mary was shocked to learn that Katherine did not come to England to marry her father but the older brother she didn't know the king once had.

"You were married to someone else?" Mary asked, incredulous.

"Yes, my child. Although, it was not a true marriage. You see, your father's older brother, Prince Arthur, was meant to be king one day. The prince and I married when we were 15. Your father was a boy of 10 at the time, but the sweating sickness took poor Arthur just a few months after we married."

Mary knew all about the sweat. It came out of nowhere and didn't discriminate which lives it took. She heard it said how a man could be healthy in the morning and dead by supper when he was cursed with the sweat.

"Were you sad?" Mary felt a surprising bereavement for the uncle she'd never met.

"Oh, I was very sad and very homesick. I was ready to go back to Spain. But my parents knew I had more to accomplish in England, and it was decided I would marry your father, who had become heir to the throne after Arthur's passing."

Katherine left out several details she did not want to burden her young daughter with. They included her father-in-law's poor treatment of her and the torment she went through when, at first, no one believed that her marriage to Arthur was unconsummated. Not to mention the years she spent in a state of limbo, unsure what would become of her, unable to pay her servants, put food on the table, or purchase new clothes. Eventually, those circumstances changed, and the pope issued the dispensation allowing Henry to marry his brother's virgin widow. Katherine fervently believed that nobody would dare question the validity of her marriage now—despite the angry words her husband screamed during their recent fight.

It hurt her to live so far from her only child, and Katherine soon had to leave Ludlow. As Mary bid farewell to her mother, she drank in every feature of the queen. Her red gold hair that poked out from her gable hood, her beautiful brown eyes, and the sweet rosy smell of her perfume. Mary wanted nothing more than to remain in her mother's loving embrace.

CHAPTER 2

1523-1527

Seven-year-old Princess Mary stood waiting with her parents in St. George's Hall of Windsor Castle. It was magnificently decorated with tapestries, paintings, and brightly colored curtains. Mary was there to welcome Charles V, the queen's nephew and both the King of Spain and the Holy Roman Emperor. The 22-year-old Charles was now Mary's betrothed. Henry had broken off the French engagement in 1521 because of another falling out with the King of France, and now, much to the queen's elation, Mary was affianced to Spain.

Charles was an impressive young man with dark hair and eyes and the prominent, square, pronounced chin of the Royal House of Habsburg. It made it difficult for Charles to close his mouth, but his thick black beard helped hide the deformity, which didn't appear to impact his speech.

He swept an exaggerated bow before the king and queen, looked down at Mary, his child bride, and exclaimed, "Is this the Princess Mary? She is too beautiful, and I am unworthy to marry such a charming creature."

Mary smiled, thrilled at the compliment and youthfully oblivious to the courtly and clever game Charles was playing. Henry, a seasoned champion, however, was all too aware. He looked at this young rogue, who had the nerve to refer to Henry as "my dear uncle," with suspicion.

Uncle, Henry thought sourly as he mused that he was only 31-years-old and still in the prime of life. He could dance, joust, ride, and hunt with ease. The only thing Henry could not do, it seemed, was sire a legitimate male heir, but the fault could not be his own. Henry believed this at his very inner core. After all, had not his mistress Elizabeth Blount given birth to a healthy son just a few years earlier? Henry toyed with the idea of legitimizing the boy, but he still believed he could get a healthy and trueborn male heir. Although he wondered if his current wife would be that child's mother.

The festivities arranged to celebrate Mary and Charles' engagement lasted more than a month and included jousting, tournaments, plays, feasting, and dancing. The princess was excited to have many fine new dresses made for the occasion— her favorite was one of crimson-satin, lined with cloth of gold. Mary shone at court, dazzling the English courtiers and visiting envoys with her elegant manner, gift for languages, beautiful dresses and jewels, her dancing ability and her affinity for music. She played the lute and virginals for a captivated audience on the final night of Charles' visit.

•   •   •

The following morning, Charles and Mary were permitted to walk in the gardens with the Queen and her ladies in attendance as chaperones. As they walked, Charles held Mary's little hand and she pointed out different aspects of the gardens — fountains and sweet-smelling roses as they walked.

Even though he enjoyed his time with the girl, Charles had doubts as to the reality of their marriage. He needed an heir now and knew it would be years before Mary would be old enough to wed, let alone consummate their marriage. The perils of childbirth claimed many adult women's lives, so how could a mere girl be expected to survive the ordeal? And to many, Mary appeared small for her age.

If he admitted it, Charles knew their marriage would not happen. Besides, England was not a very wealthy country, and older, more eligible and more affluent royal brides were to be had in Europe. But Charles would play the game. Not wanting to insult his aunt and needing to keep King Henry on the hook, he presented himself as an eager groom.

"You know, princess," Charles said, "these gardens and palaces you have here in England are very fine, but you would marvel at the magnificence of the Alhambra. When we marry, I will show it to you."

She listened intently as Charles told her of the Alhambra with its reddish walls, stunning frescos, and Moorish architecture. "The palace sits at the top of the hill al-Sabika, where you could see the entire city of Granada."

"Will I get to live there?" she asked, her eyes twinkling with anticipation.

"Of course, my sweet one," he said. "It is my home in Spain, and as my wife it will be yours too. You will be the queen of a great empire."

• • •

The visit was over before Mary knew it, much to her regret. Watching Charles' ship sail away, Mary was excited about her future as Empress of the Holy Roman Empire, but once again started to feel uneasy about eventually leaving England. She was fully aware that there was no greater match to be had in all of Europe than Emperor Charles, and knew she had to keep her feelings and reservations to her self. She dare not even mention them to Lady Pole. After Charles departed England, Katherine began training her daughter to become Queen of Spain.

Over the following years, Mary's education intensified. She prepared for the day she would have to say goodbye to her home country and her parents. But it all came to nothing.

"That whore's son," Henry screamed as he burst into the chamber where Mary and her mother were reading. "That he could think of doing this to me!"

"What has happened, Your Majesty?" the Queen asked, both terrified and concerned.

"Jilted! He jilted her, that pig-fucker you call your nephew," Henry hollered at his wife. Mary remained in her seat, terrified to move. "The emperor has married! He jilted my daughter, my princess! He has spit in my face. He thinks there are better alliances to be had. The scum! Damn him and his kin to hell; damn them all!"

Katherine did not speak. She did not move when her husband hurled a cup at the window, shattering the glass behind her head. But while Katherine was calm, Mary was terrified. Henry stormed from the room, and Mary ran to her mother. Climbing into her lap, she cried her eyes out. While relieved that she did not have to leave England, Mary was trembling. Her father's rage had frightened and unsettled her in a way she had never experienced.

Unwilling to wait for Mary to come of age, Charles wed another in 1525, the beautiful and wealthy Princess Isabella of Portugal. The princess was Katherine's niece and Charles' cousin, and he wasted no time in getting a son from his fertile, young bride.

It was an offense Henry would not stand for. How could that man insult him by jilting his daughter? Was Mary not the greatest prize in all of Europe? Henry blamed Katherine—

again—for what he viewed as her nephew's betrayal, dealing yet another blow to their marriage.

As for Mary, she was beginning to understand that destiny was a fickle thing.

•　　　•　　　•

In the late spring of 1527, Mary was happy to find herself back at court. She had last seen her mother and father over Christmas, and things had felt normal. But on this visit, she noticed the court was strangely tense. The usual feasts and dances were held, but on the brink of adolescence, Mary was more aware of her complicated world and the unsavory intrigues of the adults who inhabited it.

She enjoyed a pleasant conversation with the French Ambassador Charles de Solier. The possibility of yet another French marriage was in the air. Cardinal Wolsey had been working tirelessly for the last two years—since the Spanish engagement ended—to bring about another French alliance. Mary was once again at the center of it.

As the dances began, Ambassador de Solier requested Mary be his partner. Mary was delighted to accept, and they headed out to join the rest of the dancers. She didn't realize the ambassador was covertly scrutinizing her. He took note of her every feature, including her thin and young frame which the ambassador believed would take many more years to develop. He conceded she was tall and graceful with a beautiful face, though her voice was hardly feminine.

Mary noticed that King Henry did not ask Queen Katherine to be his partner for the first dance. Instead, the king chose a lady whom Mary had never seen before. When the king took the hand of the elegant young woman, with her raven-colored hair and dark eyes that appeared to hook the soul, Mary could not help but notice the sideways glances the woman received. Whispers started among the courtiers. Something this unknown woman had done was causing a stir.

Why was anyone taking such notice of her? Mary had seen the king dance with other ladies before, as the queen had danced with other gentlemen of the court. There could be no harm in the king offering this lady a dance. Or could there? Usually, the king did not ask another to dance until he had first danced with her mother, the queen.

She told herself to pay no consideration to a lowly maid or the whispers of others and proceeded to enjoy the dance. But she could not help but look at her father and his partner.

She was not beautiful, this mysterious woman. Indeed, she had sallow skin and a hooked nose. But one couldn't deny there was something alluring about her. She had long slender fingers, and dark enchanting eyes. She moved with a unique kind of grace that was lacking in the other ladies of the court. Mary noticed something in the way she and her father danced. Mary had never witnessed the intensity emanating from them, had never seen her father look at her mother in such a way. Yet, Mary could not put her finger on exactly what was happening. At 11 years old, she was still too young and innocent to understand.

After the dance, Mary spotted her paternal aunt, another Tudor princess named Mary. Beautiful and young, her aunt had once been married to the late King of France, and after he died, she wanted to return to England.

King Henry sent his closest friend Charles Brandon, Duke of Suffolk—a tall, robust and incredibly handsome man—to fetch his younger sister home. King Henry was furious when he learned that Charles and his sister Mary returned to England having married, doing so without his permission. Henry had plans to marry his sister off in another political match, but his spirited sibling wouldn't be a pawn in these games any longer. She and the Duke had long loved each other and took the grave risk of marrying while still in France.

King Henry banished them from court for a time. But Cardinal Wolsey spoke up for them and instead imposed a crippling fine that would take the couple decades to repay. But it was better to begrudgingly accept the financial burden than have the King follow through on his threat to remove the duke's head.

Now the French queen—as the elder Mary was known—was back in her brother's good graces, although the look on her face told young Mary that her aunt was none too pleased with her brother. She stared daggers at the king and the woman with whom he was dancing and laughing. Mary joined her aunt, who was sitting alone. Her already tipsy husband had gone to fetch more wine. Mary knew her aunt would tell her what was happening as the French queen was never one to hold her tongue, despite her father's insistence that that is what a woman should do. Of course, Mary had some idea that her father had dalliances with other ladies that were not her mother. Mary knew that another woman bore Henry a son, the half-brother she never wanted to meet. When the boy, called Henry Fitzroy, was created Duke of Richmond, Queen Katherine became concerned the King would name him his heir over Mary.

"That boy is a bastard, Mary, and he can never inherit the throne," Katherine told her daughter one night a few years previously, as she tucked her into bed. "You are the fruit of a lawful and loving union, you have royal blood on both sides, and you are meant to rule after your father. I am sure of it."

At that time, the Queen ordered Lady Pole to instruct Mary's household to show even more reverence to her as the sole heir to the English crown. For Mary, it wasn't easy to understand how and why her father might want to lay with another woman. Mary had only the vaguest idea of what it was to share a bed with a man. Her mother and Lady Pole had given her some idea of what a woman's duty was when married. But, if she were being honest with herself, Mary found the entire concept unappealing, awkward, and frankly, something she'd like to avoid.

"You'll understand when you're older," her governess told her. "When some handsome lad catches your eye and you get that warm feeling in your cheeks, you'll see." But Mary didn't think that would ever happen.

"Your Grace," Mary said to her aunt with a bow, which the French queen returned. "Who is the woman my father is speaking to? She is the same woman he danced with earlier, and I noticed murmuring when they took to the floor."

The French queen looked uncomfortable. She did not think it proper to burden her niece with details of her father's latest affair—especially if rumors of what the king intended were true.

There was more to the French queen's hesitation. How could she tell her precious niece that her father was considering putting her mother aside? Rumors swelled the court of Cardinal Wolsey's secret investigations into the validity of the royal marriage. Mary stared at her aunt, waiting for a response, when the French queen finally broke the silence. "That is Mistress Anne Boleyn, the daughter of a diplomat, Sir Thomas Boleyn, and a maid of honor in your mother's household."

"Why should her dancing with my father cause such a stir, surely my father has ..." Mary paused, "*danced* with other ladies before."

"Yes, he has," the French Queen responded. "But I think Mistress Boleyn is after more than just a dance."

CHAPTER 3

1530 - 1533

Princess Mary awoke one morning retching into a basin beside her four-post bed. Her head and stomach were in agony, and the pain in her temples was so sharp and constant the fourteen-year-old could hardly open her eyes. When she did, Mary became so dizzy the room appeared to be going around in circles. The knots in her stomach made her feel as though it may burst like fireworks. Day after day passed with no change.

On the eighth day, Lady Pole came in carrying a tray with bread coated in a bit of butter and sage and a small goblet of ale to try and tempt Mary into eating. But the Princess could not stand the sight of even such a small meal. "Please take it away," Mary said, barely opening her eyes.

"Your grace must try and eat," Lady Pole urged. "It has been days since your last real meal. Perhaps we should fetch back the physician?"

Mary was sick of physicians. Her father had sent his personal doctor to visit her after the previous physician failed to cure her pain. But even Henry's doctor could only prescribe rest. Mary was thankful Doctor Butts didn't suggest bleeding her to remove the toxins causing her illness. Though not a doctor herself, Mary thought it absurd that the cure for many ailments was to be sliced with a knife.

Lady Pole pulled a few letters out from her pocket and told Mary there was word from court. Her curiosity piqued; Mary sat upright. She tried to blink away her pain, but it persisted, every sound like a knife in her temples. Lady Pole handed Mary the letters, but the words danced on the pages. "I can't," she said, "Please, tell me who they are from and read them to me."

Lady Pole held three letters, one from the King, one from the Queen, and the third from the Imperial Ambassador Eustace Chapuys. The ambassador was a familiar face at Henry's court and had become more of a friend and ally to Mary and her mother as King Henry sought to annul his marriage to Queen Kathrine.

Henry had made his intentions clear: he would marry Anne Boleyn after the pope granted the annulment declaring his marriage to Queen Katherine null and void. The rationale was Katherine had been married to and lay with Prince Arthur, the king's late brother. Henry told himself Katherine's marriage to his dead older brother had in fact been consummated. He could think of no other reason why God saw fit to deny him legitimate sons, despite the queen swearing before God that she was a virgin when she and Henry wed.

"When you had me at first, I take God to be my judge, I was a true maid without touch of man. And whether it be true or not, I put it to your conscience," Katherine had said to the king the previous year before a tribunal at Black Friars. The couple had been called to address the validity of their marriage. The king spoke of his troubled conscience and noted a passage in the Bible. Leviticus 20:21 reads: "If a man takes his brother's wife, it is an impurity. He has uncovered his brother's nakedness; they shall be childless." The king said it spoke to the justness of his cause, but when it was Katherine's turn to speak, she fell to her knees before her stunned husband and pleaded her case.

She then rose and walked out of the hall, refusing to heed the call to return, as she believed there would be no fair trial for her in England. Katherine had commended her case into the hands of the pope and would only abide by his judgment.

Mary was firmly on her mother's side. How she wished she could have been at Black Friars to see the queen in all her glory, defending herself so well that even those closest to the king could not help but support her. When she left the courtroom, the crowd gathered outside erupted in cheers of "God Save the queen!" and "Long live our true queen!" Katherine thanked the people of England for their support and climbed into her coach.

"My mother is the bravest woman alive," Mary told Lady Pole after she learned what happened. Mary knew her mother was right. Almost all of Europe—except some of those horrid Lutherans in Germany, heretics the lot of them—supported Queen Katherine and believed Henry was only acting out of lust for his mistress.

Indeed, it was said that Mistress Boleyn and her faction, who went about the court as though Anne were already queen and enjoying the king's unending favor, were secret Lutherans. Mary was further shocked when she heard this.

It was unthinkable that her father would repudiate her mother, but for one who was not only of low rank but a heretic too was too much. To think that her father would debase himself with a woman who denied the pope's authority and the miracle of the communion was unconscionable. Though, it was said Mistress Anne attended Mass daily with the king and took the Host. Mary and those who supported the queen believed Anne was placing evil and heretical thoughts in the King's mind. Mary heard she even resorted to witchcraft to make Henry fall so deeply in love with her. Mary decided that witchcraft was the only way another could truly take her father from her divine mother.

Lady Pole read the queen's letter first. Katherine was concerned about Mary's health, but wrote, "I dare not leave court should that woman take advantage of my absence." But the queen assured Mary of her love and reminded her daughter to trust God in all things and that the king could take no action without the approval of the pope. Fortunately, the emperor was firmly on their side. Finally, her mother wrote, "Obey the King, your father, in everything, save only that you will not offend God and lose your own soul." Accompanying the letter was a gift from Katherine, a beautiful golden set of rosary beads, which Mary tenderly clutched as her governess read the letter.

The note from King Henry was brief and surprisingly lacking in affection. The King said he hoped "his entirely beloved princess" was in better health. But what he wrote next shocked both Mary and Lady Pole. He reminded Mary of her duty as his daughter and subject, noting he was God's anointed sovereign, and his word was God's law.

Etched on Mary's face was the question she dared not voice. How could the king think to put his authority above that of the pope?

"This is appalling," Lady Pole said, her voice overflowing with agitation. "It has to be that whore who has put such vile ideas in the king's mind. She and that devil, Cromwell."

Thomas Cromwell was now the King's closest adviser, much to the chagrin of the nobility, since he was a simple blacksmith's son. He'd worked closely with Cardinal Wolsey, who, as a butcher's son, saw something of a kindred spirit in the intelligent, young lawyer. Cromwell was firmly situated at the King's side now that the Cardinal was gone. Wolsey failed to secure the king an annulment and fell out of favor, dying on his way to London from Leicester Abbey to answer charges of treason.

"It was his staunch loyalty to the king and low birth that did him in," Lady Pole had said after they learned of his death. But since the king trusted Wolsey implicitly, his failure allowed Anne and others who hated the cardinal to step in and take advantage."

Everyone knew of Anne Boleyn's hatred of the Cardinal. It had flourished ever since he interfered in her marriage plans with Henry Percy, heir to the Earldom of Northumberland. Wolsey scolded Percy, a page in his household, and made him break off the engagement because Anne was not of sufficient enough rank to marry him. It seemed Mistress Boleyn had the last laugh.

After folding up the king's letter, Lady Pole said, "I heard after the cardinal died *that woman* staged a play which depicted Wolsey descending into hell." She leaned into whisper even though no one else was around to overhear. "My daughter Ursula was there and said it was as tasteless and vulgar as the woman herself. The king was said to be furious over the spectacle and people thought Henry would come to his senses and send that shameful creature from court."

But it would seem that Anne was able to work her charms again on the King and draw him back to her. If only the play had been an end to all of it, Mary thought as she lay in bed one night. She stared at the intricate magenta canopy above her bed, willing sleep to come, missing the security she once felt. It wasn't long after this that her illness began.

The letter from Chapuys held the information Mary was most eager to hear. Chapuys did not sugar-coat the goings on at court. Despite Katherine's hope that Mary would not be tainted by what was happening, he kept Mary informed of who was on whose side and did not hide his hatred of Anne Boleyn, referring to her only as "the concubine."

It seemed that Anne was queen in all but name. She was ordering everyone about and took great offense that the king still allowed the queen to make his shirts, since such a task was an intimate duty of a wife to her husband. Henry and Anne were heard arguing, and Anne shouted their marriage bed would be too crowded, demanding the King send Katherine away. Chapuys warned Mary that should an annulment be granted, though he doubted the outcome fully, Anne would be no friend to her. He wrote that she should "consider the concubine your greatest enemy."

Chapuys didn't mention a far more disturbing fact about Anne. Having the king send Katherine away was not enough. She wasn't shy about her desire for the king to have Katherine and Mary put to death.

He had eyes and ears everywhere. "I care nothing for Katherine," Anne had supposedly told a group of women at Windsor Castle one morning as she went to see the king. "I would rather see her hanged than acknowledge her as my mistress."

But Chapuys reported to Mary that the women were shocked and disgusted. With just a few words, Anne had successfully turned every lady at court against her.

"I do not expect I will ever be able to call Mistress Anne my friend," Mary told Lady Pole after she put away the letters. "Chapuys is a good friend to my mother and I long for the pope to make his decision and bring about the day Anne Boleyn's name will be forgotten. My father must come to see sense."

Mary felt woozy but told Lady Pole she wanted to visit the chapel so she may ask Jesus and his mother, the Blessed Virgin, to intercede on her behalf. She would add a pray for her parents as well as the whole of England.

•   •   •

When February arrived, the pope sent word that the King must leave Anne and treat Katherine as his proper wife until a final decision on the annulment was made. But Henry didn't listen.

It was a bitterly cold winter, which didn't help Mary's health. She was having trouble keeping food down again and her monthly courses were causing her agony when they arrived. But, in a rare act of love and kindness, the king allowed Mary to visit the court at Windsor so she could be with her mother.

Mary was hesitant. She did not want to watch Mistress Anne parading about while her mother suffered. But her intense desire to be with Katherine won out, and when she was well enough, she made her way to court.

Mary was determined to arrive as befit her station as princess and heir. She wore a magnificent gown of scarlet velvet and donned stunning diamond earrings that had been a gift from the King of France during one of her marriage negotiation sagas. Her father's emerald necklace ringed her throat accented by a stunning ruby broach at the dress' low square neckline. A silk hood lined with pearls completed the ensemble.

Wrapped in an ermine fur cloak, she exited the carriage, very glad the long and miserably frigid journey was at an end. Above all, she would make no acknowledgment of Mistress Anne— unless of course her father commanded her to do so.

Mary was led through the long corridors to the great hall at Windsor where a bustling court was making merry. One of the grooms stood at the opening and shouted for those gathered to "make way for her grace, the Princess Mary! Make way!"

Mary handed her cloak to one of her ladies, smoothed her skirts, straightened her back, lifted her head up, sniffed her orange scented pomander, and prepared to enter the court. Clasping her hands in front of her waist, Mary walked into the great hall, and everyone bowed in reverence. She made her way to the center of the hall where she stopped and bowed low to her parents who were sitting at the dais at the head of the room.

She rose, walked closer, and bowed again, doing so one more time until she was directly in front of the king and queen. She was surprised but glad to see her mother and father sitting next to one another. She had not noticed if Mistress Anne was around and would not flatter that woman by looking for her.

I am the Princess of England, Mary thought. *She should be bowing at my feet —or burning at the stake, the proper fate of witches and heretics.*

Mary scolded herself. She should not have such dark thoughts. It did not suit a princess to plan the downfall of others, nor to wish someone dead, even an enemy. Did not Jesus say we must love our enemies?

Loving Anne Boleyn was something Mary knew she could never do. She also knew that for the first time in her young life, she was truly feeling raw, genuine hatred for another person. She hoped that confession and prayer would calm the storm in her heart, but deep down she knew her enmity toward Anne was a raging fire.

Henry bid Mary rise from her bow. "Welcome, my Princess Mary," Henry said. "I am glad to see you doing so well after your illness." Then he kissed her lovingly on each cheek.

Mary was comforted by her father's show of affection and wondered how so loving a man could think of putting away her mother and declaring herself a bastard. But if the pope granted the annulment, she knew this to be her fate. Although with all her heart, she believed His Holiness would never come to that conclusion.

But how could Mary not wonder? With the King already ignoring the pope on the issue of removing Anne, how likely was it he would listen if the Pope ruled against him? She felt torn, once again, by the Great Matter, as the King's nullity suit was being called.

Queen Katherine rose to greet her daughter in a loving embrace, the king smiled and left the mother and daughter alone. As he exited the hall, he bid the musicians to play on, and the court went about its bustling. Everyone knew to whom he was going.

"I cannot tell you how happy I am to see you," Katherine said, holding both of Mary's hands tightly in her own. "I wish I could see you more, but with things being as they are..." her voice trailed off.

"I understand mother," Mary said. "Are you well? I worry for you and pray that God will put an end to all of these troubles soon."

Katherine smiled lovingly. She really was much comforted by Mary's presence, but she, too, was wracked with worry. Katherine could feel in her bones that Mary could and should rule England one day. But with her husband—for that is what he was, despite Henry's fuming he was not and could never be her husband— bent on divorce and his growing resentment of the pope, Katherine didn't know what would happen. But her daughter would be an innocent casualty in these schemes, of that she was certain.

After vespers were heard that evening, Mary stayed behind in the chapel for further prayer. She begged God and His son Jesus Christ to help the pope come to a decision—the right decision— and declare her parents' marriage valid. She pleaded with St. George to help the king see his error and send that harlot away so things could be as they once were during Mary's golden childhood.

As the princess prayed at the altar, she realized someone was beside her. When she opened her eyes, she was stunned to see the king standing in his magnificent attire. The jewels inlaid in his garments twinkled and shone in the candlelight.

"Your Majesty," Mary said as she moved into a hasty bow, "forgive me, I didn't realize you had come in." Henry smiled reassuringly at his daughter, then took her by the hand and led her to a pew.

"Mary," Henry said as he placed a loving arm around her shoulders. "I know all of this must seem confusing and uncertain to one of such tender years, but you must never doubt my love for you or the justness of my cause."

So this was why the king came to speak to her. It dawned on Mary in that moment that the King needed to win her to his side. If he could do that perhaps the Pope would cease these endless delays and rule in his favor. Mary didn't know what to say. She loved her father dearly and knew that as his daughter and subject, she was duty bound to obey him in all things, but in her heart, she knew she could not obey him in this.

"Sir," Mary ventured hesitantly, "if the Pope had issued a dispensation allowing you to marry the queen, my mother, then surely there can be no impediment to your marriage? And what of Matthew 22:24? Did not Moses say that if a man dies with no children his brother must wed his widow?"

Henry's face grew red. He couldn't believe his daughter would presume so far. His look turned stern with a dead coldness in his eyes Mary had never seen before. It frightened her. Shaking, she wished she hadn't said anything.

"Who are you to question my wisdom?" Henry screamed at his daughter. "Am I not God's anointed sovereign? Who better than I to determine what spiritual laws are being broken in my own kingdom? How can the pope, who is just as corrupt a man as any other politician, decree that I may marry my brother's widow when the Bible itself says such a thing is unnatural? The passage you so ignorantly quoted, daughter, does not apply to Christians! I know my cause to be just as I have no son to succeed me. I might as well be childless!"

Mary was on the verge of tears but fighting with all her might to keep them back. She stared in horror, trembling, as her father railed against her. Never before had she been on the receiving end of his rage. Venturing to speak in her own defense, Henry stilled her with a wave of his hand and stomped out of the chapel. She could still hear him yelling as he made his way out. An eternity passed efore the sound of his shouting faded away.

How would she be able to get up and walk out of the chapel? One of her maids had been waiting outside while she was at her prayers but didn't dare enter until after the king had gone.

"Your Grace," the sweet-faced girl in a simple black velvet gown ventured. She smiled when the Princess finally looked at her. "Shall I escort you back to your chamber?" Mary offered a small smile. She was grateful to this maid, called Margaret, for her kindness.

"Don't fret, princess," Margaret said. "I'm sure the king didn't mean those horrid things. The whole world knows he's been seduced by witchcraft and evil ministers." It took courage for Margaret to say such a thing, but Mary knew she could not let a servant speak of her father thus, no matter how right she was.

"You must never say such a thing again, do you understand me?" Mary gently scolded. Margaret lowered her head and nodded in shame, but Mary placed a hand on her shoulder. "Thank you for trying to comfort me."

They walked back to Mary's chamber in silence, and when Mary was left alone, she gave way to a torrent of tears. She could not stop them; she was so full of fear, anxiety, and sadness. She wanted to run to her father's chambers and beg him to forgive her, and for the briefest of moments, Mary considered capitulating to the King's will. Then she wondered if her father's outburst may have another cause.

Henry had never behaved like that with her before. Never in her wildest dreams could Mary have imagined the king, her kind, generous, and magnanimous father, acting in such a way. She thought about what Margaret said, about the world knowing the king had been seduced by witchcraft. It must be the spells of that whore, she thought. Don't people act out of character under some kind of enchantment? This must be the cause, there can be no other explanation. If only there was a way to break these charms.

As Mary lay awake watching the flame melt the wax candle on her bedside table, the door to her chamber slowly opened. She looked up to see Queen Katherine Only a single maid holding a candle was with her. The queen took the light and dismissed the maid. She walked over to Mary, who sat up in her bed. Mary was expecting to hear her mother say she was disappointed in her for being so disrespectful to the king.

Katherine placed the candle on the table and cupped her daughter's face in both hands. "You have your grandmother's bravery, child," Katherine said. With that, Mary began to weep again.

The queen sat on the bed with her daughter, folding Mary into her arms, silently stroking her head as Mary cried. They said nothing, but the queen spent the night comforting her daughter, who held on so tightly to her mother, as though she were a shipwrecked sailor clinging to the wreckage.

The next day as Mary was making her way down to the stables—she wanted to ride out into the park to clear her head— she was stopped cold by the sight of Anne Boleyn standing next to her horse.

"Princess," Anne said with a smile and no curtsey. "I am so pleased to have run into you. I had been hoping we'd have a chance to speak during your visit."

Mary stayed silent.

"It is my dearest wish that you and I become friends," Anne said. "I know your father is not pleased with you at the moment. It was quite foolish to question the king on the justness of his cause, but I will use my influence with His Majesty to bring you back into his good graces. After all, princess, I am about to become your stepmother, and I will always look out for your interests."

"I'm not sure what you are playing at Mistress Boleyn, but I am not some foolish girl, despite what you may think," Mary said. "I know you have only your own interests at heart. You covet a king and a crown, despite both of those things belonging rightfully to my mother, Queen Katherine. Perhaps you should just come to your point."

"Such a proud and haughty child," Anne responded with a conniving smirk. "You do your Spanish relations proud. Believe it or not, I did genuinely hope you and I could build a friendship. After all, you'll need all the friends you can get once your mother's marriage is annulled for the incestuous farce it is. It would do well for the king's bastard daughter to be gracious and warm to her future queen."

"You will never be Queen of England," Mary said, trying to hide the quake in her voice. "My parents were granted a dispensation to marry, and His Holiness knows my father is being bewitched by his mistress and her family of grasping schemers. You should enjoy your time at the king's side while it lasts."

"Oh, you poor, misguided girl. Before long, the pope's authority will be abolished in this realm, and only the king's word will matter. And when I give my Henry the son he has so longed for, I know what fate will befall you and the barren old crone you call a mother."

Mary nearly struck Anne over the insult to her mother. She could feel the flame in her cheeks, her hand involuntarily ballooning into a fist. Anne gave Mary a conniving smile and nodded toward her balled fist as if she were daring the princess to strike her. That would be all the ammunition Anne would need to turn the king entirely against her Mary knew. She could picture Anne spinning a story of how his ungrateful daughter struck his mistress unprovoked. God only knew how the King would punish the princess for that. Mary lowered her hand and did nothing.

As Anne walked away, a gaggle of ladies trailing in her wake, Mary felt her heart pound hard and fast. She leaned against her horse's neck, burying her face in its mane, tears streaming down her face. Her own ladies were at a loss of what to do. But Margaret, the young maid who comforted Mary that night in the chapel, stepped forward. In a move many of the higher-ranking women felt was out of turn, she reached out and touched Mary's hand to give her a reassuring squeeze and a smile. Mary gratefully returned the gesture.

The next day, Mary's distress worsened. The king left Windsor with Anne without saying a word to the queen or the princess. Katherine was deeply hurt that Henry would go without saying goodbye, but she and Mary knew it was Anne's doing.

Mary believed Anne would take advantage of the rift that had been opened between father and daughter. She was sure that Anne was filling Henry's head with negative thoughts about his ungrateful and disloyal daughter.

Over the course of several weeks Mary and her mother spent every possible moment together sewing, riding, walking, dining and praying. They were determined to soak in as much of each other as they could, neither daring to admit what they were both feeling—that things were about to get much worse. Mary was heartbroken when the time came for her to return to Ludlow. As she said her farewells to her mother, Katherine pulled Mary close and whispered in her ear. "You are the King's trueborn daughter, the granddaughter of Ferdinand and Isabella of Spain, the greatest monarchs this world has known. And you are the only heir to the English throne. It is your destiny to be Queen of England."

CHAPTER 4

1533 -1535

Mary sat in the lush gardens of her establishment at Beaulieu where she had been living for some time after the king recalled her from Ludlow. She was trying to enjoy a cool, late September afternoon; she had a book of psalms in her lap but couldn't focus on it. She was too preoccupied with everything that had been going on, hardly knowing what to think.

Earlier in the year, her father had sent her mother from court and claimed to have married Anne Boleyn, who was going around styling herself as Queen of England. The king declared that as Prince Arthur's widow, Katherine must now be referred to as the Dowager Princess of Wales, a title she refused to acknowledge.

The king even had a coronation ceremony for Anne where she was anointed with Saint Edward's Crown which was typically only placed on the head of a ruling monarch. The whole of England—and the world—believed this meant it was Anne who truly ruled the king in all things. Being big with child at the time, it seemed all but certain Anne would deliver the king his much-desired son. Then Mary and her mother would be truly lost.

But at the start of September, Anne gave birth to a daughter at Greenwich. "It seems God did not see fit to answer the concubine's prayers," Chapuys wrote to Mary.

"It appears I have a sister called Elizabeth. My father must be bitterly disappointed," Mary said to Lady Pole, a hint of triumph in her voice. "Although, Chapuys writes that he is showing no outward signs of it."

"A half-sister," Lady Pole reminded Mary. "Remember, she is a bastard, born of a woman who is the scandal of Christendom. She will never succeed to the crown. That is yours, by right. Even the pope agrees."

Indeed, after years of delays, the pope finally made a decision on the king's divorce. His Holiness was furious when he learned the king took Anne as his wife without waiting for a judgment from the Holy See.

The pope issued a decree that coincided with the birth of Anne's child, proclaiming that Henry and Katherine's marriage was true and valid, and the king's new marriage was null and void. The pope made it clear the child of Henry and Katherine was born of a true marriage and therefore stood lawful and legitimate. In contrast, any children born of this second union were illegitimate.

But it was too late. Though this was a moral victory for Mary and her mother, the king had already taken the extreme step of denying the authority of the pope. Henry declared himself Supreme Head of the Church of England, making it illegal for any English subject to appeal to Rome on any matter. Henceforth, the pope would be referred to as the Bishop of Rome and stripped of all authority in England. The king would answer to no higher power, save God, whom he was sure was firmly on his side. Although the birth of another daughter must have somewhat clouded this view, Mary thought.

Mary looked up from her book to see her maid Margaret walking toward her. Margaret had become more of a friend to Mary over the years. She enjoyed the lively girl's company. Margaret was easy to talk to, outspoken, probably more than

Mary should allow, and fiercely loyal to the princess and her mother.

"Princess," Margaret said with a bow, "your chamberlain, Mr. John Hussey, has returned from court and seeks an audience with Your Grace."

Mary entered the parlor where a weary John Hussey stood. The look on his face told her he had nothing good to report. Mary stood in stunned silence as Hussey told her the king had commanded him to inform her she must abandon her pretensions and recognize she was no longer Princess of England.

Her bastard status meant she was not entitled to such recognition. Hussey added that no one would be allowed to call her princess in the future, and she must abandon her apartments at Beaulieu to go to Hatfield, where the infant Princess Elizabeth would soon be residing.

To make her new status clear to Mary and the world, the king ordered Mary to go live in her baby sister's household, where she would serve as a maid. This meant her own household would be dissolved, and her servants—her dear Margaret and her beloved Lady Pole—would have to return to their families or find new positions.

It was unthinkable that this would happen, that the king would order it. Despite everything that was happening, Mary believed it was all Anne's doing and the king would never humiliate her so. It occurred to Mary that she only had Hussey's verbal communication, which could have come from one of Anne's cronies under the pretense of being from the king.

"As I have had no written notification from my father, the king, or his council, my conscience will in no way suffer me to take any other name for myself other than princess," she declared loudly. "I will happily obey the king in moving residences to any he should like, but to acknowledge this false title will dishonor my parents and the deed of our mother, the holy church, and the pope who is judge in this matter and none other."

Hussey returned to court to deliver Mary's response. She immediately wrote to her mother who was residing at the Bishop of Lincoln's palace at Buckden in Huntingdonshire, a poorly cared for residence meant to bend Katherine into submission. She told the queen what had just happened and vowed to never acquiesce to the king's demands that she renounce her title and place in the succession, no matter what. Katherine replied lovingly, saying how much she wished she could be with her daughter and reminded Mary of her rights and the many influential friends who were supporting them both.

Days later, an official written command arrived. The king ordered Mary to leave her establishment and move to a smaller residence, one which was in bad repair and exposed his often ill 17-year-old daughter to the poor autumn weather. In his command, Henry referred to his daughter as "Lady Mary, the King's daughter."

Mary was hurt and angry when she saw that. She wrote back to her father pretending to believe his omission of her proper title of princess was an oversight.

"I could not a little marvel," Mary wrote in reference to the title the king used. "For I doubt not that Your Grace does not take me for your lawful daughter, born in true matrimony."

It was a brave but futile response on Mary's part. She heard nothing from the king after that and quietly moved to her new home. Beaulieu was given as a gift by the King to Anne Boleyn's brother George, who wasted no time moving in once Mary had vacated.

Mary and her mother faced similar struggles. Katherine refused to cease calling herself the king's true wife and the true Queen of England. She had also refused, for a time, to give up the jewels of the Queens of England. But she was forced to relinquish the precious items so Anne could wear them for her false coronation.

Before Elizabeth was born, Anne had been proclaiming to the world she would be delivered of a prince. She demanded Katherine give up the christening robe and bearing cloth she had brought with her from Spain to use at the baptisms of her own children. Both Mary and Katherine's deceased Prince Henry had been christened in those garments, and Katherine said she would rather be torn apart by dogs than give them up. Henry didn't press again after her initial refusal.

Mary now fully understood how this game needed to be played. She knew she had to be careful in everything she said and did. The slightest misstep could have disastrous consequences for her and her mother. Soon after her move, she was visited at her new home by a team of commissioners, similar to the ones who had gone to see her mother in an attempt to bully Katherine into capitulating. When they arrived, Mary summoned her entire 160-person household to bear witness to the exchange, knowing that so many witnesses would force her visitors to treat her with at least minimal respect.

They came expecting to find a weak girl, ready and willing to bend to their might and accept her new lot in life. They promised her a return to the king's favor and a place at court with the king and queen.

"Sir, I cannot return to a court with the king and queen since the queen, my mother, currently resides in Huntingdonshire, though why I cannot understand. The pope himself declared the validity of my parent's marriage."

One of the commissioners, a short, stocky, balding man with a red nose that betrayed a dangerous love of ale, stepped forward to scold Mary that the pope held no authority in England. "The Archbishop of Canterbury proclaimed your parent's marriage incestuous and null, making you a bastard and leaving the king free to marry Queen Anne," he said. "I suggest, madam, that you make peace with this and bow to the king's will, as any loyal subject and daughter ought to do."

Mary shook her head. She had nothing but contempt for the archbishop, a man called Thomas Cranmer. Chapuys had warned Mary that Cranmer was fully in the pocket of the Boleyns, and he was also believed a secret heretic, being that he was a good friend to that devil, Thomas Cromwell. It was the idea of Cranmer and Cromwell that the king canvas the universities and get the opinions of scholarly men studying the scriptures to determine the validity of his marriage to Queen Katherine. Neither Katherine nor Mary would accept their views that the marriage was null, knowing that the reading and interpretation of scriptures was meant only for the clergy.

But what did Mary expect from a pair of heretics? She knew that once her father was brought back to reason, Cranmer, Cromwell, and that witch would be among the first to rightly suffer the king's punishment. How Mary longed for that day.

When the commissioners left Mary, they were exhausted and frustrated as their threats and persuasions failed them. Mary was as immovable as her mother.

•　　　•　　　•

In early December 1533, the Duke of Norfolk, Anne Boleyn's uncle, arrived to inform Mary she must make ready to leave for Hatfield where she would reside in the household of the infant Princess Elizabeth. When Mary heard this, she once again responded that she would happily move to any residence the King commanded, but she could not be made to wait upon the princess as "that is a title which belongs to me by right, and to no one else."

"I did not come here to argue with you, my lady," Norfolk responded. "I am here only to see the King's wishes accomplished."

None of Mary's servants were allowed to accompany her to Elizabeth's residence. They had been dismissed in the previous weeks for encouraging Mary in what the king called her "persistent disobedience." This included her sweet Margaret, who protested vehemently at the thought of being parted from her mistress.

When Norfolk told Mary that Lady Pole may not accompany her, it felt like she was punched in the stomach. Lady Pole protested, shouting that she had been with the princess since she was a small child and raised Mary like her own. She even offered to pay her own way to continue to serve Mary and fund the wages of any other servant the princess may need.

"Princess Elizabeth has no need of more servants beyond the ones the king and queen have already appointed," Norfolk responded. "That must be of whom you are speaking madam, since the king claims only one legitimate daughter."

Lady Pole attempted to protest again, but Norfolk cut her off. "Two maids of honor will be a sufficient retinue of the king's bastard daughter," Norfolk said. "They will be appointed by the queen herself. I suggest you ladies make ready to leave."

A few weeks later, just before Christmas, the king sent his good friend and former brother-in-law, Charles Brandon, Duke of Suffolk, to escort Mary to Hatfield. Mary loathed to see the duke. She thought it scandalous and disgraceful that he remarried only a few months after the death of her beloved aunt, the French Queen.

Charles wed his wealthy young ward Katherine Willoughby, the daughter of Queen Katherine's closest friend Maria de Salinas. Despite her annoyance with the duke, Mary couldn't help but laugh at the wedding itself and the thought that the king's staunch supporter married a girl whose mother was firmly in Queen Katherine's corner.

But the duke wasn't there to act only as an escort. He had one other task he was dreading to perform.

"Madam," he said to Mary, "I have come on the king's orders to conduct you to Hatfield. It is the king's pleasure that you act as a maid to his entirely beloved daughter and heir, Princess Elizabeth."

Mary couldn't help but wince at the duke's description of the baby girl.

"Additionally, it is the king's desire that you have few visitors at Hatfield and send no letters. You will be stripped of all jewels and property. You must also give up your horses and fine clothes."

The Duke swallowed apprehensively before he spoke again. "The king also forbids you to communicate with the dowager princess, your mother."

Mary could have dropped to her knees and wept until her heart gave out. How could the king be so cruel as to separate mother and daughter completely? It was bad enough they had not been allowed to see each other for what seemed like endless months—but now this?

Mary's mind raced and her heart was beating so hard it hurt. Her knees felt weak, and she began to swoon. Lady Pole was there instantly, supporting her charge one final time.

Forgetting all formality, Mary and Lady Pole clung to each other in a loving and desperate embrace. Mary buried her face in Lady Pole's shoulder, who promised to visit Mary at Hatfield as soon as possible. She whispered in Mary's ear that she would be going straight to see Queen Katherine and make her and Ambassador Chapuys aware of what had happened.

"Stay strong, Your Grace," she told Mary. "All will be well in time, you'll see. Remember, always, that our Lord and Savior, Jesus Christ, went through many trials and suffering before ascending into Heaven. He has not forgotten you."

When Mary arrived at Hatfield—a beautiful red brick building with four lavish wings surrounded by several acres of gardens—she was greeted by a sour-faced woman in a gray damask gown and a French hood. The woman had an evil look, like she should be in a school room threatening some poor unsuspecting pupil with a rod. She was Lady Anne Shelton, aunt to Anne Boleyn and therefore, Mary concluded, no friend to her or her mother.

Mary stepped out of her carriage, the Duke of Suffolk and his retinue behind her. No doubt they would be glad to be rid of her. The king and Anne would not be pleased when they learned of what happened as they were conveying Mary to Hatfield. Though their orders were to keep the windows of the coach covered, it did little to hide the identity of the person they were transferring from the common people.

As Mary traveled, throngs of ordinary people from the villages came to see her. Cries of "God save your grace!" and "Long live our true princess!" greeted them along with cries of support for Queen Katherine, all of which touched Mary deeply. She barely had a chance to acknowledge the people for their esteem before the duke chided her for looking out the windows.

All the way to Hatfield the people came out for Mary. They cheered as her party drove by. She would slyly peek out of the window, then quickly close the flap when she was scolded. She could not suppress her smiles when the crowds would chastise those conveying her to her new home. They used foul and unseemly language, yet Mary was grateful to know she and her mother were so loved and respected by the people. They would win out in the end. She knew it.

Lady Shelton did not bow when she addressed Mary. "Welcome to Hatfield, Lady Mary," she said in a tone that was as cold as ice. "You are about to be presented to her grace, Princess Elizabeth. You will then be shown to your quarters and will begin your duties attending the princess in the morning after prayers."

Mary was resolved, even in this strange place without a friend in sight, to stand her ground and make it known to all attending her infant sister that she would not be bullied into submission.

Stiffening her back, Mary responded, "I am glad to meet my little sister, for although she was not born in a true marriage as I was, I will be happy to lavish as much sisterly affection on her as I might possess."

It was hard for her to say the words. Mary had no intention of paying this child any mind, just as she paid no mind to her half-brother, Henry Fitzroy, the King's other bastard child.

Without a word, Lady Shelton walked up to Mary and slapped her across the face. Mary wobbled on her feet after the blow, mainly from the shock of it.

"How dare you presume to strike the king's daughter!"

Bang, another hit on her other cheek. With that, Mary fell to her knees, her face throbbing from Lady Shelton's cold hands. They were surprisingly rough for a noblewoman. As Mary stared down at the cobblestones of the palace courtyard and tried to regain her senses, Lady Shelton towered over her.

"You should know that Queen Anne has instructed us that should you not comply and accept your position and renounce your false claim as princess and heir, we are to beat you for the cursed bastard you are," Lady Shelton said.

Mary stood up and looked at the woman she now understood to be her jailer and tormentor square in the eye. "There is only one true Queen of England and one true princess; my mother and I rightfully hold those titles."

Mary remained on her feet when the third strike from Lady Shelton came, despite the woman's emerald and diamond encrusted ring catching her cheek. She had turned it around for that purpose, and a small trickle of blood rolled down Mary's face. But she would not break eye contact.

At that moment, a tall, matronly woman of advancing years wearing a simple black gown, with not a strand of her auburn hair out of place under her pearl-lined French hood, appeared. It was Lady Margaret Bryan, Elizabeth's governess.

She didn't look at Mary, but thanked the duke and his men for delivering her safely. Not one of them had intervened when Lady Shelton began her assault. Lady Margaret Bryan instructed Lady Shelton to go and attend to the princess, and before Mary could protest that title, Lady Shelton went off into the house.

Lady Bryan then turned to the maid standing behind her and instructed the girl to take Mary to her room and give her the details of her duties. To Mary's intense relief, the young maid taking direction from Lady Bryan was her own dear Margaret.

Mary's heart leaped with joy. She had to restrain herself from running and hugging her friend whom she had not seen for many weeks. Mary was glad there would be at least one person at Hatfield she could count on and confide in, even if it had to be done in secret.

The look on Margaret's face told Mary she was just as happy to see her, but Margaret was aware of the eyes all around them. A happy reunion would have to wait until they were alone.

Margaret led Mary into the house, through the long gallery, and down into the servants' quarters where Mary was to lodge in the smallest room in the palace. No doubt this was another one of Anne's punishments.

To think a king's daughter should languish in such a room, with no windows and space only for a small bed, which might fit if she slept curled up. A single chest of drawers was the final piece of furniture, not that Mary had much to store away these days. The king and Anne had repossessed many of Mary's fine dresses and jewels — which Anne paraded about on her person. She even gifted some to the ladies and maids attending her at court.

All Mary had left were a few special pieces she managed to keep the king's henchmen from finding. Most of the pieces were gifts from her mother, but Mary was allowed to keep the emerald necklace her father had given her as a child. How Mary longed for the days when she was his beloved child and her mother his adored Queen.

When they entered the room, Margaret shut the door and sank into a low bow, waiting for Mary to bid her to rise. After she did, the two young women hugged, both with tears streaming down their faces. Mary's tears burned as they reached the cut on her cheek.

"Princess, I am so glad to see you, and so sorry you have come to this place in such a way," Margaret said, almost whispering. She and Mary knew the walls had ears.

"Worry not, dear friend," Mary said, clutching her golden rosary. "For I know that the best road to Heaven is one paved with troubles. I believe with all my heart that God has a purpose for sending my mother and I such sorrows. Though, I confess, I wonder when they will end."

"You have more friends than you know of, Your Grace," Margaret went on. "My sister Jane was made to serve *that woman* at court when I was made to come here after being forced from your household. Jane tells me there is tension at court between the King and *that woman* over the birth of their bastard. It seems when she was with child, the King took a mistress. When *that woman* confronted him about it, the King told her she must shut her eyes and endure, as more worthy and honorable ladies had done before her."

Mary was glad to hear the King had compared Anne to her mother and found Anne wanting. Perhaps this meant the King was tired of her and would eventually recall her and her mother, putting Anne away.

As Margaret tended to the cut on Mary's face, Mary thought of her mother. Would she have any word about her here in this grim place? Then an idea struck her.

"Margaret, I would ask a thing of you," Mary said. "I understand what I am asking you may put you and your sister in a difficult position, so if you say no, I will understand."

"Anything for you, Your Grace," Margaret said stoutly. "My sister, mother, and I are with you and the queen. My father, like most men, is for the king. But that is mostly because he knows agreeing with the king means advancement and preference."

"Can you get a letter to your sister without anyone here seeing it?"

"I believe I can, Your Grace."

"Then write to your sister Jane and ask her to tactfully seek out the Spanish Ambassador Chapuys the next time he is at court. Have her tell him of my plight here and that I have been cruelly separated from my mother's loving embrace and denied the comfort of her words in writing. Tell him of Lady Shelton's malice and beg him for his advice on this matter. But mostly, ask that he get word to the queen, telling her only of my love and resolve, and that I am well and pray for her every day."

Margaret agreed, bowed, and left the room to complete her task. Mary wasn't bothered by Lady Shelton or anyone else in Elizabeth's household the rest of the day, so she decided to somewhat explore the palace.

Walking through the long gallery, she made her way upstairs to a series of fine bedrooms, each inhabited by the ranking members of the child's household. There, at the end of the hall, was Elizabeth's nursery. Mary ventured quietly down the hall, which was chilly from the December air, and slowly peered into the room where a sleeping young maid was neglecting her duties. Mary rolled her eyes and tiptoed into the room. A loud creak of the wooden floor stopped her cold, but when she saw the maid was still sleeping, Mary kept going.

She looked into the cradle to see her little half-sister, wide awake and fussy. The small cooing creature looked at Mary, her brown eyes wide and curious, a mess of thin red hair atop her head. Mary stared at the baby, willing herself to hate the tiny bundle who usurped her place in her father's affections, and whom some were going around calling heir to the throne.

But she couldn't. Mary took one look at Elizabeth and saw an innocent, as she herself had once been. She could not blame this child for the actions of her mother and their father. She ventured to gently caress the baby's face with her finger. Elizabeth wiggled with excitement then grabbed Mary's finger with her full fist, squeezing tightly and making happy gurgling sounds. Mary smiled at the child then paused as an ugly reality hit her.

At her age, she should be cradling her own child, the first of many sons and daughters born to some great prince. But in her current situation, it seemed that fantasy would never come true.

For the first time, Mary realized how much she wanted to be a wife and mother — despite her lack of worldly knowledge, she dreamed of some handsome young man who would take her into his arms and call her his own. Together they would fill a nursery with royal children and rule over some great principality. Snapping back into reality, Mary fled from the child's room. As she rounded out the door, she heard Elizabeth begin to cry. She wanted to go back but forced herself to keep going. She went straight for the chapel and spent the next several hours on her knees in silent, fervent prayer.

•   •   •

The first eight months of Mary's time at Hatfield were the most difficult. Mary objected every time Elizabeth was called princess. Every time she was addressed as Lady Mary, she would remind the speaker that she did not recognize that title, that she was England's only true princess and her mother its true queen.

With each argument came the inevitable blow from Lady Shelton. When it came to mealtimes, Mary would eat alone in her rooms, because Elizabeth was given the chair of honor in the dining hall. Lady Shelton told Mary she was to sit in an inferior place. Again, when Mary refused, Lady Shelton would strike her, but it would prove useless. Mary refused to give up, no matter how many humiliations and scare tactics they threw at her.

But as strong as Mary's spirit was, her body was not cooperating, and she fell dangerously ill again. Margaret was at her side, knowing she was a poor substitute for Lady Pole or Queen Katherine. The girl did her best to nurse her friend and mistress back to health. Mary spent days in her uncomfortably small bed in agony, her head and stomach in more pain than any other illness.

"They have poisoned me," Mary said as Margaret tried to coax her into taking some warm broth.

"No, madam, don't say that," Margaret said. "They could never."

"*She* could," Mary said. "She has. Remember what happened to Bishop Fisher?"

"That happened in the early years of the Great Matter, Princess, because the bishop spoke out against the king and his harlot. Things are different now, and the bishop survived. Not even that woman would stoop so low as to poison the king's own daughter," Margaret said, trying to comfort Mary but not entirely believing her own words.

Margaret's sister Jane had been writing to her, both girls acting as a go-between for Mary and Ambassador Chapuys. Anne's hatred of Mary and her mother had intensified dangerously since Elizabeth was born. Perhaps, Margaret contemplated, that woman had actually made a move against the princess.

After a few more weeks, Mary began to improve. Margaret vigilantly took charge of preparing Mary's food, the princess urging her to be careful not to be discovered. Mary was worried she had pulled Margaret in too deep, that if she were found out, she could be removed from Elizabeth's household. Margaret and Jane would be punished severely.

But Margaret insisted she was being careful and that no one was paying her much attention. Margaret proved to be a capable spy, getting letters out and in without anyone noticing. Mary was glad to learn that Kathrine was not giving in, despite the king's and Anne's efforts to break Katherine's spirits by continually moving her to dilapidated houses further and further from London.

The queen was fighting for her and her daughter's rights, refusing to acknowledge the title of Dowager Princess of Wales. She would state over and over that her marriage to Prince Arthur was never consummated. Katherine, Chapuys wrote to Mary, was constantly petitioning the king to be allowed to see her child.

When Katherine had gotten word of how sick Mary had been, she begged the ambassador to urge the king to allow her to comfort their child. But Henry, it seemed, was too fearful of Mary and her mother reuniting. The king believed mother and daughter would conspire against him to bring the might of Spain down on England by inciting Charles V to make war on their behalf.

"My mother loves her adopted country and her husband the king. She would never ask such a thing of her nephew, the emperor," Mary told Margaret after reading one of Chapuys' letters.

"The king does not see reason these days, Your Grace," Margaret said, dabbing Mary's sweaty head with a damp cloth. "As long as *she* holds power, I fear he never will."

•　　•　　•

Mary was resting by a crackly fire in a humble parlor at Hatfield working on her embroidery when Lady Shelton came storming into the room. Two guards in green and white Tudor livery followed beside her.

"Take her to her chamber!" Lady Shelton commanded. "And keep her there."

"What is this?" Mary demanded to know.

The guards moved toward Mary as though they were about to manhandle her out of the room. "Why must I be removed to my chamber?" Mary asked again. She jumped up from her chair and backed away from the two men.

"Stop this, how dare you," Mary shouted as the guards grabbed her by her arms. "What do you think you are doing? Answer me!"

"Lady Mary," Lady Shelton screeched, "the king will be here any moment to see his daughter, Princess Elizabeth. You must be removed and kept out of the king's sight, by his own orders."

"No, I don't believe you," Mary flung back. "I know the king, my father, would want to see me, as I am his only trueborn child." Mary couldn't stop her voice from cracking, tears running down her face.

"Remove her," Lady Shelton said and swept out of the room.

Mary yelled and protested as one of the guards stood behind her and wrapped his steel-like arms around her, pinning her arms to her sides, and lifting her up. The other guard took her by the legs, though she managed to kick him in the face before he could fully subdue her.

"Stop this! I can walk by myself. How dare you! Get your hands off me; you cannot do this!" Mary yelled the entire time the guards carried her through the palace and down into her chamber.

They dumped her onto her small, uncomfortable bed, its sagging mattress swallowing her up and making it difficult to stand quickly. When she finally got up, the guards had already hurried out of the room, locking her in behind them. Mary vigorously banged on the door, demanding she be let out, but no one was outside to hear her. She slid onto the floor and wept uncontrollably, pausing only briefly when the sounds of commotion above her head told her the king had arrived.

The king's visits to his infant daughter were a new kind of torture. Each time Mary was locked away, and after each visit, the pains in her head and stomach returned. Mary wondered if this was all part of a plan to hasten her into an early grave.

· · ·

One day, a few weeks after the king's most recent visit, Lady Shelton appeared to say Mary had a visitor of her own. She was confused, but made her way to the long gallery where Anne Boleyn was waiting for her. Anne had been to Hatfield on several occasions before to visit her daughter, so why now, Mary wondered, did she want to speak?

The two women had not seen one another since the confrontation at the stable. A thousand different questions ran through Mary's head. Why did Anne want to see her? What latest humiliation would she inflict? Was Mary about to be arrested and taken to the Tower? Was Anne here to gloat? Did she feel remorse for the hurt she had been causing Mary and her mother—a woman she once served loyally?

When face to face, Mary did not bow to Anne or show her any respect as Queen of England—for that she could never be. Yet here she was, the woman who was causing such scandal across all of Europe, a woman hated by every good and true Catholic in England.

Mary thought back to that evening many years ago when she first saw Anne and her father dance. Back then, Mary thought Anne was graceful and intriguing, but the woman standing in front of her had changed drastically. The events of the last few years were etched on her face, as were signs of anxiety and exhaustion. Her once ebony hair had streaks of gray, and she seemed to have lost her infamous charm. Yet, she still moved with an unmistakable grace.

She handed the infant Elizabeth back to Lady Bryan while looking down at the child with what Mary instantly recognized as a mother's love. She had seen that same look in her own mother's eyes. There it was, Anne's one redeeming quality, Mary thought.

Anne turned toward Mary. "Stepdaughter," Anne said when she and Mary came face to face. Mary was surprised by the greeting.

"Madam," Mary responded coldly. "You asked to see me?"

The meeting started off civilly at first. Anne was there to offer Mary an olive branch. She would welcome Mary back to court and pay her respect as the King's daughter, granting her a royal title and any worldly goods she could want. There was, of course, a catch.

Mary must accept Anne as queen, acknowledge Elizabeth as the rightful heir, and pronounce her mother's marriage invalid. In return, she would be treated as a princess in every way but name and be reconciled with her father.

This had to be some sort of jest, Mary thought. How on earth could this woman believe that after all this time, she would just capitulate and betray her conscience, her mother, and the Holy See? The world knew Katherine and Henry's marriage was valid and that Anne was nothing more than a well-dressed, heretical whore, Mary told herself. She would never risk her soul for worldly goods.

"We have been here before, madam. I know of no Queen of England but my mother, and I acknowledge only she as my father's true and lawful wife," Mary said. "But, Lady Anne, if you would intercede with the king on my behalf, I shall be forever grateful."

It was a cold and political response, but enough to bring out Anne's temper.

"You ungrateful, little bastard," Anne fired back. "The universities, parliament, and his grace the Archbishop of Canterbury all agree the king's first marriage to that ancient, sterile relic was incestuous and invalid. You cannot marry your brother's widow! The Bible itself says so."

"And what does the Bible say about marrying a woman whose own sister was previously known carnally by her husband?"

That stopped Anne cold, and Mary thought she might strike her from the fiery rage coming from her eyes. But Anne did nothing.

It was common knowledge that Anne's sister had been mistress to King Henry in the early 1520's. It was even said that the other Boleyn woman's daughter was not her husband's child, but the king's. It was yet another reason that Mary, her mother, and all their supporters believed the king's divorce suit was just a convenient excuse to remove his wife and marry his mistress. After a moment, Anne took a step closer to Mary so she could whisper in her ear.

"This can only end one way," Anne said with an unparalleled coldness in her voice. "It will be with my death or yours. But I promise you, I will bring down the pride of your unbridled Spanish blood if it is the last thing I do."

•　　•　　•

The daily struggles of living in Elizabeth's household were taking their toll on Mary. The continual battles over title and place of honor accompanied by Lady Shelton's unending lectures, threats, and strikes. But it seemed for the moment that Henry and Anne were leaving Mary alone. They were focusing on cementing the king's authority as head of the Church and reforming what they called the abuses of the clergy and the pope.

Chapuys' letters detailed what the King and Anne were doing, and each letter broke Mary's heart a little more. Monasteries were being dissolved, and the money from each was transferred to the royal treasury. Mary said a prayer for the monks and nuns living in the different religious houses who were now being displaced. And the poor, unfortunate souls who sought guidance and relief in those places—where would they turn to now?

As the months dragged on, more and more disturbing reports came in. Back in January 1534, Parliament passed the Act of Supremacy, which declared King Henry Supreme Head of the Church and officially named Mary a bastard. A year later in 1535, he formally accepted the title. Now the king's subjects were required to take an oath acknowledging this title, his marriage to Anne, and any children they had as the lawful and legitimate heirs to the throne. Those who refused to take the oath were imprisoned or worse.

Knowing this, Mary refused to take the oath. Lady Shelton wasted no time reminding Mary that she should take warning from the fate of others. "You are a superfluous nuisance, who has long ago been marked for death," Lady Shelton told Mary after a visit from Archbishop Cranmer.

He had come to Hatfield to get Mary to swear the oath, even going so far as to lie and say Mary's mother finally capitulated and signed it herself. Mary didn't believe him, and the Archbishop left agitated and defeated.

Most of Henry's nobles and ministers happily took the oath. But two prominent men were refusing. Bishop Fisher and Sir Thomas Moore had always supported Mary and her mother and, being devout sons of the Church, would not—rather they could not—accept the king as head of the Church in England. That title, they adamantly said, belonged only to the Holy Father. As the pope already ruled on these matters, they could not accept the judgment of the king or parliament.

In April of 1534, Bishop Fisher and Sir Thomas Moore were arrested and taken to the Tower of London, where they had languished for over a year. Fisher's arrest came as no surprise, but people were stunned by Moore's imprisonment.

Moore had been as close to Henry as any man could be. Yet his support of Mary and her mother, as well as his religious convictions, angered Henry and Anne. Moore refused to attend Anne's coronation a few years earlier and would make no formal acknowledgement of Elizabeth. He never ceased to refer to Mary as princess and Katherine as queen. The lengths to which the king and Anne were willing to go seemed limitless to Mary. In July 1535, Moore and Fisher were tried for treason and condemned to death. Their executions were carried out to the shock of the nation and the world. Their deaths delivered a morbid message about who the King of England was becoming.

But Moore and Fisher wouldn't be the only ones to die for refusing to take the oath that year. When Mary learned of the fate of the Carthusian monks — an order typically held in high esteem and having considerable influence among the English people — she fell to her knees in prayer.

Three Carthusian monks, one Bridgettine monk of Sion, and another priest refused to accept the King's title or his marriage to Anne. They were tried and convicted of treason, and their executions were carried out in front of a horrified crowd at Tyburn. Dressed in their religious garb, the men were hanged, cut down from the gallows while they still lived, then had their torsos sliced open. They screamed in agony as the king's butchers carelessly removed their organs. Finally, they were beheaded, and their corpses were paraded through the streets before being burned. Their severed heads and feet were displayed at the city gates.

Mary felt the vomit rising in her throat as she learned of the fates of these holy men. Retching into a basin, she began to wonder if the king would indeed proceed against her and the queen in the same way. She wondered if she and her mother would be allowed to lodge together in the Tower. She pictured herself on trial, sitting before judges who would have already made up their minds as to her guilt or innocence.

She could see herself walking from the courtroom with the axe turned towards her—showing all the world she had been condemned to die. Would she be brave and composed as she mounted the scaffold steps, or would the sight of the ax, just waiting to slice through her slender neck, cause her to lose her never? Who would go first, mother or daughter? Mary gave way to tears, thinking about her mother having to lay her head on the block. She wondered if the emperor's support was all talk. Would he invade if his aunt and cousin were sentenced to death? Would he arrive in time to rescue them, or would he instead be avenging them?

For the first time, Mary understood that her death and that of her mother would—in the king's mind—mean an end to her father's troubles. With her and her mother gone, no one would dispute Anne as queen or Elizabeth as heir. Mary shuddered.

She contemplated reaching out to Chapuys and asking him to hatch a plan of escape. The emperor's sister, another Mary, was regent of the Netherlands and very vocal in condemning the King's treatment of her aunt and cousin. She may be willing to offer us sanctuary, Mary thought. But she also knew it would be difficult to convince the Queen to abandon England. This course would need considerable thought.

"It is all her. Only the spells of that woman could have forced my father to act so recklessly against a prince of the Church and a man who had been his friend and mentor," Mary said to Margaret one morning while they were made to mend laundry in Elizabeth's nursery.

Margaret was on the floor, mending linen while Mary sat on a small chair. Margaret handled all the chores she and Mary were assigned together, agreeing that it was beneath the dignity of a princess to perform such menial tasks. So far, the young women had been lucky, nobody had discovered the true depth of their friendship. But they both worried it would come out someday.

"What happened to Moore, Fisher and those monks is a travesty," Margaret said. "Those behind their deaths will have much to answer for when they come face to face with our Lord. No doubt you have heard what the people are saying about Fisher?"

"No, what now?"

"Well, my sister writes that the Londoners say the King murdered a saint! After he was killed, Fisher's head was impaled on a pike on London bridge, but it would not decay. Every day, passers-by said the head was wearing the same sad expression Fisher wore in life. It was as though Fisher were keeping a reproving vigil. The miracle of it so frightened the king that he had Fisher's head taken down and tossed into the river.".

Mary said nothing. She crossed herself and said a silent prayer for Fisher and the others. Suddenly the women heard the sound of little feet quickly heading for the nursery. Standing before them was an almost two-year-old Elizabeth, who clearly moved faster than her governess.

Margaret stood up and bowed to the little girl. She had no choice. Mary remained in her chair. The child had a handful of comfits, which she was happily munching on as she toddled over to a small oak chest, lifted the lid and pulled out a doll.

"What are you doing, little one?" Mary asked, "and where is Lady Bryan?"

"Lady Bryan told me to go to my room," the aggravated child said.

"And is she coming?" Mary asked.

"Lady Bryan says I am sick, but I feel fine. And anyway, she shouldn't be allowed to tell me what to do. I'm a Princess."

Mary couldn't help but laugh. She marveled at how forward and advanced her sister was. She thought for a moment about scolding the child on her title, but despite her sharpness, Mary knew Elizabeth was too young to understand. Did she know they were sisters? Mary wondered. What had the girl been told about Mary, and who did the telling?

"Come here, child," Mary beckoned with the wiggle of her finger. Elizabeth waddled over, and Mary placed a hand on her head.

"Elizabeth, you have a fever," Mary scolded. "I want you out of that dress, into your night rail, and tucked under those covers immediately."

Elizabeth tried to protest again that she was fine, but Mary stilled her. "To bed, now, no more arguing." Defeated, Elizabeth did as she was told.

"Go fetch Lady Bryan, tell her to hurry. Elizabeth needs an herbal mixture of sage, lavender, and marjoram," Mary told Margaret. She remembered the many times her loving Lady Pole had made the same simple mixture to cure her illness. How Mary missed her. A word from her former governess was all too rare. But Mary took comfort in knowing Lady Pole was safely home at her estate, enjoying time with her children and grandchildren.

"Is this wise, Your Grace," Margaret asked in a whisper. "Leaving you alone with her, they could accuse you of something. Poison, perhaps."

"You're right. I will go myself to Lady Bryan. Stay here with Elizabeth. Be kind. She is not the cause of my troubles, though her existence does add to them."

"What are you two whispering about? Where are you going?" the child demanded.

"Now, listen, little one, lay back on the pillow and close your eyes, and all will be well soon."

"Yes, sister," Elizabeth said as Mary walked out of the room. She did know.

Elizabeth was ill for days. Her fever raged, and she couldn't keep any food down. One thing the child made abundantly clear—she wanted to be comforted by her older sister.

"Get her. I want her now," she demanded when Lady Shelton protested.

Mary stayed with her sister, comforting her the way she was comforted when battling her many illnesses. Mary decided that when the king finally sent Anne away — a naive hope she still held onto, despite everything—and recalled her and her long-suffering mother back to court, she would ask her father to be good to Elizabeth.

Anne, however, could go to hell, she thought, remembering her threat. But to her sister, she would be loving and kind. Tending to this child, whom she still wanted to hate but couldn't, Mary was once again struck with a yearning to be a mother herself. At almost 20 years old, Mary knew she was too old to still be unwed. She wondered if she would ever know true joy and happiness again. Still, the specter of the ax clouded her thoughts.

One evening while Elizabeth suffered, she and Mary were left with only another of the young maids of the household in attendance. Mary listened with care as Elizabeth wheezed and moaned from her illness, tossing every which way as she was unable to remain comfortable for long.

"Do you think our mother the queen will come soon?" she asked Mary.

"What did you say?" Mary was shocked. Did Elizabeth really believe they shared a mother? She and Anne were only a decade or so apart in age. But Mary supposed that to a child it would be difficult to see.

"Will our mother come soon?"

"Elizabeth, you and I..." Mary trailed off. Why was it her responsibility to tell Elizabeth the true nature of their relationship? The situation was difficult enough to understand as a young adult. How was a child supposed to comprehend it?

Finally, Mary decided she would respond tactfully, again resolving to spare Elizabeth the ugly truth in a way never done for herself.

"Elizabeth, you and I share a father, the king, but our mothers are different ladies," Mary said as her sister tilted her head in confusion.

"Your mother loves you very much," Mary almost choked on those words, "but she doesn't love me, and I do not love her. She and I are not friends. She would not be pleased to know that you and I are so close. These are heavy matters for one so young. Just focus on getting better and all will be well, eventually."

Elizabeth was silent. Her quick mind was working to understand what Mary had just told her, and her feverish words tumbled from her lips.

"Why don't you and mama love each other," Elizabeth asked. "Queen Anne is such a loving and kind mother. You are a wonderful sister, so warm, and sweet."

Mary was silent. She was trying to think of something to say. *Your mother is a whore, who usurped the place of my mother, the rightful Queen of England,* seemed too harsh, Mary thought.

The silence lasted a little longer until, finally, Elizabeth spoke again.

"Well, I love you, sister."

Mary's eyes filled with tears as she kissed the little girl's head. "I love you too."

Not long after Elizabeth recovered, King Henry paid another visit to his youngest daughter. Mary was once again shut away in her room, but this time her jailers did not see fit to lock the door behind them.

Mary seized her chance. Slipping out of her room, Mary made her way up to the leads of the roof, hoping to catch a glimpse of her father as he exited the palace courtyard. As she stepped outside, she saw her father for the first time in years.

She spotted one of Henry's courtiers attract the King's attention and point to where Mary was standing. Seeing her father again, Mary realized she never stopped loving him. For all the pain he was causing her, she saw him as the father he once was—the man she would run to as a little girl, the loving father who would scoop her up into his arms, laughing heartily.

"The pearl of my world," Henry used to call Mary. How she missed that loving name, the sound of her father's voice, and the wonderful feeling of being wrapped up in his affectionate embrace. Tears formed in Mary's eyes as the king finally looked at her. They stared at each other, for how long Mary could not say. Finally, she decided to bow ever so slightly, lowering her eyes and joining her hands together in prayer, hoping her father would show some sign of affection.

Henry looked at his daughter longingly. He bowed to Mary, touching his bonnet, and each of the courtiers accompanying the King followed suit, respectfully saluting the young woman whom some once thought would eventually be their queen. Henry then mounted his horse and left Hatfield. As he looked back while he rode out of the gate, Mary thought she could spot tears in his eyes—but perhaps it was just wishful thinking and a momentary illusion.

CHAPTER 5

1535-1536

That summer Henry and Anne were setting out on a royal progress, a tour across the country. Elizabeth's household was moved to Eltham Palace, just ten miles outside of London, where Henry and Anne would pay another visit to their child before embarking on the months-long journey through the realm.

Once again, Mary was told to stay out of sight of the king. She didn't expect another chance to show herself to her father; the guards watching her appeared to have doubled since her journey to the roof that day.

She found it strange there was no other move against her as punishment. Not even Lady Shelton had anything to say about it. Mary was allowed to be present while the king, Anne, Elizabeth, and the court heard Mass in the chapel. She was, however, regulated to the back, where one of her guards was waiting patiently to hasten her out of the church at the conclusion of the service. The king would not lay eyes on her again.

Going through the motions of Mass, Mary kept trying to subtly get her father's attention, but he would not turn his gaze to her. It frightened Mary how changeable her father could be. While she stared at him from the rooftop, he was his warm and loving self. But now she was looking at a man with ice in his heart.

As Mass came to an end, the guard made his move toward Mary. She stood up, exited her pew and bowed to the altar before making her way out of the chapel. As she was being escorted back to her room, suddenly rushing footsteps came up behind her.

"Wait, My Lady, please," cried Madge Shelton, Anne's cousin and the daughter of her jailer Lady Shelton. Madge was a stout young woman with her cousin's dark eyes and hair, but she didn't seem to have the same grace as Anne. She was huffing and puffing after chasing Mary.

"The queen salutes your grace with much affection and begs your pardon. If she had seen you curtsey toward her, she would have responded in kind. Her Majesty hopes this can be the beginning of a new and loving friendship, which the queen heartily embraces on her part."

Mary stood there stunned as Madge grinned foolishly. Anne honestly thought Mary was acknowledging her as Queen of England. Why would Anne believe she would ever betray her mother, her conscience, and God? Or perhaps her father orchestrated this to remind Mary of her options.

"The queen could not have sent me such a message since she is so far away from this place," Mary responded coldly. "I believe what you meant to say was that Lady Anne has sent word, for there can be no other queen but my mother. As for the reverence that I made, it was made only to He who is the creator of us all. Lady Anne should not be deceived to think otherwise."

Then Mary turned her back and left, feeling a little sorry for Madge, who must now tell Anne and the king that Mary again refused her olive branch. As she made her way back down the corridor, Mary wondered what fresh punishment would come her way now.

The Christmas season of 1535 was as miserable for Mary as the last few seasons. She missed her mother terribly. Chapuys was still writing to Mary. He told her the queen had been getting sick but not to worry and that Katherine's thoughts were always of her daughter.

But the truth was the ambassador was worried for the Queen's life, not wanting to express in writing his fears that Katherine was being poisoned. The queen's own maids, the handful that remained, shared the same fear. They took to preparing Katherine's food themselves, not allowing the cooks at Kimbolton House to touch anything she may eat. But even taking this step, the queen's illness persisted. Those around her were worried she may not be long for this world.

In early December, Elizabeth and most of her household left Eltham Palace for the borough of Richmond, where the court would celebrate the holiday at the king's magnificent palace of Hampton Court. It once belonged to Cardinal Wolsey, the late clergyman who had given the palace as a gift to King Henry when he lamented about having nothing as fine as the palace the cardinal had built.

Once the cardinal had vacated, Henry and Anne wasted no time in refurbishing Hampton Court to their liking. Lady Shelton was one of the members of Elizabeth's household who went to court, much to Mary's relief. Mary and only a handful of servants were ordered to return to Hatfield, where Elizabeth would reside again after the holidays. The servants mostly left Mary to her own devices. Sadly, Margaret was among those who would be spending Christmas at court.

In late December, Mary was stunned to receive a visitor to Hatfield. It was Maria de Salinas, Queen Katherine's most loyal supporter and her longtime friend. Maria had come to England in Katherine's train all those years ago when Katherine's future in England was filled with hope and promise.

Maria had been forbidden by the king to visit Katherine, but the brave woman she was ignored that command. After seeing the state her dear friend was in, Maria knew immediately she must get to Mary. Maria did not care if Henry found out she visited Katherine, but she knew her visit to Mary had to be done as tactfully as possible, as did the next part of her plan.

"Your Grace," Maria addressed Mary when they were alone in a parlor, "I am here to bring you to your mother, Queen Katherine."

Mary couldn't believe it. "How can that be? We are forbidden to see one another!"

"I don't care, princess. Your mother is very sick, and I fear she may not be with us much longer."

Maria noticed the horrific shock on Mary's face. "I'm sorry, princess, I know Ambassador Chapuys has been getting letters to you. I thought he would have told you."

"I think he did not want to worry me," Mary said, tears welling in her eyes. "Even so, I don't see how we may pull this off. Even with so few people here, I am constantly watched and would be recognized on the road."

"We will say you are sick again and must retire to your chamber, then I will return tonight after midnight with one of my maids. She will take your place in your bed, refusing entry to anyone. We will disguise you in plain servants' garments and take my coach to your mother, who is only a few hours' journey from here. Two of my late husband's most loyal men will be with us for protection."

Mary's head was spinning. She thought she might be sick after all. Her mind racing, she wasn't sure what the right decision would be. Her instincts told her to run to her mother and see her one final time.

Perhaps a visit would even restore the queen to health. But what if her father, or worse, Anne, were to discover what she had done? Mary's fears of her father and Anne had flourished during her time in Elizabeth's household. Some even said the king contemplated putting Mary to death over her refusal to take the oath and accept all the king had been demanding of her. But after consideration, Mary realized she already knew what to do.

"I will go to my mother, the queen. We will do our best to keep this from the king, but if he learns the truth of it, I will beg for mercy, and should he not grant it ..." Mary couldn't finish.

Maria went to Mary and hugged her tightly, which the young, frightened woman welcomed with all her heart. "All will be well," Maria said. "I will see you tonight, princess."

With that, Maria was gone, and Mary began to feign her illness, telling those remaining in the house she was going to bed and was not to be disturbed. Around midnight, she slipped out of her room and went through the kitchens to let Maria's maid in. The girl looked similar to Mary, though their voices were very different. The maid's voice was mellifluous and smooth, while Mary's was deep and gruff.

There was no time to quibble about that though. Mary led the maid to her room and instructed her to keep the door locked until she returned. "The house is deserted save a few servants. They should leave you alone."

Mary handed the maid her own night rail, and she slipped into the simple, black dress Maria had told the girl to bring to her. Peering out into the hall, Mary saw that no one was coming and made her way toward where Maria and her men would be waiting. As she was about to round the corner Mary spied a pair of guards making their way toward her. Mary's heart leapt into her chest as she quickly ran back to her room.

She knocked on the door softly, "Girl, let me in quickly," she whispered.

"Madam, what is the matter?" The servant asked.

"There were guards blocking my path. I thought they would have made their rounds by now," she said, slightly out of breath. "I don't know if I can do this."

The maid simply stared at her with pity and confusion. It made Mary long for Margaret. Her help would be invaluable at this time. Before venturing into the hall again, Mary poured herself some wine and took a large, un-ladylike gulp to settle her nerves. She bolted quickly out the door, afraid if she didn't move as fast as her legs would carry her, she would succumb to her fear and abandon the chance to see her mother. Mary made it out of the palace, but Maria and her carriage were not waiting at the agreed upon spot. Mary began to panic, wondering if the delay caused Maria to leave or worse, if she was caught waiting for her. Mary made her way toward the road, hoping for some clue as to what happened. There she saw the coach approaching. Maria had also been delayed. When she came upon Mary, she found the girl trembling with fear.

"We'll never get away with this, Maria," Mary said.

"Calm yourself, princess, you cannot appear before the queen in such hysterics. All will be well. It is after midnight; nobody will be on the road. Come now, we must move quickly."

The ride to Kimbolton was frigid and long, lasting about five hours. It was nearly dawn when they arrived. Mary couldn't believe how close her mother had been this whole time. She was terrified they would be discovered and hardly spoke to Maria beyond chit-chat during the trip.

She kept picturing Katherine's jailers stopping them before they got through the door. She could see herself being dragged kicking and screaming back to the carriage, her mother hearing her cries, unable to do anything about it.

"How will you get me in?" she asked Maria.

"We're going to walk right through the front doors."

Mary was shocked. "Are you mad? We'll be stopped and hauled off to the Tower!"

"Princess, do you know the queen's jailer, Sir Edward Bedingfield?" Mary shook her head. "Exactly, you have never met him, and he has never met you. Nobody is going to recognize you as the princess in those clothes. I will walk up and tell that jellyfish he must let my servant and me in to see the queen."

Mary was full of terror. She was certain Maria's plan was doomed to fail, but if she could see her mother for just a moment before they dragged her away, it might be worth it.

The carriage stopped out of sight of the gatehouse, part of Maria's plan. "We'll walk from here," she said.

The door opened, and one of Maria's grooms extended his hand to help Mary out of the carriage, a young man she heard Maria call John. When she looked at him and placed her hand in his, Mary was filled with a sensation she had never experienced before. There was a warm tingling feeling spreading in her chest.

This simple groom was the most beautiful human being Mary had ever seen. His eyes were a deep honey color, inviting and warm. He was tall, with a heart-shaped face. He had brown-reddish hair and a beard.

John's beard must tickle when he kisses a woman, Mary thought, then immediately scolded herself, wondering what kind of thought was that to have at such a time. John helped Mary down and then Maria. Mary hoped he did not notice the blush in her cheeks when their hands touched. If he did, she prayed he'd think it was due to the cold. The kind smile and nod John gave her suggested otherwise.

When Maria exited the carriage, she tore at her elegant skirt, messed up her coiffed hair, and tossed her hood to the side. She did the same to Mary's clothes and hair. Mary looked at her, puzzled. "You'll see, princess." She instructed Mary to stay behind her. "Remember, you're supposed to be my maid. Keep your eyes downcast. And you two," Maria said, pointing to the grooms, "stay close but don't be seen. If this goes wrong, we'll need to move fast."

They approached the house and Mary did as Maria said. When Sir Edward came to greet them, he seemed annoyed to see Maria again. Sir Edward told her he had no word from the king about Katherine having a guest. She had already been allowed entry and would not be allowed in again.

"Sir, my maid and I had trouble along the way. We were tossed from our horses, and the poor scared creatures ran off. You can see from our torn clothes it was a bad fall. I lost the papers giving me permission from the king to see the dowager princess."

Maria had warned Mary she would use the false title they imposed on Queen Katherine to play the game and gain access. But it still hurt to hear one so loyal to Katherine use that title.

Sir Edward looked at Maria with suspicion, but to Mary's shock, her ploy worked, and Sir Edward let them in the house. "Keep your hood up until Sir Edward leaves us alone with the queen," Maria whispered. "We don't want your mother to get too excited when she sees you."

When they entered the poorly lit room, Maria made it clear to Sir Edward that he was no longer needed. She also dismissed Katherine's few servants, and when they all left the room, she locked the door behind them. Across the small room Queen Katherine was lying in her bed. She looked pale, exhausted, and worn. Each breath she took was a struggle.

She turned to look at Maria and began to cry. Katherine couldn't believe her old friend had defied the king's command and come to see her twice.

"I have brought someone else to see you, my lady, but you must remain calm. Your excitement cannot betray our ploy."

Katherine was confused. She watched a tall, slender girl in a black cloak make her way from the shadow of the door and come into the room. She drew back her hood and looked directly at Katherine. "Sweet Jesus child, is it really you? Are you here or do I have a fever?"

"I'm here, mother," Mary said, running to Katherine's bed. Feeling more strength in that moment than she had in weeks, Katherine flung herself toward Mary, enveloping her dear child in a loving embrace. For the first time in years, mother and daughter were together again. They both wept uncontrollably until finally Katherine broke away.

"How is this possible? The king will be furious. Child, your life is in danger. You must go! Maria, take her back. I command it!"

"No, mother, I will not go, not yet at least."

Katherine was stunned by the strong young woman standing before her. Her convictions that Mary should rule after her father grew stronger at that moment. Seeing Mary this way reaffirmed to Katherine she was doing the right thing in refusing to compromise her conscience and bend to the king's demands. She thought about what a glorious queen Mary will make, wishing she could live to see it.

Mother and daughter spent several glorious hours together discussing how much they missed each other and praying for the day when the king would relent and see the light. Mary kept her answers vague when Katherine asked about life at Hatfield; she did not want to burden her mother with the full depth of her troubles.

"You are truly content living in that child's household?" Katherine asked Mary.

"Yes, mother, as content as I can be. I am left to my own devices, and my dear maid Margaret was sent to live there as well, so we have each other for company. Truly, mother, you must not worry. Concentrate only on getting better. You will need all of your strength when we return to court."

"My sweet, innocent girl," Katherine said, cupping Mary's face.

Mary laid her head down on Katherine's lap, and Katherine began to gently stroke her hair. At that moment, Mary realized how exhausted she was and began to drift to sleep. She was holding her mother's hand tightly. She wasn't sure how much time had passed when she woke up to her mother looking down at her lovingly. Katherine was exhausted too but refused to take her eyes off her beloved child, even for a moment.

The entire time they were together Mary couldn't help but notice the change in her mother. She was older, frailer, and Mary wondered if this would be the last time she and her mother would see one another.

"Your Majesty, princess," Maria said softly as she slowly cracked the door to Katherine's room. She had been standing guard outside. "We haven't much time left."

"I cannot leave you now," Mary said to her mother.

"You must, child," Katherine replied lovingly. "I know God is on our side. He will not abandon us. This isn't goodbye."

"He has already abandoned us," Mary said, agitated and shocked at her blasphemy.

Seeing the look on Katherine's face, Mary quickly apologized. "I am sorry, mother. I did not mean that. I know it is not my place to question God's judgment. He must have his reasons for sending us these troubles."

"Of course, he does, my darling girl," Katherine said, tears welling in her eyes. "For how can you be a great Queen if you have led an easy life? You are no spoiled heir, my girl. You will fight for your place in this world, and when the day finally comes and the crown is placed on your head, you will understand God's reasoning."

When it came time to say farewell, Mary and Katherine couldn't let each other go. When they finally broke away from one another, Katherine reminded her of something she had once written in a letter.

"Obey the king in everything, my child," she said, "except that which would offend God and imperil your soul."

Katherine kissed her daughter on the head and watched Mary leave, knowing she would never see her beloved girl again.

CHAPTER 6

1536

It was early January, and most of Elizabeth's household had returned to Hatfield after the Christmas celebrations, but Elizabeth, Lady Bryan, and a few maids were staying behind at Hampton Court for a little while longer. Much to Mary's dismay, Lady Shelton would soon return to Hatfield, but Margaret would also be with her, offering Mary some bittersweet excitement for their arrival. Mary was eager for Margaret to let her know what was happening at court and what advice Chapuys was sending along with her.

Sitting alone in a parlor one afternoon, Mary sipped some warm pear cider while enjoying the last few precious moments of solitude before the household filled again. A fire roared, yet the chill January air was still felt, leaking in through a crack in one of the windows overlooking the snow-covered gardens.

She heard clamoring in the halls and outside the window, telling her Elizabeth's household was returning. She remained in her seat, watching the fire devour the logs in the hearth, when Lady Shelton came stomping in.

"Lady Mary," she started. Mary just looked at the fire. "You should know that Mistress Margaret Groby has been dismissed from Princess Elizabeth's household."

Mary turned to her in shock and anger. "You should not be so surprised! How long did you think you two could keep up your charade? Mistress Margaret was seen conspiring with her sister and the Spanish Ambassador Chapuys. They have been sent home to their family in disgrace, and you all should count yourselves lucky that the king and queen chose not to proceed further against you! When will you learn that you have no place in this world save for what their majesties decide for you? You would do well to remember that you are nothing more than the king's bastard, a person of no importance who none would miss if some mishap were to befall you."

"There will come a day when you will regret your words," Mary said coldly.

"I doubt that very much, Lady Mary. When the queen, who is again with child, is delivered of a son, we know what shall befall you."

Lady Shelton turned away, walking out of the parlor. But she stopped at the doorway. Looking over her shoulder she had one last blow to deliver to Mary.

"Oh, I had almost forgotten. Lady Katherine, the Dowager Princess of Wales, died at Kimbolton four days ago." With that, Lady Shelton swept out of the room.

Mary spent days closeted in her room in an inconsolable state of grief and depression. She felt as though she wasn't inside her own body anymore. The weight of losing her mother was like a stone around her neck. She thought she would drown in her own tears and, for the briefest of moments, welcomed the idea of never waking again. Food held no interest. When Lady Bryan attempted to rouse her for morning prayers and duties, Mary stared blankly at the wall, unable to perceive the woman in her room. She knew Lady Bryan was speaking, but she couldn't hear anything. She held so tightly to the rosary her mother had given her as a gift that the beads began to cut into her skin. It burned, and she could feel the trickles of blood seeping from her hand, but still, she didn't move. Mary slept all day and was awake all night. She would howl her heart out as she thought of her mother's final moments.

She wanted to know who was there when her mother died, what caused the queen's illness, and if it were possible that Anne and her faction had hastened Katherine's death by foul means. What she learned chilled her to the bone.

The embalmer's report —of which Chapuys had gotten a copy and sent to Mary—showed that all of the late queen's organs and tissues were normal, except for her heart. It sported a large, hideous black growth that no amount of washing would remove.

Mary believed it could only have been caused by poison. With her mother out of the way, Mary was certain Anne would be coming for her next. She wondered if her mother had been in much pain. Would death by poison be a better way to die than by the ax? Surely the pain would not be as great, she thought.

Mary also wondered what the emperor was thinking. Would her cousin move to avenge his aunt? Mary knew he was busy with his war with the Turks, but the insult done to his family by King Henry might be too much to ignore.

Mary knew that if the emperor was to move against England, he would have supporters here. Chapuys kept her abreast of what the people at court and the realm at large were saying about the King's religious reforms.

While the King and his mistress had their supporters, the majority of the realm, especially those in the north and the old nobility, were staunchly Catholic and believed the King and his kingdom were being led into sin by an evil council. The people, Chapuys wrote to her, looked to Mary as a symbol of the true faith. Nobody would rally in Elizabeth's name to challenge Mary's claim to the throne were God to call away her father. Mary was sure Henry and Anne knew this too. If they were to secure the future of their issue and the son Anne believed she was carrying, Mary would have to go. The thoughts threw Mary into a frenzy.

Night after night Mary cloistered herself away in her room, going over and over her precarious situation. When she finally drifted off, she was tormented by horrid dreams.

She found herself exiting the White Tower, the cold winter wind stinging her face as she attempted to adjust her eyes to the sunlight. It had been dark and grim in the dungeon where she was being kept. Walking a few yards through a crowd of angry onlookers shouting obscenities at her, Mary mounted the scaffold. It was tall and seemed to reach the sky. Looking out at the crowd who'd come to witness her death, it was as though the entire world came to see the princess meet her fate. When she finally reached the platform, Mary looked across and saw Anne. She was sitting on a golden throne smiling from ear to ear. The king was sitting at her feet. She was stroking his head as though he were a dog. Mary tried to speak, but no sound would come. Then suddenly she was forced down onto the block, and that is when the blow came. The ax was so sharp, the impact crushing, the pain excruciatingly real. Mary woke from her nightmare screaming, sweat pouring off her face, and panting uncontrollably. At that moment, she knew it was time to put an escape plan into motion.

Her pen flew across the page faster than her mind had time to form the words she wanted to write. She needed to get this letter to Chapuys. The ambassador was able to buy the services of a page in Elizabeth's household. As long as the money held out, he'd happily dispatch letters for them and keep Chapuys updated with the goings-on around Mary.

My most loyal friend, Mary wrote, *it is out of haste and mortal fear that I am begging you most urgently to think over the matter of my escape. Otherwise, I consider myself lost, knowing they desperately want me to be keeping company with my late mother, the queen."*

Weeks went by with no reply, and Mary fell further into despair, becoming violently ill again. She could not take much food or drink, vomiting up what little contents her stomach could hold. She wrote again to Chapuys, begging him to seek the emperor's help and spirit her out of England and into safety.

Finally, she received word from Chapuys that a plan was taking shape. The emperor had contacted his captain-general in the Netherlands, who was sending his most able man to England to rescue Mary.

By this time next month, your grace will be living safely in Flanders, under the protection of the emperor, Chapuys wrote to Mary. Laying on her side in her bed, the coverlet pulled up to her cheek, Mary slipped the letter under her pillow and began to weep.

Chapuys' letter brought her more comfort than she had felt in weeks. But her relief dissipated quickly and was followed by an unbearable wave of guilt.

Mary chided herself for her cowardice. Running away was never an option for Queen Katherine, Mary thought. I will not be seen as a weak and feeble woman who abandoned her rights, her people, and her supporters. History will not call Princess Mary Tudor a coward. As quickly as she decided to flee, Mary decided now the right move was to stay, even if it meant her death. She wrote to Chapuys again.

I must remain in England. Who am I to decide otherwise if it be God's will that I suffer martyrdom? I will not dishonor the memory of my mother, who suffered many troubles with courage and grace, by running away. Whatever God has planned for me, it must play out here.

Mary sealed the letter and slipped out of her room to find Chapuys' spy. She went to the stables where the boy peacefully slept on a tall stack of hay bales. She paused, looking down at the letter in her hand, her heart pounding quickly. Maybe this is wrong, she thought. Living in Flanders might be the best choice after all.

She spent endless minutes trying to decide what to do. Every second that ticked by made her heart break a little more. Finally, she decided. She walked up to the sleeping page and cleared her throat loudly. The boy jolted awake.

"See that this letter gets to Ambassador Chapuys without delay," Mary commanded. The boy nodded, and she turned on her heel and hastily fled back towards the house. She spent the rest of the evening in the chapel praying.

Mary was shocked when she received word from the king that she would be removed from Elizabeth's household in late March. No reason was given, only that she must go to Hunsdon House in Hertfordshire within the week. Additionally, none of Elizabeth's household would be there attending to her, meaning Mary was finally to be free of Lady Shelton.

But she wondered if she was exchanging one hell for another. What would be waiting for her at Hunsdon? Would the king and Anne be appointing someone worse than Lady Shelton? Mary shuddered at that thought. Was Hunsdon just a stop before the Tower? No doubt the King would again demand Mary sign the oath of supremacy, and again Mary would refuse.

Mary left Hatfield with little ceremony; none of Elizabeth's servants or attendants were allowed to bow to Mary as she made her exit. Elizabeth was the only one sad to see her go. No doubt those who had been her jailers were happy to see the back of her, glad to be rid of their unwanted burden.

"Why must you go, sister?" Elizabeth asked.

"The king, our father, commands it," she replied. "And the king must always be obeyed."

Mary could feel Lady Shelton roll her eyes when she said that. Tears welled in Elizabeth's eyes as she said goodbye to her older sister. Elizabeth had been oblivious to what life was like for Mary under her roof and believed Mary was just as sad at her departure as she was. Mary mounted her horse; two of the king's men were there to escort her to her new residence.

As they reached Hunsdon, Mary could hear a commotion ahead of her. Her heart started to beat harder at the sound of a large crowd. Slowing her horse to a walk, she saw a great throng of people in front of her new residence. When the people saw Mary coming, they went silent and fell onto their knees in front of her. When they heard she was coming to Hunsdon, the people wanted Mary to know they loved and supported her as they did her mother.

Flocked by people on either side, Mary slowly walked her horse toward the great house, nodding in gratitude at each person. She smiled as a little girl boldly darted out to attempt to hand Mary a bundle of flowers. When the child was stopped by one of her guards, Mary quickly dismounted her horse and demanded the guard let the girl go. Mary walked over to the child and knelt beside her, placing an arm on her shoulder and wiping away the girl's tears.

"What is your name, dear one," Mary asked.

"Katherine," she responded, "My mother named me after the queen."

"I am sure my mother would have been most honored by that gesture," Mary said as she took the flowers from the girl.

The guards behind her were agitated by Mary's interaction with the people. But they were quick to notice that some of the men were carrying scythes, pitchforks and other farming tools that could quickly become weapons. They decided to let the situation play out.

Taking little Katherine by the hand, Mary led her back to the woman she assumed was the child's mother. "God bless your grace," the woman said with a bow before taking the child's hand.

"God save you, Princess Mary," someone in the crowd shouted, and soon the entire congregation joined in the cheer.

Mary remounted her horse, made the sign of the cross, and blessed the gathering.

"I am overwhelmed by your love and support," she said, trying to hide the emotion in her voice. "May our Lord and Savior, Jesus Christ, and his blessed mother keep and watch over you."

Mary continued on her way, nobody from the crowd leaving until she was out of sight. Life at Hunsdon was not as stifling as Mary had expected. She was allowed more attendants—almost as many as she had during her tenure as England's only princess. She could also receive visitors and the freedom to write letters without secrecy. The months went by without incident, and Mary allowed herself to feel hopeful that she'd get to enjoy a pleasant spring. The best part about her move to Hunsdon was that Margaret had been allowed to rejoin her household.

When Mary and Margaret were first reunited at Hunsdon, they abandoned all formalities, hugging as though they were long lost sisters, their eyes filled with tears. Mary was as delighted to see her dear friend as she was confused by her presence in her household again.

All Margaret knew was that her father received word from Lord Cromwell that she was to go to Hunsdon where she would attend Lady Mary. Even though he was wary of his daughter returning to Mary's service, he did not want to insult the king and fall further from favor by refusing.

On their first evening together, Mary and Margaret stayed up all night talking. They drank spiced wine and enjoyed candied fruits as they caught up on their time apart. In between bouts of laughter and tears, Mary and Margaret lamented that they were both in their twentieth year and still unmarried.

Margaret spoke of her sister Jane, who had married a handsome young gentleman of means. The man worked closely with Cromwell. Margaret's father worked hard to regain favor after his daughters' espionage on Mary's behalf was discovered.

His efforts appeared to pay off with his eldest daughter's marriage. It was a lucky match for her sister, and Margaret expected news of Jane being with child before her first year of marriage was complete.

Feeling grateful that Margaret and her sister were not punished too harshly for their actions, Mary felt the familiar pang of jealousy as Margaret spoke of her sister's happy life. She wondered again what it would be like to be loved by a man and was transported back to that day she had met the groom John on her visit to her mother.

She would often revisit that memory, thinking of the spark she felt when John took her hand and helped her down from the carriage. She wondered how such a brief moment could stay with her so firmly. She could remember every feature of his face, warm eyes, and kind smile. She wondered how it would feel to kiss him, his beard tickling her face.

What went on between a man and woman beyond kissing was still a mystery to Mary. She understood it took two people to create life, but an understanding of the passion and excitement of the act still eluded her.

As peaceful as this new living arrangement appeared, Mary knew she was by no means secure, though the incident with the crowd told her the king may be fearful of the people's reaction should he make a move against her. She still had doubts, fears, and concerns. There has been no word from the king since being told she was moving out of her sister's household, no threats from the court, no demands that she sign the oath. Too much had happened over the years for Mary to think her father and Anne had simply relented.

"My lady, Ambassador Chapuys is here to see you," Margaret said with a curtsey.

Mary shielded her eyes from the sunny May day as Margaret made her exit so she and Chapuys could speak in private. As he walked toward her, Mary noticed an air of triumph about

Chapuys. His smile stretched from ear to ear, and when he came up to Mary, he bowed so low it was as though she were the Queen of England herself.

"My friend, what has you in such a jubilant mood?" she asked, gesturing for Chapuys to take a seat on the bench beside her.

"My lady, it has finally happened," Chapuys exclaimed. "The concubine and her faction have fallen! She and her whole cursed family are out of favor with the king. She is utterly ruined!"

"What are you talking about?"

"Two days ago, the concubine was arrested for treason and taken to the Tower."

Mary's eyes widened as she crossed herself. She was trying to wrap her mind around what Chapuys had just told her.

"It seems that on the day of your mother's funeral, the concubine miscarried a son. Afterward, the king was heard to berate her and exclaimed that God would permit him no male children if he continued their marriage.

She fired back that the miscarriage was the king's fault because she had walked in on him with one of her ladies in waiting, a mistress Jane Seymour."

"This is unbelievable," Mary said. "Yet how did charges of treason spring up months after her miscarriage?"

"Well, at first, it was believed that mistress Seymour was just another of the king's passing fancies, but it seems that is no longer the case. The king means to marry her once Anne is out of the way. Master Cromwell set his spies to work and discovered," Chapuys paused to take a breath, "the concubine had been unfaithful to the king with five men, one of the five a lowly musician and another her own brother!"

"Good God," Mary exclaimed. "Her own brother! How could *she* even stoop so low?"

"There is more, Your Grace," Chapuys said. Though Mary didn't know if she could handle any more news.

"They say her daughter is not the King's child but was fathered by one of her lovers, though the King has not acknowledged this."

At that, Mary felt dizzy. Elizabeth, not her father's child. Could it be?

"What is to happen to Elizabeth?"

"The king's previous relationship with Anne's sister has been cited as the reason their marriage is null. Elizabeth will finally be known for the little bastard she is," Chapuys said.

Mary knew she should have chided him for speaking of an innocent child thus, but she also thought of how she was treated in the same manner, with no one there to defend her.

"The concubine is to be tried on the fifteenth of May and her accomplices as well. The charges are to also include accusations of plotting the death of the king," Chapuys continued. "It is said that she wished to have the king killed and then marry one of her lovers and rule the kingdom through her bastard daughter."

"I.. I.. I don't ..." Mary couldn't find the words for several moments. Chapuys just regarded her patiently, waiting for it all to sink in. Finally, Mary started to sob.

"It's over. It is finally over," Mary cried. "I have prayed so hard for this. If only it could have come to be before my mother departed this life. When will I be summoned back to court? Surely the king now sees this was all the doing of that adulteress witch? He must know of the love I bear for him, and now he can restore the true faith to England, and all will be set right!"

Chapuys looked at Mary with pity in his eyes. After all this time, she still could not see that the King would never admit he was wrong, only that he was *wronged*. Not wanting to dull Mary's joy, he simply offered her muted reassurance.

"I would not expect anything just yet, Your Grace. The king will no doubt be preoccupied at this time. Yet I am told this new lady, mistress Seymour, is of the true faith and inclined to restore you to the king's favor."

Mary breathed a sigh of relief so deep it was as though she had just emerged from the depths. She knew it wouldn't be long now. Soon she'd be back in her father's loving embrace. She would willingly forgive him for everything. She told herself once again that none of the torment she and her mother had suffered could have been the king's doing. It was Anne and those devil's servants Cranmer and Cromwell. If only they were joining in her fall.

· · ·

On the morning of May 19th, Mary woke before dawn. She tried to stay quiet, not wanting to alert any of her household that she was up. She made her way over to the casement window and flung it open. She knew that Anne Boleyn was greeting her final sunrise, miles from Hunsdon.

A pitcher of wine sat on the table by the window. Mary poured a cup but couldn't drink it. Her stomach was in knots, and her breathing was shallow. Her nerves were on edge, but she didn't know why. It was not as though she were about to face the headsman's sword, Mary thought.

Still, Mary was feeling unsettled. As she became lost in her thoughts, they turned to her baby sister. "Is she my sister?" Mary wondered aloud. But the girl was about to lose her mother, and she felt pity for the innocent child. At that thought, Mary did something she never expected she would do. Crossing herself, Mary began to pray.

"Blessed Virgin, Mother of God, allow *her* end to be quick and with no pain. God in Heaven, you know she deserves her fate, yet I would ask you to grant this small mercy, not for her, but for her child. Dear Jesus, please give me the strength not to feel vengeful toward my enemy, though she would have done so to me with no compunction."

Tears streamed down Mary's face as she was flooded with relief after finishing her prayer. She knew that soon her troubles would end. As she watched the hands of the clock tick slowly toward the appointed hour, she strained toward the open window, hoping that even so far away, she'd hear the Tower cannons announcing Anne's death.

CHAPTER 7

Summer 1536

Mary sat staring at the blank parchment, her heart lurching at the thought of what she was about to do. It had been almost a month since Anne's execution, and still, the king had not seen fit to recall Mary to court. He had married his new queen, Jane Seymour, eleven days after Anne went to her death.

Chapuys had visited Mary shortly after Anne's execution with a slightly changed tone. "God knows the concubine deserved her fate for her past transgressions," Chapuys said. "Yet now it seems there was something malapropos about the accusations against her."

Mary didn't care to listen. She was dismayed to hear him speak of Anne in a somewhat friendly way.

"Has she finally worked her spells on you, ambassador?" Mary barked at Chapuys as they walked in the gardens at Hunsdon. "It is a shame her enchantments did not take hold before her justified end!"

Chapuys stared at her dumbfounded. "Madam, I didn't mean to suggest I believe her to be an innocent victim, just that there may have been more to her fall than appears. She long deserved a meeting with the headsman. It just seems strange that a woman who spent more than a decade chasing a king and a crown would stoop so low as to sleep with a lowly musician. Mark Smeaton, her personal musician, was the only one of the five men she was accused with to confess his guilt. And that only came after Cromwell's men tortured the poor wretch. I think Cromwell may have concocted the entire thing to be rid of her."

"Nonsense! She was a whore!" Mary shouted. "She was an adulteress witch who used her charms and enchantments to lure my father from my sainted mother! She tried to torment the queen to death, and when that didn't work, she resorted to poison! She wanted to do the same to me and may have succeeded had her contravention not been discovered!"

It was only shortly afterwards when he informed her of the new marriage. He delivered the news with little explanation but a disapproving face.

Snapping back into the present, Mary dipped her quill in ink and began her letter to Cromwell. It galled her to beg for the help of such a notorious heretic, but she was feeling desperate.

Master Secretary,

I would have written to you sooner to ask you to intercede on my behalf and bring about a reconciliation between my most illustrious father, His Majesty the King, and myself. Yet I knew nobody would have dared speak for me as long as that woman lived. Thankfully she is now gone, and I pray our Lord in His great mercy to forgive her. Please, I humbly ask you to plead my case to the king. Begging that he remember I am his most loving daughter. I beg for his blessing and forgiveness for my past transgressions in as humble and lowly a manner as a child can.

Cromwell's response was prompt. He drafted a letter of submission to the king, which Mary merely had to sign and return. Cromwell assured her that all would be well again between her and the king if she did that. Reading over Cromwell's letter, Mary felt a pang of regret. The king still wanted her to admit her mother's marriage was unlawful, and that she is a bastard with no legitimate claim to the throne. It was something Mary knew she could never sign the submission with a clear conscience.

Taking up her quill she made alterations to Cromwell's original draft and returned it. In a covering letter Mary thanked Cromwell for his efforts and told him she would follow his advice, but only so far as God would allow. *I have done the utmost my conscience will suffer me,* she wrote, *and I can do no more.*

Cromwell fired back an angry response.

I warn you, my lady, that should you not comply, you will find me a friend no more. You do not seem to comprehend how perilous your situation truly is. Do not mistake the king's silence for absolution. His Grace will not hesitate to proceed against you should you continue your obstinace.

Feeling defeated, Mary copied Cromwell's letter of submission again and sent it back with no changes. Cromwell was thrilled that Mary had finally capitulated. He sent word that she should expect a visit from members of the king's privy council.

Mary was intent on receiving the king's counselor in as royal a manner as possible. She had her maids dress her in a French-style gown of crimson satin with pearls lining the square neckline and trailing down the long bell sleeves. She added a large ruby brooch, which her late aunt, the French Queen, bequeathed to her in her will. Her hair she wore loose and, as a final touch, wrapped several stands of pearls around her neck with large emerald, sapphire, and other precious stone rings on her long, slender fingers.

It had been many years since Mary had last seen these gentlemen. She tried to shake away the memories of being removed from her home at Beaulieu to serve in Elizabeth's household. She shuddered to think of the men's cruelty, of their indifference as Lady Shelton struck her for standing her ground. She knew this exchange would be different.

She received the king's commissioners in the great hall at Hunsdon; the Dukes of Norfolk and Sussex and the Bishop of Chester had all come on the king's orders. When they entered the room and saw Mary in all her finery, they made only the slightest of obeisances. Puzzled, Mary spoke first.

"My lords, I am so glad you have come to see me."

"Lady Mary," Norfolk said coldly, "we have come here to present you with the oath of supremacy, which declares the king as Supreme Head of the Church of England, denies the authority of the Bishop of Rome, and recognizes that as the king was never lawfully married before his union with Queen Jane, any issue from those couplings are illegitimate and incapable of inheriting the English crown."

Mary was stunned. She did not expect the king to proceed in such a way, not after she signed the submission sent by Cromwell. Thinking of her mother, Mary stiffened and replied in her old, familiar way.

"As I love my father and am a dutiful subject to him, I still cannot risk my soul by going against what I know in my heart to be the true faith. The faith of my mother, the late Queen of England."

"You do not love your father and king, my lady," Sussex barked. "You cannot, as you insist on denying his true authority and refuse to acknowledge the incestuous nature of his union with the Dowager Princess of Wales!"

"We will return to the king and tell him how unnatural and monstrous a daughter you are," Norfolk added. "Yours is such a freakish departure from the natural obedience of a daughter to her father that I marvel the king can still hold any love for you in his heart."

"Madam, you must submit to the king," the bishop added, more warmly than her other guests. "You must swear to submit to him, his laws, and all official declarations as they relate to his union with Lady Katherine. The king will forgive you for everything if you do this. After all, he knows you are only a woman, incapable of understanding the true weight of these matters, as you are being advised by those hostile to the king."

Mary was fighting back tears as they berated her. "I will obey my father in all things, save that which will touch my conscience and imperil my immortal soul."

"You ungrateful little bastard," Norfolk screamed. "I tell you plainly that I doubt you are even the king's child, for no child of his, not even a bastard, could be as willful and obdurate as you! If you were my daughter, I would beat you to death, and no man could call it unjustified! I would bash your skull against a wall until it was as soft as a boiled apple!"

Mary spent five days after the commissioner's visit sick in bed. The familiar pains in her head and stomach had returned. She could keep down no food and hardly drank anything. She would not have risen from bed at all had Margaret not burst in on the fifth day to say she must rise and receive Ambassador Chapuys.

Whatever it was he had to say could not wait. Weakly Mary held out her hand so Margaret could help her up. When she met him in the parlor, Chapuys could not hide his dismay at her appearance. He had seen Mary when she was ill, but never looking so worn and wasted. Her pale face made her red hair stand out more, though it was soaked with sweat. Not bothering to invite Chapuys to join her, Mary took a seat near the open casement window. She was sweltering from a fever, and the June heat was too oppressive. She prayed for a cooling breeze.

"You have something urgent to tell me?" she said coldly, looking out the window.

"My lady, you are in the most extreme danger, and I am here to implore you to submit entirely to the king's will. The king is having his council investigate a charge of treason against you. If they find any evidence, the king will not hesitate to instate an act of attainder against you. If you do not submit, you will surely face the ax!"

Mary buried her face in her hands. "No, he will not. He could not!"

Abandoning protocol, Chapuys joined Mary at the window, wrapping a loving arm around her. "My dear lady, he can and he will. Please hear me. I understand the scruple of conscience you feel. I admire your strength and courage. You are your mother's daughter through and through. But please, listen to me. Your mother fought to the death to ensure you always remain the king's only trueborn child and heir. She died believing you can and should rule England after your father. The people know this. They believe it too. If you suffer martyrdom, no one will be left in England to pull it back from the brink. You have been placed here to save England from sin and restore the true faith. The king has had little luck in siring sons. There is no guarantee his new queen will provide him with a male heir. You must be ready to take your place on the throne if God should call away the king."

Mary was trembling. Chapuys pulled a document from his coat pocket. The heading was written in an elegant and large script: *The Submission of the Lady Mary*. She choked back a sob when she saw it. Chapuys startedto open it, but Mary stopped him.

"What does it say?"

"It acknowledges your parents' marriage was never legal. It denies the authority of the pope and recognizes the king's supremacy. Cromwell also says the king will forgive your past transgressions and welcome you lovingly back to court, but only if you swear to these truths with all your heart."

"I cannot," Mary said, tears streaming down her face. "I might as well spit on my mother's grave and our holy mother church!"

"Madam, please, sign this earthly document. God knows the truth inside your heart. His plan for you is much greater than you know. You will be Queen of England. You can right the ship. But only if you submit. Please."

Mary stared at Chapuys, the gravity of his words weighing heavy on her. She rose from her seat by the window and gently took the paper from Chapuys. Unfolding the document with trembling hands, Mary walked over to the desk at the opposite window. Refusing to read the submission, she dipped her quill in ink and signed the submission. Handing it back to Chapuys, Mary asked him to beseech the pope for absolution, though she knew it would not assuage her guilt.

"I have betrayed my mother," Mary said, though it was barely a whisper.

•   •   •

When Cromwell handed King Henry Mary's submission, the king stood in stunned silence, glad it was only he and his most loyal adviser in the room. He would hate if any of the court saw him cry or read the relief on his face to finally have Mary back. Henry would never admit it to anyone, not even himself and especially not to Mary, but he missed her beyond the measure of words.

Every act of defiance, every prod by Anne to have Mary sent to the block, chipped away at him more and more. By the time Anne fell, Henry wasn't sure if there would be anything of his old self left to keep going. But now that Mary had come to see reason (as he believed it) he could regain something of his former self. Henry felt more hopeful than he had in months, maybe even years. The future seemed bright, and all that was left was to get a son from his new bride.

•　•　•

Mary woke one morning to loud commotion coming from the courtyard. She heard excited voices from beyond the window and the sound of chests and trunks being unloaded. Confused, she rose from her bed and called for her attendants. Margaret came excitedly flying into the room, waving a letter in her hand.

"My lady," she addressed Mary with a curtsey. "You have a letter here from the king! His majesty has also sent you gifts. There are trunks of beautiful fabrics for new gowns and a chest of jewels!"

Mary was too excited to speak. She motioned for her ladies to help her dress and quickly took the letter from Margaret. She was moved by the king's words of love and devotion. He told Mary how much he missed her and longed to see her again.

The king promised her she would return to court, where she would be welcomed by the queen, who was eager to be a loving mother to her. But Mary already had a loving mother. Seeing Mary's expression suddenly change, Margaret recognized the look on her mistress's face as the one she made when thinking of the late queen.

"It is time to move forward, my lady," Margaret said. "The future is brighter than the past."

"I know it is what I must do," Mary replied. "I just don't know if it is something I *can* do." Giving Margaret a reassuring smile, she said, "But I will try. Come, ladies, let us look at the fine gifts the king has sent!"

As the months went by, Mary eagerly awaited her summons to court. The king sent gift after gift, expanded her household and sent warm, loving letters. She was beset with visitors at Hunsdon, including Cromwell and Queen Jane's brother Edward, now Lord Beauchamp, who arrived with a gift of a beautiful horse and saddle. Filling her days with riding, writing, and entertaining her many guests, Mary was happier than she had been in years.

She requested that Lady Bryan bring Elizabeth to visit her so they could discuss the child, who was just turning three. When Mary learned that Lady Bryan had written to Cromwell to request more money to buy the fast-growing girl new clothes, Mary decided she would also contribute. She was taking a warm interest in her sister. Elizabeth was now aware of her new status and her mother's death.

Mary wondered again why she should be so concerned about Elizabeth, as she may not even really be her sister. That woman had been with five men, anyone of whom could be Elizabeth's real father. Mary prayed to the Blessed Virgin that she could find it in her heart to let go of her resentment of Elizabeth.

Perhaps things might be easier if she now thought of Elizabeth as her adopted sister. Mary knew she loved the child, thinking back to her time at Hatfield when Elizabeth was sick and wanted only Mary for comfort. Now that Anne was gone, Mary told herself she had no reason not be a kind and loving sister to the girl. Thinking of that precocious little redheaded girl, Mary couldn't help but smile.

When Elizabeth arrived at Hunsdon, she greeted Mary with a low bow, as instructed by Lady Bryan, but when she rose from her curtsey, Elizabeth broke protocol and stretched out her arms in excitement, leaping into her sister's arms.

"It is wonderful to see you again, little one," Mary said with genuine affection. "How is my sweet sister?"

"Very well, sister," the excited child exclaimed. "I must thank you for the beautiful doll you sent me for my birthday! I wanted to bring her with me on this visit, but Lady Bryan said I should leave her safe at home."

Elizabeth's visit lasted several days. She and Mary went riding, played music, and Mary helped Elizabeth with her lessons, though the child hardly needed any assistance. Mary was impressed by the girl's aptitude; Elizabeth was an outstanding pupil at such a young age. When Lady Bryan and Mary were alone one evening after Elizabeth went to sleep, Mary asked how Elizabeth fared after learning of her mother's treason and death.

"It tormented the child for days. She woke up every night screaming from nightmares," Lady Bryan said, and Mary crossed herself. "She couldn't understand what her mother did or why the king sentenced her to die. She doesn't appreciate her demoted rank either. Then one day, she just stopped asking questions and went on as though everything was normal. She hasn't mentioned her mother since."

"Perhaps that is for the best," Mary said. "The less she thinks of her mother, the sooner she will forget her. It's best she's never reminded of her, and one day Anne Boleyn will just be a name to her and nothing more."

The day Elizabeth left Hunsdon, she seemed to be putting on an air of strength. Mary could tell she didn't want to go, and though it was hard to admit, Mary wanted Elizabeth to remain with her for a while longer.

As the sisters said their goodbyes, Mary promised to tell the king of Elizabeth's accomplishments and that he would have much cause to be proud of her. She told Elizabeth that soon she would be invited to court with Mary, where they would be presented to the new queen.

A few weeks after Elizabeth went back to Hatfield, Mary received word from Cromwell that soon the king and queen would be paying her a private visit, before her formal return to court. Mary felt ecstatic.

She set out immediately to see that her household got to work in preparation for the king's visit. She hired musicians and dancers to come for the evening's entertainment and ordered meat and ale to be served for supper. Mary told her seamstress to take some of the bolts of fabric the king sent and fashion a gorgeous new gown. She went through her jewels with Margaret, trying to pick just the right pieces to wear. She wanted to look stunning but not overdo it, she told Margaret.

"It's been five years since the king and I last spoke to one another," Mary said to Margaret as she rummaged through her jewel chests. "I hardly know what I will say to him. Or what he will say to me. And what of the queen? Chapuys said the queen is eager to be my friend, yet how can I be sure? She'll surely be with child soon, so why would she want to champion my rights over that of her own children?"

"Madam, you have this way of assuming the worst before it happens," Margaret told Mary, who gave her a sideways glance. "Things between you and the king have improved, and I am sure this meeting will go well. You'll see."

CHAPTER 8

1536 - 1537

Mary kicked off her velvet slippers, tossed her hood to the side, and flung herself down onto her bed, exhausted and exhilarated at the same time. Margaret followed in her wake, stumbling slightly and flushed from all the wine she drank that night. The meeting with King Henry and Queen Jane could not have gone better.

The small royal party arrived around ten o'clock that morning, and it was well past midnight before they departed. Mary didn't know what to expect when the king and queen arrived.

She was surprised to see the king being driven to Hunsdon in a coach rather than riding on some magnificent horse. The king exited the coach first. Mary's entire household assembled in the courtyard and made a deep reverence to welcome the king. He had grown stouter, Mary thought.

Her once muscular father now had a surprisingly noticeable gut growing beneath his doublet. His once slender legs were now rounder, and Mary noticed a red stain on his hose. She would later learn that before Anne's fall, the King had an accident while jousting. He was crushed under his horse and knocked unconscious for several hours. The fall opened up an older jousting wound the king suffered as a younger man, and now Henry was plagued by a recurring ulcer.

Mary could see the five years that separated them had not been kind to her father. As Henry approached his daughter, she thought she caught a slight foul odor emanating from the king's wounded leg.

Henry ambled to where Mary was situated. She was holding her low curtsey, with her eyes downcast. As Henry stopped in front of her, he brushed his rough hand against her cheek, sliding his finger under her chin and lifting it so Mary would look at him.

"Rise, daughter," Henry said and Mary obeyed.

•   •   •

Mary wasn't the only one surprised by the change the last five years had brought. When he looked at his daughter, Henry remembered the little girl she had once been and marveled at the woman standing before him.

He had last seen Mary as a thin and sickly child of fifteen. Now here was a tall, intelligent-looking woman of trim build standing before him. Henry was startled by how similar to himself Mary looked. Her heart-shaped face was very pleasing, he thought, and her gray eyes were becoming. Her high forehead was made to look more prominent thanks to the smoothed hairstyle and domed headdress Mary chose.

What was perhaps most startling to Henry was Mary's deep, rough voice. Henry would later remark to his wife how much deeper Mary's voice was than his own.

•   •   •

When Mary rose to her feet, she looked her father right in the eyes. Mary could tell his emotions were overwhelming him, just as her own were overwhelming her. She wondered how she could feel so much love for the man standing before her, the man who put her mother away and hounded her to death, the man who stripped her of her rights and bastardized her, and who only weeks before was considering signing her death warrant.

Yet somehow, none of that mattered now. Anne was gone, Mary was back in her father's good graces, and there was a new queen to befriend.

Henry, Jane, and Mary spent hours conversing pleasantly, feasting, playing music and in the evening, Mary and her stepmother danced the Cinque Pas to Henry's delight. An unknowing bystander might have mistaken the scene for one of pure family bliss, ignorant to the fears swelling within each of them. At one point during the visit, Henry asked to walk privately in the garden with his daughter. He was loving at first, speaking to Mary with genuine affection about life at court, his latest hunt and how he was certain that soon the queen would be pregnant with his son.

He assured Mary of a magnificent return to the court and public life, making brilliant promises for the future. When he brought up the possibility of negotiating a marriage for Mary, her heart leaped in her chest. Mary still felt she should have been married a long time by now, surrounded by beautiful children, her eldest son Henry's recognized heir. Silly dreams, she thought.

The pleasantries didn't last much longer. As Henry and Mary walked along, the king's leg began to bother him, and Mary insisted they take a seat on a bench. Henry gingerly lowered himself down to his seat and turned toward his daughter.

"Mary, I'm so pleased with how I find you," he said. "You have more courage in you than most of the soldiers I have known. And I know from…" Henry paused to find the right words, "from past unpleasantness, that you are strong in your convictions and would not lie to please anyone, not even your father and king."

Mary stared at her father nervously, unsure where he was going with this; she played with the sapphire ring on her right hand.

"Tell me truthfully, daughter," Henry continued, "Did you sign the submission willingly, because you know the truth of what it said or merely as a ruse while you maintain contrary and fallacious beliefs."

Mary stiffened her back and took a deep breath. She knew what she had to do. She had done it once before. Slipping from the bench, Mary kneeled at her father's feet. She kept her eyes downcast knowing she had no other choice than to continue down this path. The threat of the headsman's ax loomed if she didn't, the fate of her faith in England too.

"Your Majesty, I am your true and loving daughter and subject," she started. "I am sincere in my submission. I have seen my error and want nothing more than to forget the unhappy past. I beg your majesty humbly and from the very bottom of my soul to believe the sincerity of my repentance. I am your most humble, faithful, and obedient child."

Henry seemed satisfied with Mary's response, yet he had another demand to make of his daughter. She must write to her cousins, Mary of Hungary, regent of the Netherlands, and Emperor Charles.

Henry wanted Mary to make it clear to her powerful relatives that she came to the correct conclusions about her mother's marriage, her bastard status, and her inability to inherit the throne, all of her own free will. Mary agreed without hesitation. She had already written to her cousins telling them of her true beliefs and that any letters in her hand that said the contrary were a ruse to please her father.

Once again, Henry was underestimating his daughter. Though he was a master dissembler himself, Mary was quickly becoming his match.

Henry raised Mary from her obeisance and drew her to him in a warm embrace. Mary rested her head against her father's chest, and for a moment, she was transported back to her golden childhood, filled with nothing but her parent's love and admiration.

If only, Mary thought, her mother could be here. It seemed to Mary that this reunion was happening five years too late.

Before the royal couple's departure, Henry again promised to bring Mary to court soon and handed her a note for 1,000 crowns. Mary bowed gracefully, and Henry kissed his daughter on the cheek. Before climbing into the coach, the king presented Mary with a final gift, symbolizing his daughter's submission. Mary opened the leather pouch to find a gold ring with portraits of himself, the queen, and Mary on top. Latin verses from the Magnificat were inscribed on the sides celebrating obedience and humility. Henry wanted his daughter to know her dutifulness was divinely ordained.

Mary bid farewell to Queen Jane as well. In their short time together, Mary knew she had found a true friend. Jane promised to tell Mary of her time as maid of honor to Queen Katherine when they had more privacy and asked Mary to write to her often.

·   ·   ·

When the summons to court finally arrived, Mary spent days agonizing over what dresses and jewels to bring. She had every intent on arriving in as glamorous a style as she could exude.

When she finally arrived at court, Mary felt triumphant. Nobody could keep their eyes off her as she made her way through the courtyard and up toward the banquet hall. The doors to the hall were shut and Mary gave the guards standing by instructions to announce her arrival. Looking back at Margaret, who gave her friend and mistress a reassuring smile, Mary turned to the doors where she was about to be announced to the king, the queen and their waiting court.

It was a frigid December day, and Mary wasn't sure if she was shivering from the cold or her nerves. Flanked by her ladies, who were almost as gorgeously attired as she, Mary nodded toward the guard who called loudly as he opened the doors to the great hall at Windsor: "Make way for her grace, the Lady Mary Tudor!"

Mary reached back for Margaret's hand and squeezed it tightly, her friend returning the gesture. When the doors opened and Mary saw the great crowd of people, she dropped Margaret's hand and started toward the dais where her father and stepmother were seated.

The hush that descended over the room was as uncomfortable as it was long. All Mary could hear echoing in her head was the sound of her heart banging against her chest and the clacking of her shoes on the floor. After an agonizing walk, she made it to the dais and bowed low, waiting for the king to bid her to rise.

Henry stepped down slowly to greet his daughter, his ulcerous leg causing him intense pain as he moved. Taking Mary by the hand, he lifted her up and kissed her on both cheeks. Both Mary and the king expected the court to react to this loving display, but they remained silent, not knowing what to do. Mary looked around the room and immediately spotted Cromwell and Archbishop Cranmer.

Those devils, she thought. They looked as uncomfortable as she felt. Mary noticed a strange expression on her father's face as he stretched out Mary's hand, seemingly presenting her to the court so they could get a better look at her. Then he finally broke the silence.

"I remember a time not so long ago when many in this room were desirous that I should put this jewel to death," Henry bellowed. The silence continued with many of the court—

Cromwell and Cranmer in particular—looking down at their feet, embarrassed.

"It would have been a great pity to lose your chiefest jewel of England," Queen Jane exclaimed as she broke the silence and made her way over to her husband and stepdaughter. Jane moved faster when she noticed it was all becoming too much for Mary, who began to swoon and collapsed at the king's feet.

Without thinking, Margaret moved toward her friend but was stopped by another of Mary's ladies, an older woman who reminded Margaret of her place. The queen knelt to help Mary, but the excruciating pain in Henry's leg forced him to remain standing.

Mary opened her eyes, feeling a pounding pain in her head. She slowly rose to her feet and looked at her father, who was staring at her with genuine concern in his eyes. A look Mary had not seen from him in some time.

Wrapping a loving arm around his daughter, the King told Mary "to be of good cheer, for nothing now will go against you." With that, Henry motioned for music to be played and the court slowly went back to its bustling. Henry placed Mary's hand in Jane's and left his wife and daughter to talk.

Jane led Mary to a pair of seats near a fire in the back of the room, which would allow them some privacy. Mary took a seat, and Jane gave her a cup of wine, waving her maids off. Jane lovingly cupped her stepdaughter's face, and Mary closed her eyes and enjoyed the first scrap of motherly affection she'd felt since that final meeting with Queen Katherine.

She drank in the scent of Jane's perfume, which was so similar to her mother's. When Mary opened her eyes, tears were threatening, but they subsided when Jane smiled.

"It's going to be all right, Mary," Queen Jane said. "There is much darkness in the past to haunt you. But I promise if you look forward to the future, it will be bright."

"It is a difficult thing to believe, Your Majesty," Mary responded.

"Yes, I understand. I cannot imagine the torment you have been through. But I can see your mother in you. She is in your spirit, your courage, and your faith, which is also my faith. You are stronger than you know, Mary, and you have a friend in me. I will not forsake you. When I was removed from her household, I promised your mother that if it ever lay in my power to be of service to you, I would not hesitate. It was a great honor to serve such a kind and virtuous queen. And now I serve her still, not only because I feel it is my duty, but because of my genuine affection for you. You are my daughter now too."

Her conversation with the queen had Mary feeling more secure about her familial and personal life than she had in years. Jane told Mary that noises had been made about a potential marriage negotiation.

"With all due respect, Your Majesty, I have been down this road before, and I think it best not to get my hopes up," Mary said. "With whom is this negotiation supposed to be?"

"Your cousin Charles is pressing the suit of Dom Luis of Portugal, younger brother of the King of Portugal. They say he is very handsome," Jane said, smiling as she noticed Mary blush.

Mary awkwardly cleared her throat. "Well, we'll just have to wait and see what my father the king decides."

As the women chatted, Mary noticed a man staring at her. She asked her stepmother if she knew who he was.

"That is Robert Aske," Jane said. "He is the leader of the northern rebellion. The king invited him to court for Christmas to negotiate a peace and learn more about what the rebels are demanding."

"Why is he looking at me that way?"

"Well," the Queen hesitated and began to whisper, "it appears the northerners are also angry about your situation. Mr. Aske and those who follow him believe the king was mistaken to declare you illegitimate. They believe you to be the king's only legitimate child and say you should be restored as heir, until a son is born."

Mary held her breath as the queen continued.

"Those who wish for a return to the true faith are looking to your influence to bring it about. Your former steward, Lord Hussey, is among the rebels. He and Mr. Aske exchanged many letters, now in the hands of Master Cromwell, in which they discussed how you come from the greatest blood in Christendom on your mother's side. The rebels believe that the statute declaring you illegitimate was framed more for some displeasure toward you and your supporters than for any just cause."

Mary had heard about the uprising in the north and the great army of over 30,000 people who marched from Lincolnshire and Yorkshire, but she wasn't aware they were angered by her situation. It began in October when a spontaneous protest erupted in the town of Louth after the people heard reports that royal commissioners were making their way there to continue the king's program of shutting down the monasteries and confiscating the treasures of the parish churches. The people in the north had had enough. Not only did they want the king to end the suppression of the monasteries, but they also wanted Cromwell and Cranmer, as well as some other bishops and members of the privy council, removed and punished for their heretical practices.

The queen told Mary the king was livid when he heard of the uprising and that he wanted to hang everyone marching under their banner, which showed the eucharist host, a chalice, and a figure of Christ bearing the five wounds of the crucifixion. Mary noticed a shadow go across the queen's face.

"Are you alright?"

"Yes, yes. I just pray for a peaceful end to the rebellion. I hate to burden you with the truth after finally reaching a bit of peace. But when the rebels' demands were made known, I went before the King on my knees, begging my husband, in the presence of his court, to reconsider the fate of the monasteries and asked for the restoration of some of the smaller ones. I suggested that God allowed the rebellion to go on as a punishment for the deliberate destruction of these holy places."

Mary gasped. "You didn't!"

The queen nodded and relayed how for the first time since their marriage the king erupted in anger against his new queen. He ordered Jane to rise, grabbing her by the arm and scolding her that she should not meddle in his affairs.

"My last Queen paid the price for involving herself too much in my business," Henry hollered at his frightened wife. "You had best attend to other things. Busy yourself with domestic affairs and matters concerning your estates! Leave the business of my realm to me!"

Jane looked around to make sure no one had overheard her frank confession. "I have not brought up the subject of the monasteries again." She squeezed Mary's hand and wiped her face of all distress, smiling as if all was well. "Come, let's enjoy the pleasures of court life."

The rest of Mary's first evening back at court passed without incident. She even found she was beginning to enjoy herself, participating in several dances and partnering with a few handsome gentlemen. She relished the feeling of their hands around her waist.

"Who was the attractive young man you were dancing with?" Mary asked Margaret when they returned to her apartments. "He couldn't keep his eyes or his hands off you all night." Margaret was flushed from the wine and a little embarrassed by Mary's question.

Mary, on the other hand, felt jealous that her maid was attracting the attention of such a charming man. None of the young men Mary danced with had looked at Mary the way Margaret's partner did at her.

"His name is Piero Manetto," Margaret responded. "He is an Italian and came to England to be a lawyer. Master Cromwell is his sponsor."

"He's Cromwell's man?"

"Yes, madam, although I don't think in the way you mean," Margaret was slightly panicked and babbled as she explained the situation to Mary. "I didn't take him for a spy, which was my first thought. He didn't ask me much about you or the goings on in your household. He seemed genuinely interested in me, and we talked about our families. I told him of my sister Jane's twins, a boy and a girl, and how I am excited to see them in the new year."

Mary looked at her friend with disappointment and wondered how she could think to trust a man loyal and indebted to Cromwell. But another thought occurred to her. About to go into their twenty-first year, she and Margaret should have both been married for a long time by now. Both women spent long nights talking about the day they would finally wed.

Margaret mentioned how her father didn't seem too interested in finding her a husband after he married off her sister Jane. Margaret spoke often of how Jane was their parent's favorite, and now that she had a son, her father had the heir he'd always wanted. He doted on the boy, forgetting he also had a granddaughter and another child of his own.

Each letter to Margaret from Jane was a knife in her heart and often led to late-night discussions over wine and candied fruit between her and Mary. With a twinge of guilt, Mary realized she was feeling the same jealousy toward her friend that Margaret felt towards her sister, and so she relented a little.

"Please be careful, Margaret. Take note if this Italian presses too hard for information he doesn't need to know."

Margaret bowed in silence and left the room, leaving her usual duty of helping Mary prepare for bed to another of her ladies. Both women knew there had just been a fundamental shift in their friendship.

Mary was delighted when a week after she returned to court, Elizabeth arrived for the Christmas season. This would be Elizabeth's formal return to court as well, and Mary knew the vipers would be waiting to see how her father would welcome Anne Boleyn's child. If Elizabeth was worried about coming face to face with the man who ordered her mother's death, a deserved death in Mary's mind, she showed no outward sign of it.

Mary lavished gifts on her little sister, fine furs, dolls, material for new dresses, and a new saddle for the pony the king and queen gave her for Christmas. She also gave Elizabeth's chaplain some money to put toward the girl's religious education.

Mary understood that Elizabeth would be brought up under her father's reforms. But she wanted to be sure the child got a fundamental Catholic education, even if it had to be kept secret. Though the child's religious instructor Father Parker was grateful for Mary's gift, he had no intention of instructing Elizabeth in the popish faith. Having served Anne Boleyn as her chaplain, Father Parker was determined to keep his promise to the late queen and care for Elizabeth's soul.

Mary was relieved when she saw the affection the King was giving the little girl. She wondered if the King had the same doubts about Elizabeth's paternity as she did. If he did, Mary doubted Elizabeth would ever feel it, not if the way the king was treating her now was any indication.

However, watching her father whirl Elizabeth in the air and show her off to his court, Mary couldn't help but feel that familiar resentment arise. Mary hated that she could still feel that way towards the child. She pacified herself by remembering her love for Elizabeth outweighed her resentment. Mary prayed it would stay that way. She was lost in thought when she heard a familiar voice behind her.

"My Lady Princess," Lady Pole said in a whisper so low only Mary could hear. "I am so pleased to see you."

Mary turned to see her former governess in a stunning crimson gown trimmed with ermine. She bowed low to Mary who could not hide her joy. She embraced her dear Lady Pole, hugging her so tightly that Lady Pole might burst, but neither cared.

"I have missed you so much, my sweet girl," Lady Pole said. "To lose you was to lose one of my own children. "

That was a sensation Mary knew Lady Pole was too familiar with. Her son, Reginald, a clergyman, was in exile; he fled England when he spoke out against the king's reforms, his marriage to Anne Boleyn and the issue of the supremacy.

When they finally let go of one another, both women were aware of the court's eyes upon them. But again, they didn't care. Finding a quiet corner, they talked for the rest of the night, not noticing when the crowds dissipated and finally realizing how time had flown by when the sun began to pierce the window glass. Reluctantly, Mary bid goodnight, or rather good morning, to Lady Pole. They promised to dine together while they were both at court, and Mary even offered to speak to the king about Lady Pole's son.

"Thank you, dear princess, but I fear no amount of persuasion will move the king to change his mind about my Reginald," Lady Pole said. "Especially not after the pope appointed him a cardinal and commissioned him as legate to come to England and raise support for the rebels. I would not have you risk the king's displeasure again on what would be a fruitless mission."

CHAPTER 9

Fall 1537

Mary and Margaret knelt together at the chapel altar in fervent prayer, so long their knees ached, and their arms throbbed from tightly clutched their hands together. Margaret was exhausted, but she was determined to remain at Mary's side.

Their friendship was still warm and loving, but Margaret could tell Mary stayed wary of her relationship with Piero, whom Margaret was positive would propose soon. She made sure not to discuss Mary with her lover and planned to tell him she would not leave Mary's service if they married, unless Mary or the king commanded it. Margaret was determined to prove her unwavering loyalty to Mary.

But Margaret's beau was not Mary's only concern. When she learned how her father defeated the northern rebellion, or the Pilgrimage of Grace as it was being called, Mary fell to her knees and wept. The uprising was crushed and 216 of its leaders were executed. Though she abhorred treason against her father, the king, she could not help but sympathize with what the pilgrims demanded.

Mary, too, wanted the monasteries restored and England's return to Roman obedience. If she could have lent her voice to the growing crowd, she would have. Under her father and his ministers Cranmer and Cromwell, the Catholic faith was being attacked. She and the queen discussed it at length when they visited, promising never to put their concerns in writing for fear their letters would end up in the wrong hands.

Mary was convinced Cromwell was reading her correspondence. If Chapuys could employ a spy when Mary was in Elizabeth's household, she was sure Cromwell could have one of his own in hers.

As Mary and Margaret prayed, Mary thought back to a recent, unexpected visit she had from those demon heretics, Cromwell and Cranmer. They had come to question Mary and members of her household about any possible involvement with the rebellion.

"You insult me, gentleman," Mary said in a tone so similar to her father that both men flinched in fear, which didn't go unnoticed by Mary. "How could you think that I, or any member of my household, would have any involvement with traitors and rebels?"

"My lady," Cranmer responded, "the rebels were known to be sympathetic towards you! The king himself sent us here to get to the truth of these matters."

"The truth, Archbishop, is that the king has evil counselors about him offering him false and heretical advice," Mary said.

As angry as she was with Cromwell, Mary hated Cranmer even more. It was Cranmer who declared her parents' marriage null and was the one who convinced the king to canvas the universities, rather than heed the pope and Church.

"I do not believe you are here by his command. I believe you are looking for something that does not exist to build a case against me. I know that it would have been to both of your benefits had my mother and I been executed when *that woman* was alive and pretending to be queen. Now you use the tragedy of rebellion to once again remove me from my father's good graces. Well sirs, you may look around and speak to as many people in my household as you like. I swear before Almighty God that I am ever the king's true loyal subject and daughter. I would rather be torn apart by dogs here and now than ever betray him."

After their scolding and without any evidence against her, Mary's interrogators went back to court, crestfallen.

"A day will come when they meet their much deserved ends," Mary said to Margaret, after Cromwell and Cranmer rode off. Her face was as stone as she spoke. "They deserve to burn. If I could, I would light the pyres myself."

Mary was even more convinced that the interrogation from Cromwell and Cranmer was not her father's idea when a few weeks later, she was invited back to court to await the birth of the next royal child. When the hour finally arrived, Mary listened outside the queen's chamber as Jane screamed in pain. As an unmarried woman, she was not permitted to attend to the queen as she labored to bring her child into the world. Mary toyed with her rosary as the queen's cries pierced the palace's thick walls. Mary thought of Eve and her sin of tempting Adam with the fruit from the tree of knowledge. That all women should suffer for the folly of one and endure such extreme pain to bring life into the world seemed cruel and unfair.

"Who am I to question God's judgment?" Mary whispered to herself as the queen screamed again.

"Did you say something, madam," Margaret asked as she nervously played with her engagement ring.

Margaret timidly approached Mary back at Hunsdon to tell her Piero had proposed and wished to formally ask Mary for her permission to marry her maid. At first, Mary had every intention of saying no. It was out of a mix of distrust for the man and, if she were being honest with herself, jealousy of Margaret's happy situation.

But when Piero fell onto his knees before Mary, she was astounded by what he had to say. Piero was truly in love with Margaret. But confessed that he had not expected to find himself in such a state. It was not part of his mission.

Mary had been right. The Italian was sent to England to spy at King Henry's court, but not on Mary. Piero was the pope's spy.

His holiness wanted someone in Cromwell's household to keep him abreast of what was happening in England and how far Henry's heretical policies were going. The pope wanted to know how the people truly felt about the king's religious policies and whether or not the king still planned to proceed against his daughter. Piero expressed his unending loyalty to Mary, the Catholic faith, and the pope. He also swore never to take Margaret from her service and apologized for placing any doubt about Margaret's loyalty in Mary's mind.

Stunned, Mary agreed they could marry, yet she was uncertain about knowing Piero was indeed a spy. She knew it was her duty as a good and loyal Catholic to keep the pope's secret, yet as a good and loyal daughter to the king, she owed it to him to make her father aware of Piero's true purpose at court. She was torn but ultimately decided the Holy Father had a good reason for sending Piero.

"My lady, did you say something," Margaret asked Mary again, who then snapped back to the present.

"Only that I think we should go to the chapel and pray for the queen."

Jane cried out again.

The queen's ordeal lasted three days and three nights. Mary was terrified the doctors would have to follow through on their plan to cut the queen's child from her womb.

Finally, at two in the morning on Friday, October 12, Queen Jane gave birth to the king's long-desired son. Born on the Feast of Saint Edward the Confessor, the child was named after the holy English king. By eight o'clock, all of London knew of the prince's birth, and soon the news would spread through the country and onto the continent.

Three days later, Mary stood as a proud godmother to her little brother in the Chapel Royal at Hampton Court. She held the tiny bundle as Archbishop Cranmer performed the rites of baptism over the infant prince. Staring down at Edward, Mary was filled with familiar emotions of pain and regret, mixed with mild joy. It pleased her that Edward seemed so comfortable in her arms. He hardly made a sound when Cranmer poured the warm water over his head. He kept his little eyes fixed on her the entire time.

Mary looked over and saw her four-year-old sister held by the queen's brother, Edward Seymour, Earl of Hertford. She had been the one to convey the baptismal chrism into the chapel, a task she was proud to perform, though she was too little to do it on her own, so the queen's brother carried her in his arms.

Mary could tell Elizabeth was basking in the attention she was receiving; the little girl was happiest when receiving the admiration of others. But she kept her eyes fixed on the baby when the ceremony started. Looking at her younger siblings, Mary knew her duty was to protect them. Not just from physical danger but from those who would seek to corrupt their souls. Mary knew Elizabeth was already in danger, having had Anne Boleyn as a mother and Matthew Parker as her chaplain. Now, Mary worried that the prince, too, was in danger.

She knew the earl and those around him were keeping the true depth of their heresy from the king, who was still teetering on the brink. Standing in the chapel, holding her brother and watching her sister, Mary made a vow before God to protect her siblings from heresy and safeguard their immortal souls, no matter what it may cost her.

When the ceremony was over, Mary handed Edward to his nurse, took Elizabeth from the earl, and led her by the hand to the queen's chamber, where their father and stepmother were waiting to receive their guests. Mary presented the queen with a golden cup and gave a gift of thirty pounds to Edward's nurse, midwife and cradle rockers. The streets of London were jubilant. People lit bonfires and drank to the prince's health while bells rang out across the country.

But the celebratory mood was about to shift drastically.

Mary refused to leave the queen's side as she suffered through an illness, which many were now convinced was childbed fever. A hush descended over the court as everyone feared for the queen's life. The king, ever fearful of death and disease, kept his distance from his wife, confident his daughter would make a suitable substitute at the queen's side until she recovered.

"Majesty, please try and eat something," Mary pleaded with Jane, offering her some warm broth.

"No, I cannot. Please, it is so hot here. Open a window," Jane commanded. She was feverish, drenched in sweat, and writhing in pain.

Mary instructed Margaret to open one of the windows, despite the complaints from a midwife. How fresh air could be bad for someone was a mystery to Mary. Jane seemed to settle a little as the chilly October air filled the room.

The queen laid in delirium for three days, making little sense when she spoke. Sometimes she didn't know where she was or what was happening to her.

Mary grew annoyed with the flotilla of people going in and out of the queen's chamber. She'd finally had enough and lost her temper when she saw the queen's doctors huddled in a corner, whispering and glancing at the queen. They went silent when Mary looked at them.

"Get out, all of you!" Mary hollered. "You are all useless! And you as well," Mary yelled at the other maids and servants and noble ladies in the room. "I shall have none but myself and the queen's confessor, the Bishop of Carlisle, here. Remove yourselves before I have the guards drag you all out by your ears!"

Chastised, the flock of people bowed and withdrew one by one. As Margaret made to leave, Mary stopped her and told her to go to her sister Elizabeth.

"Tell her governess that I sent you to keep Elizabeth company since I cannot," Mary said. "I don't want her to learn of the queen's...situation from anybody but me."

"Mary, where are you?" Jane called out.

"I am here madam. Shhh, try and rest."

"I cannot, I cannot until I know he is safe. Where is my boy?"

"The prince is in his nursery. He is surrounded by people who would never allow any harm to come to him. I believe his uncles, your brothers, are there too."

"You must promise me you will watch over him, Mary, please. My brothers and the king, all of them will raise him as a heretic. He must be brought up in the true religion. You are the only one who can ensure that happens."

"Of course, of course, madam, I will make sure the prince knows God's truth," Mary said, though she knew it would be difficult to keep her promise to the queen. But she still had to try.

"I will never see my boy again. This is my punishment for my great sin," Jane said.

"Madam, you are confused. What possible sin could you have committed?"

"Her blood is on my hands." Jane was taking gasping breaths between each word. "I stepped over her corpse on my way to the throne. I tried to be better than she was, to be as good as your mother, but I failed."

"Hush now. There was no sin in what you have done," Mary said as she tried to comfort the queen. "You unseated an adulterous witch, who in all likelihood helped my mother into her grave. You have done God's will, he is with you now and will not abandon you, Your Majesty. You will be delivered and see your son grow."

As the queen drifted in and out of consciousness, Mary sent word to her father that he should be at his wife's side. Despite her attempts at comforting Jane, Mary knew it wouldn't be long now. Jane was holding Mary's hand so tightly when the king arrived that she could not rise to bow, but he didn't seem to notice. The king dismissed all those in the room whom Mary had allowed back in; he wanted only Mary with him at the queen's side.

Henry sat beside his wife, taking her free hand and bringing it to his lips. His eyes were full of tears. Mary wondered if he cried over her mother when he learned of her death. It amazed Mary how a man with such a capacity for cruelty could be so vulnerable and show such genuine grief.

Jane stared at her husband, and Mary wondered what she felt when she looked at him. Did she even know he was there, or was she too consumed with thoughts of little Edward?

The Bishop of Carlisle offered her the last rites, and again Jane drifted off to sleep, still holding her husband's and stepdaughter's hands. Mary and Henry were silent, each offering up useless prayers that Jane may somehow recover.

Then, in a moment both Mary and her father seemed to have missed, Queen Jane slipped from their world.

Henry could not remain in the same place as his wife's corpse. When the sun rose that morning, he fled from Hampton Court to Windsor, leaving a grief-stricken Mary and the Duke of Norfolk in charge of arranging the funeral. Mary abhorred the idea of working with Norfolk, but she knew this wasn't the time for such animosities.

Mary could hardly stand when they came to take away the queen's body. She was seized with a tightness in her chest when Jane's corpse was wrapped in linen and taken away by the embalmers. She cried so heavily she realized she was heaving. She'd become dizzy and needed to steady herself on one of the queen's bed posts. She could have collapsed right there as she had done when her own mother died. To lose Jane was to lose a friend so special that Mary felt there could be no solace. Then she thought of her sister who must be told of their stepmother's death.

When Lady Bryan welcomed Mary into Elizabeth's rooms, her face told the governess everything she needed to know.

"That poor boy, never to know his own mother," Lady Bryan said.

"Is my sister awake? She needs to be told, and it should come from me."

Mary walked in to find her sister on the floor with Margaret. They were giggling as they played with Elizabeth's dolls. Margaret looked up at Mary and her expression immediately changed. She excused herself, and she and Lady Bryan left the sisters alone.

"Mary, you're crying? What's wrong?" Elizabeth asked, springing to her feet and running to her sister. Mary scooped her up and held her tightly.

"My sweet Lizzie," Mary said, she was the only one to call Elizabeth by that name, and her sister loved it. "I have something unfortunate to tell you." Elizabeth just looked at her. She was nervous but curious. Mary tried to be gentle.

"Our most gracious stepmother and queen has gone to heaven to be with Jesus and his mother the Blessed Virgin, Lizzie. Do you understand what that means?"

"You have to die to go to heaven," Elizabeth said. Mary knew Elizabeth had learned a hard lesson about death only a year before.

"Yes, Lizzie, the queen has died."

"But why?"

"It is a perilous thing for a lady to give birth, and our queen did not survive the effort."

"Having a baby killed her?" Elizabeth asked, shocked and confused.

"Yes, sweetie, and now we must have a funeral and say our goodbyes."

"But why did she have to die? Why did having a baby make her die?"

"It is God's will that childbirth is a great trial for women. It is our punishment for Eve's sin of tempting Adam. Sometimes God wills it that the lady gives up her own life when bringing new life into the world."

"That's ridiculous," Elizabeth shouted angrily. "Why should every woman suffer just because of another woman's mistake? Why did the queen have to die?" Her little face became red, and she started to cry, falling into Mary's arms. The sisters held each other tightly as they cried together, each fully aware that this was the second time they'd lost a mother.

Jane's funeral was a magnificent affair. In helping to arrange it, Mary wanted to honor the queen and make up for the coronation she never received. Mary acted as chief mourner. She and other noble ladies were dressed in black mourning habits with white headdresses—a symbol the queen died from childbirth.

Jane's corpse was dressed in a robe of gold tissue with a crown on her head and beautiful jewels on her neck and fingers. Mary followed the coffin. Her cousin Frances Brandon, the daughter of the king's good friend Charles Brandon and Mary's late aunt, the French Queen, carried her train.

Following prayers, the queen's body was left to lie in state overnight. A grief-stricken Mary kept vigil by the queen's side the entire time. Margaret wanted to stay with Mary while she prayed, but Frances dismissed Margaret for the evening with an unapproving wave of her hand.

"That maid of yours is too familiar, my lady," Frances said. "You should surround yourself with noble ladies, not low-born maid-servants."

"Margaret has been my most loyal companion for years, cousin," Mary said as she stroked the dead queen's hand. "She is the only constant in my life."

Frances rolled her eyes as she stood behind her cousin. Mary wanted to change the subject. She knew Frances as a woman who disapproved of many things, including her friendship with Margaret. Frances never made eye contact with her servants and berated them for the most minor infraction.

"Cousin, tell me, how have you been feeling since your daughter was born? You and your husband, Henry Grey, must be thrilled," Mary said.

Frances made a sour face. "Yes...my daughter...Jane, we named her after the queen. I pray that she will soon have many brothers for company in the nursery."

Mary turned back to look at her stepmother's lifeless body, her heart aching even more. Frances displayed that same fervent desire for a male heir that brought her mother and stepmother to their early graves and set her father on his heretical and tyrannical path.

She thought of her brother Edward who must now grow up without a mother's love. She also thought of her newborn cousin, Jane, who it appeared would also grow up missing that love, but in an entirely different way. Mary felt sour. She thought about all the love she would lavish upon baby Jane if she were her child. It struck her as unfair that she was still unwed and childless while her obnoxious cousin was married with a child to dote on, though Mary knew she never would. Poor little Jane Grey, Mary thought.

A few weeks after the funeral, Mary took Elizabeth to Richmond to visit their little brother. Her sister was nursing another devastating blow to her broken heart, and Mary wanted to distract her. Her governess Lady Bryan had been reassigned to the prince's nursery. Her new governess, Mistress Catherine Champernowne, was younger and seemed to have more energy than her predecessor, which Mary knew her sister would come to appreciate.

If it weren't for the fact that Kat—as the governess was known—was a heretic and a former member of Anne Boleyn's household, Mary would have liked her. But Kat was just another reminder of the past and the trauma it held. Mary wondered if she would ever be free of Anne's memory and the pain it brought.

It was reliving those memories that caused Mary to unfairly snap at her little sister on their way to Richmond. Elizabeth made a comment about the incense smelling during Mass. Mary demanded Elizabeth attend Mass with her before visiting their brother. After the scolding, Elizabeth was quiet the entire journey and didn't perk up until they were presented to the baby prince.

"Welcome, Lady Mary, Lady Elizabeth," Lady Bryan said. A stung Elizabeth humphed at Lady Bryan and walked over to the cradle where Edward lay. Mary and Lady Bryan just shrugged, smiled at Elizabeth's pride, and went about their own ways.

"May I hold him?" Elizabeth asked, not addressing her question to anybody in particular.

"Of course, but you must sit in this chair and be very gentle with the prince," Mary said. Elizabeth did as she was told, and Mary went to pick up Edward, who started to coo excitedly. Her heart sang at the baby's reaction to seeing her, and she instinctively placed her forehead gently against Edward's, breathing in his scent and longing, for what felt like the millionth time, for the day she would be holding her own child. She made her way over to Elizabeth and silently reaffirmed her vow to the late queen to constantly watch over Edward.

"Like this, Lizzie," Mary said as she handed the baby to her sister. "Be mindful of his head. Good girl." Elizabeth smiled at Mary, and she knew their brief tiff was at an end.

CHAPTER 10

1539 - 1541

As the next few years dragged on, King Henry became increasingly paranoid about the prince's health, taking every precaution to safeguard his precious jewel. Mary was disturbed to get a letter from the king chastising her because he heard she had gone to visit the prince after she had been ill.

"I would never risk the prince's health," she told Margaret. "I would not have gone to visit my brother if I wasn't confident I had fully recovered. My father will keep that poor boy locked away from the world in the name of protectiveness."

That visit to her little brother had not been as pleasant as some others. The prince's uncle Edward Seymour, Earl of Hertford, had arrived a day after Mary, and a heated exchange had taken place between them over the prince's religious education and the people the earl was installing around him. More heretics, Mary realized.

Mary was sitting in the nursery holding the chubby toddler prince in her lap and reading from a book that detailed the stories of the saints when the Earl came in with a disapproving face. He admonished Mary for reading the prince what he called "popish nonsense" and the "abominable veneration of saints and false holy relics." Mary was appalled. But she kept her tone congenial for Edward's sake.

"My lord, I instruct the prince in the true faith, which was, as you are well aware of, his dear mother's faith," Mary said. The mention of his dead sister made the Earl wince, Mary noticed.

"I promised Queen Jane I would care for the prince. She asked that I protect him from all who would endanger his immortal soul through false doctrine. It was her main concern before her unfortunate passing. As Edward's sister and godmother, it is a duty I do not take lightly."

The earl smiled, but there was nothing warm about his expression. Mary knew Seymour to be cold as ice.

He reached to take the child from his sister, who looked up pensively at his uncle. Speaking to one of Edward's nurses, he told the woman to take the prince to enjoy some fresh air so he and Mary could speak.

"You think that I am a danger to my own nephew, my lady?" Seymour asked. "You, who would show more loyalty to a tyrant who calls himself the Vicar of Christ, than your own father? The king saw the Bishop of Rome for what he truly is, a corrupt, unscrupulous and perfidious devil! It seems very clear to me, Lady Mary, that it is I who must protect the prince from you and all idolaters!"

"You are a liar and a heretic! How dare you say such things to me. I am the king's daughter, and you are nothing more than a leach who grasped onto his sister's good fortune! Queen Jane would cry for shame if she knew how you planned to raise her child in heresy."

Seymour looked enraged and took a step toward Mary. She thought he may actually dare to strike her and jumped backward.

"No more!" they heard a small voice cry. Mary and Seymour looked in horror as they saw the prince who had escaped his nurse and undoubtedly witnessed the ugly exchange. The-two-year-old had tears streaming down his face.

Mary ran to him, brushing past the earl as she scooped him up. She did her best to soothe the troubled child. A fuming

Seymour left in a huff. Mary stayed at Richmond for a few days more, trying to cheer the child up. But she began to notice that little Edward was already becoming a serious young boy and wondered if the king isolating him from most of the world was the cause.

Mary thought how unfair it was that she and her siblings should be denied the one thing every child needs a mother's love. Mary took the disturbing thought home with her, where it weighed heavily.

"Piero tells me the king is in constant fear over the prince. He says Cromwell is seeking to negotiate a new marriage for the king in the hopes it will produce a Duke of York," Margaret said as she rested her hands on her growing belly.

She and Piero had been married nearly a year and they were expecting their first child. Margaret knew she would eventually need to leave Mary's service, but her mistress refused to be separated from her friend, offering her home to Margaret and her child whenever she wanted.

Mary even paid to have the best midwife in London attend Margaret. She vowed she would not lose her friend as she had lost Queen Jane.

About a month after Margaret and Piero married, the young lawyer and spy had to return to Cromwell's service, and Margaret returned to Mary. The couple had a little house in London, but Margaret preferred to stay in the country when Cromwell's business kept her husband busy long into the night or took him away from the capital on assignment.

As had been the case in the past, the two women were overjoyed to see one another when Margaret returned to Hunsdon. They dined together that first evening she had returned, which started awkwardly. Margaret felt Mary might see her differently now that she was married and no longer a permanent member of her household. Mary was hoping that her jealousy would not shine through.

Though genuinely happy for her friend, self-pity was a dark cloud that constantly followed Mary. But after the first course was served, and the wine started flowing, both women fell back into their sweet familiarity. Finally, Mary had enough wine in her to ask a burning question.

"Tell me truthfully, Margaret, what is it like…to be married," Mary said.

Margaret knew what Mary was really asking, but she wanted to ease into the details.

"Marriage is difficult, madam. Sometimes I wonder if I am truly suited to be a wife. I find there are more challenges than I was expecting," she said. "But, as frustrating as those moments can be, they are nothing compared to the tender moments we share. I have never felt as safe or loved as when Piero holds me at night. He showed me what real love feels like on the evening we were married."

Mary's cheeks burned red as she quietly sipped her wine.

•　　　•　　　•

As King Henry continued to mourn Jane Seymour, the French and Spanish were working out a truce and agreeing to peace talks, which had been mediated by the pope. The King and Cromwell had become aware that this alliance was a growing Catholic threat to England. And the King needed a new wife, someone who could bring with her strong military support and an alliance that would keep France and Spain at bay.

Moreover, the King was aware that his eldest daughter was seen as a beacon of Catholic hope, and there would always be those who would support her, especially if it meant toppling her father and making England nothing more than part of France or Spain.

Henry would always regard his daughter and those who supported her with suspicion. He and Cromwell knew they needed to keep Mary politically isolated or find her a husband who would not favor either of England's enemies.

Of course, this would be easier said than done. Cromwell and Henry also knew that any potential marriage contract negotiated for Mary would likely have to include a complete restoration of her rights and a place in the line of succession.

But it wasn't just Mary whom Henry was suspicious of. The King had begun going after the old Catholic families of England, especially those with royal Plantagenet blood who had also been supporters of Queen Katherine and Mary.

Reginald Pole was living on the continent and hadn't stopped his denouncing of the king over the years. He even boasted he would leave the Church and marry Mary, uniting the houses of Tudor and Plantagenet as Henry VII and Elizabeth of York had done.

Since the King could not get his hands on Pole, he decided to go after his family, including Mary's former governess, the Countess of Salisbury. In August 1538, Pole's younger brother Geoffrey was arrested for treason and sent to the Tower. In November of that same year, the elderly countess was interrogated, and her home was searched. Without a trial, she was convicted of aiding and abetting her sons, committing other abominable treasons, and was thrown in the Tower.

Upon hearing that her beloved Lady Pole was a prisoner in the Tower, Mary vowed to go to Whitehall and throw herself on her knees in front of the king and beg him to be merciful. She told Margaret she must make ready to go, but her friend was unsure this was the best plan.

"Madam, are you sure you should be doing this? I know how much you love Lady Pole. Indeed, I care for her too. But the king already views you and all those who support you with suspicion. If you do this, he could think you were part of this plot."

"I must trust in my father's love for his daughter," Mary said. "I will go and beg him to be merciful. He will listen to reason. I am sure of it."

But the truth was Mary wasn't sure. She knew as well as Margaret that come the following morning she could be breaking her fast in the Tower. But Mary also couldn't sit by and let her beloved Lady Pole suffer for supporting her and her sainted mother.

"Jesus, give me strength. Holy Mary, Mother of God, give me strength," Mary said as she was announced to the king, who was going over some important-looking documents with Cromwell.

"Daughter," Henry said happily, surprised and bounding to Mary as excitedly as his ulcerous leg would let him. But he stopped in his tracks as Mary fell to her knees.

"Your Majesty," she began, keeping her eyes on the ground. "I am here to beg for mercy on behalf of Lady Margaret Pole, Countess of Salisbury."

Henry was aghast, and Cromwell wanted to be anywhere else.

"You come to ask for mercy for a traitor," Henry exclaimed.

"Forgive me, Your Majesty, but I do not believe Lady Pole is guilty of any treason. I cannot speak for the actions of her sons. But I can tell you she is a good woman and a loyal subject. She is an old woman. She wants nothing more than to dote on her grandchildren and live out her days in peace."

"You are wrong, daughter," Henry exclaimed, flying into one of his rages and making Mary wince. "She wants to marry you to her milksop son, murder my son and I, then place you both on the throne! Perhaps it is what you want too!"

"Sir, please," Mary said, refusing to allow any tears. "That is the last thing I or Lady Pole would want. If you speak to her, you will get to the truth of this matter and see she is blameless."

"Lady Pole has been thoroughly examined," Henry said, forcing Mary to conjure visions of the rack in her mind. "I know the truth of these matters. You will leave my presence, Lady

Mary. Return to Hunsdon, and do not show yourself to me until you have learned some humility!"

Mary rose, curtsied, and fled from the room. Cromwell caught up with her in the hall.

"Are you mad?" he said, grabbing Mary by the arm. "After all that has been done to return you to the king's good graces and spare you from the block, you do this!"

"Take your hands off me, heretic," Mary said, wrenching her arm away from Cromwell. "How dare you lecture me. I have lost so much in my life. Do you think after all of that I am afraid of your threats! I am here because of the great love I bear Lady Pole and the love she has for me. If doing what I know is right puts my life in danger, then so be it! Not all of us act out of scheming self-interest."

"Foolish woman," Cromwell responded, stepping closer to Mary. "Be careful, my lady, my scheming self-interest, as you call it, has already cost a queen her head. What do you think it will cost some ungrateful, bastard girl?"

As Cromwell walked off, a frightened and incensed Mary called after him, instinctively yelling: "I'm not sure, Lord Cromwell. What do you think a war with my cousin the emperor will cost?"

As Henry's fears of war against him mounted, he started to take Cromwell's suggestion of an alliance with the Lutheran princes of Germany more seriously. In January of 1539, he sent the English ambassador Christopher Mont to the Duke of Saxony to discuss the prospect of a match between the king and the Duke of Cleves's eldest daughter Anna. He was also to discuss the possibility of a marriage between Mary and the Lutheran duke, Philip of Bavaria.

"Another heretic!" Mary yelled, flinging a glass of wine at the wall. "They expect me to marry a Protestant heretic? I refuse! And I am sure my cousin the emperor is as appalled at the suggestion as I am. I will never marry someone who openly defies God's word and denies the authority of the pope."

Mary looked at Chapuys as she spoke. He had heard of the marriage negotiations and immediately set out to make the emperor aware and then go to Mary and tell him herself.

"Believe me, my lady, the emperor is not pleased to hear of this," Chapuys said. "He informs me he will pressure the king not to proceed with the match."

"This is that devil Cromwell's doing. He and the other heretic Cranmer will be overjoyed if I am shackled to a Lutheran for the rest of my life. Tell the emperor that I will never abandon my faith, the faith of my mother. I would rather remain a maid the rest of my life and be known as Lady Mary, the most unhappy lady in Christendom, than betray God, my conscience, and all that I know to be right!"

By the autumn of that year, negotiations for a marriage between Henry and Anna had been secured, yet the talks regarding Mary and Duke Philip were still ongoing. Anna was expected to arrive by the end of the year, and Duke Philip was to visit England ahead of her. The King summoned Mary to court where she would eventually meet the young duke.

"I don't think I should even like to look at him," Mary told Margaret as they walked in the gardens of Westminster Abbey on a cold December day. "I am told the duke is already here and eager to meet me. Here, allow me." Mary gestured to Margaret's baby girl, whom she had swaddled in blankets to protect her from the chill air.

Margaret handed little Katherine over to her friend. She was touched when Margaret and Piero decided to name their first child after her mother and more so when they asked her to be the baby's godmother. "This entire situation is ludicrous." Suddenly Katherine began cooing vigorously. "See, even little Kate agrees. I shall never marry the Duke of Bavaria."

"That's disappointing, my lady," a heavily accented voice came from behind the women, startling them. Mary quickly handed Kate back to Margaret and stepped in front of her friend and godchild.

The dashing young man chuckled when he saw Mary's protectiveness. "There is no need to worry, madam. I am Duke Philip of Bavaria. I mean no harm to you ladies."

Mary and Margaret looked at each other bewildered and wondered how long the duke had followed them.

"Sir, this is improper," Mary said coldly. "We were not meant to meet until the banquet tomorrow night. I would thank you to be on your way and leave my good servant and me to finish our walk."

"Of course, madam, I have been very rude, and I do not wish to intrude much longer. But I had to see for myself, away from the prying eyes of the court," Philip said.

"See what for yourself?" Mary said, unaware she had taken the bait.

"I had to see if the tales of your beauty and intellect do you justice. I can see they do not. I look forward to speaking with you more tomorrow night. Perhaps I can even persuade you to dance with me." Without waiting for Mary to respond, Philip bowed and went on his way.

Mary's face was inflamed, though not exclusively from anger.

Since England was still without a queen, 23-year-old Mary took precedence over all the other ladies of the court. She sat at the king's right side, with Duke Philip on Henry's left as the guest of honor. Further down the table, Mary spotted her six-year-old sister Elizbeth eagerly drinking in the splendor of the court. Mary couldn't help but smile when she thought of Elizabeth peppering her with questions about "that handsome duke," as she called him. Mary had to agree that Philip was, indeed, very handsome.

"When will you marry? Will you have to move far away? Will they allow me to come visit you? Will you come to visit me? Why must you marry? How magnificent will the wedding be?"

"Lizzie, you are getting too ahead of things," Mary said when the two sisters spent time alone earlier in the day. "Duke Philip and I will not marry. We are not suited for each other. He is of the heretical faith, and mine is the true faith, as yours should be."

Elizabeth knew enough of her sister's beliefs to lower her eyes at that last comment. While she missed her sister dearly and loved spending time with her, even at such a young age, Elizabeth knew the conversation would eventually turn to religion and what Elizabeth was being taught.

"Religion should be a private thing," Elizabeth whispered.

"What was that" Mary asked.

"Nothing, sister," Elizabeth said, and quickly changed the subject. "I think I shall wear my blue silk gown for the banquet tonight."

Not long after the court festivities commences, the moment Mary had been dreading came. Duke Philip had asked the king's permission to dance with his daughter, and Henry obliged.

Philip offered Mary his hand and led her to the floor to a chorus of applause. Mary was stiff when she and Philip danced the Galliard but found herself loosening up as they went on.

When she and Philip danced La Volta together, Mary found that she was feeling drawn to Philip. With every touch and every look, Mary sank deeper into a feeling she had only known briefly years ago when the spark of passion flickered after encountering John, the handsome groom. But with Philip, that feeling was more pronounced. It has to be all the wine I had tonight, Mary told herself.

Before the fun died down, the king excused himself. Mary noticed he was having difficulty walking. His wounded leg was troubling him again. The king had also grown stouter since their last meeting, he became breathless more easily and his appetite seemed insatiable. She pushed the troubling thoughts from her mind and returned her attention to Philip, who was proving himself a good conversationalist and, though Mary hated to admit it, charming company.

The pair had found a somewhat secluded area near a window overlooking the snow-covered palace gardens to speak.

"I know my religious beliefs are not what you would want in a husband," Philip said. "But I would never ask you to abandon yours, even as my wife."

"There is no force on earth that could make me turn my back on the true faith," Mary said. "And in the unlikely event I were to marry outside my faith, I would work night and day to turn my husband's heart to Catholicism and save his soul."

Philip was charmed by Mary's fervent passion for her religion. "I think there are those who may underestimate you, Mary," he said.

Mary didn't know she could enjoy the sound of her own name coming from another's lips so much until now. "I believe those who underestimate you will one day regret their folly."

Without thinking, Philip leaned in and kissed Mary lightly. Neither of them expected the spark that would follow. Mary was shocked by her body's reaction. Philip pulled his lips away slightly, resting his forehead against Mary's. Both kept their eyes closed, savoring the sweet moment. Then Philip moved to kiss Mary again, this time with more passion. He placed his arms around her waist and drew her closer. Instinctively, Mary rested her hands against his chest, melting into his embrace, never wanting it to end.

When it did, Mary was captivated by his smile and wondered if marriage to this man would be so terrible after all. Then another thought hit her—Queen Katherine would never approve of this match, and Mary's heart sank.

That night, Mary slipped into a fantastic dream, the kind she'd never experienced before. As she drifted to sleep, Mary had an image of herself standing in her candle lit bedchamber wearing only her linen night shift. She was anxiously playing with the diamond and ruby encrusted wedding band Philip had slipped onto her thin finger earlier in the day. Now, she waited for her husband to come to her and truly claim her in every way.

When Philip entered the room, she stood nervously in one spot. Philip made his way to her, and it was all Mary could do to keep from trembling. Philip removed his own bed clothes and without saying a word lifted off Mary's shift, scooped her up, and placed her onto the bed.

His kiss was hard and full of passion. Mary was transported to a place of pure bliss as he moved his hands all over her. She waited eagerly for the moment he would be inside her as Philip delicately caressed the forbidden parts of her body.

Mary woke with a start, drenched in sweat and breathing heavily. There was an unfamiliar wetness between her thighs. She looked around the room, but there were no candles. When she saw no ring on her finger, the reality of the situation hit her like a stone.

Laying back against the sweat-soaked pillow, Mary looked over at the empty spot next to her and began to weep silently. She knew her dream was a dreadful sin but couldn't face the idea of discussing it in the confessional.

It had been a few weeks since she and Philip danced together. The busy matters of the court had kept both Mary and the duke occupied so often that they did not have another moment alone together before he left court. Philip was traveling with the Duke of Suffolk to meet his cousin Anna when she arrived in England.

The king would marry his new queen in the morning, though Mary knew he was unhappy about it, having found his future wife unappealing. The king was insulted when he tried to woo Anna in a game of courtly love. He arrived at the house where she was residing in disguise, hoping to win the fair maiden awaiting her king. Anna was aghast by the advances of the audacious and elderly stranger. When she slapped the king after he tried to kiss her, Henry became enraged. His disguise discarded, Anna dropped to her knees in panic and fear. She apologized in broken English, her translator attempting to explain that such romantic jests are unheard of in Germany. Henry would not hear it, and stormed back to his palace, leaving his terrified new bride unsure of what would happen next. After the uncomfortable meeting with Anna, Henry tasked Cromwell with finding an impediment to the union, but he came up with nothing.

At eight in the morning on Tuesday, January 6, 1540, Henry VIII married Anna of Cleves, henceforth to be known as Queen Anne. The ceremony was presided over by Archbishop Cranmer, both Mary and Elizabeth were in attendance, but the King wanted his three-year-old son kept far from the court.

As Mary watched her new stepmother walk down the aisle on her wedding day, she thought the queen modestly pretty, no great beauty, but not displeasing to look at. She liked Anne's dress, which was cut in the Dutch fashion with a rounded skirt and no trail. The gown was also embroidered in gold with large flowers of great Oriental pearls. Mary thought it was a strange look, but Anne seemed to pull it off effortlessly.

The wedding feast was an uncomfortable affair. Mary looked for Philip, but he was busy tending to his cousin. The new queen seemed nervous, and the king showed little interest in celebrating his marriage.

The court was buzzing the next day when rumors began to swirl that the king refused to consummate the marriage. Mary decided to return to Hunsdon and take Elizabeth with her to protect the child from whatever storm she knew was brewing. She saw Philip one final time before leaving.

Strolling through the palace gardens, Philip came upon her as he did that first night at Westminster. This time she was not afraid, signaling to her ladies that they should follow at a distance. Philip took her arm in his.

"Mary, I am going back to Germany, but I am hopeful that I will return to England soon, and when I do, it will be to celebrate our marriage."

Mary wasn't so optimistic. She knew now what it was to love someone, but the tension around the court regarding the king's marriage made Mary feel uneasy about a future with Philip. The duke cupped Mary's face with his hands and she wrapped her arms around him. She wanted to savor every moment of that kiss, knowing in her heart it was their last.

Six months after Mary returned to Hunsdon she received word that the king's marriage to Anne of Cleves had been annulled. Their marriage was terminated on the grounds of non-consummation and a pre-contract between Anne and the Duke of Lorraine's son from when she was twelve.

This confirmed what Mary had known for months: She and Philip would never be. Their letters had grown from weekly to sparse and had finally stopped before Mary received the news about the end of the royal marriage.

But there was more. The king blamed Cromwell for forcing him into the Cleves' marriage, and Cromwell's enemies capitalized on the situation. He had finally fallen. Mary crossed herself and thanked God that he saw fit to remove Cromwell from the king's side. Mary would have preferred to hear that he was burned for his heresy, but when she learned his execution was bungled, taking several strokes to remove his head, she knew justice had been done.

Mary wasn't fully satisfied. While Anne Boleyn and Cromwell were gone, Archbishop Cranmer remained, as did the Earl of Hertford. Cromwell had been arrested and taken to the Tower in early June but wasn't executed until July 28, the same day Henry married his fifth wife. The King had fallen in love with one of Anne of Cleves' maids, the seventeen-year-old Katherine Howard, one of the Duke of Norfolk's nieces and cousin to Anne Boleyn. Staring at a letter informing her of these developments,

Mary turned her eyes to the sky and asked the heavens: "How many wives will he have?"

•   •   •

Mary and Elizabeth stood outside the king's privy apartment at Hampton Court. They were waiting to be called in so their father could present his daughters to the new queen. Mary was not impressed by the woman the King had chosen as his newest consort. She was shorter than Mary and five years her junior. Looking at her father and his new bride, Mary calculated that the king must be at least thirty years older than Katherine.

The sisters bowed to their new stepmother. Mary felt a pang of resentment at bowing to a woman who was little more than a child. Mary instantly disliked the girl, looking at Katherine's innocent smile as she fawned over Elizabeth and ordered her maids to bring in some cakes. Familiar feelings started to bubble to the surface. This simple, dotty girl was married, the Queen of England and given the king's amorous attention very soon to be with child. Mary thought of Philip at that moment.

Although her affection for him had diminished and she felt relief at not having married a heretic, Mary was missing the feelings he stirred in her and the possibilities he represented. It seemed clear to Mary that her father was keen on keeping her a maid, unwed, and therefore no threat to him.

It never escaped Mary that were she to marry and have a son, his grandfather would consider him a more significant threat to his and Edward's throne than any invading army. She knew that as long as her father lived, she would remain the Lady Mary, a spinster with only her younger siblings to care for.

Queen Katherine presented Mary and Elizabeth with a set of matching gold rings as a token of her affection. Elizabeth was overjoyed to receive the gift, expressing her gratitude by breaking protocol and hugging the queen, who reciprocated in kind. But Mary just mumbled her thanks and handed the ring to her maid. Katherine was fully aware of the slight, but the king was oblivious, keeping his attention fixed on his buxom young wife.

Lately, Mary had been spending more time at court at the king's insistence. The king thought his eldest daughter would make a good companion for the queen and hoped Mary would become somewhat of a mentor to his inexperienced young wife. But the king didn't keep tabs on his wife and daughter's relationship, and Mary and Katherine were happy to keep their distance from each other.

Katherine attempted to reach out to Mary on several occasions, inviting her to supper, to go riding and to play music together. But most of the time, Mary declined. Though young and inexperienced with interpersonal politics, Katherine was not blind to how Mary looked down on her, shooting disapproving glances at her when Katherine acted in a way Mary believed to be frivolous. Katherine finally had enough and complained to the king, who agreed that two of Mary's maids should be removed from her service as punishment for her lack of respect.

Luckily for Mary, the king did not agree to Katherine's demand that he banish Margaret from court, but it was still heartbreaking for Mary to lose two loyal ladies. The parting was distressing for all involved, neither of the maids wanted to leave their mistress, and the stress caused Mary to fall ill.

As Mary lay in bed with the familiar searing pain in her head, Margaret went to find Chapuys, hoping Mary's protector could help her figure out a way to reconcile with the queen. Chapuys visited Mary when she was recovered and told her to play the part of a dutiful stepdaughter when she must be in the queen's presence and keep her distance at other times.

"I long for the day when the king tires of her as he has done so often in the past," Mary told Chapuys. "It has been many months since the wedding, and the queen still has not conceived a child. I pray the king sees this as a divine judgment that this girl is not fit to be the mother of his son."

"Perhaps, my lady, you are not aware that the queen has been very generous to the Countess of Salisbury as she still languishes in the Tower," Chapuys said to Mary, who looked at him in bewilderment.

"It is true, madam. As a member of the powerful and devoutly Catholic Howard family, the queen expressed to me in confidence that she believes the countess innocent but dare not say anything to the king. So, she is doing what she can to make the countess comfortable, sending warm clothes and blankets along with food, wine and books."

Mary was stunned. Though she wrote to and prayed for the countess often, she was powerless to do anything about her situation. Mary felt a tiny seed of respect for Katherine Howard growing. She decided she would send the queen a note thanking her for her kind treatment of the woman who was a second mother to her.

When Margaret returned with the queen's reply, it included a gold pomander to signal that their feud had ended. Mary knew she and the queen would never be friends, and Mary would never cease to see Katherine as a silly little girl. But since she was genuine in her interest in helping the countess, Mary decided she could at least be warm to the queen. But as Mary was soon to learn, even the efforts of the queen would not be enough to help her beloved Lady Pole.

Only a short time later, the tranquility of Hunsdon was shattered with the heart-rending news of Lady Pole's fate. Mary screamed and fell to the ground. Margaret rushed to her side, leaving her husband standing silently as he witnessed the aftermath of the news he had brought. When he learned Lady Pole had been executed that May morning, he knew his wife's mistress should be told in the company of those who love her. Piero managed to survive Cromwell's fall since he had established himself so well at King Henry's court, and Mary and Margaret were still the only ones who knew that Piero was a spy from Rome.

Margaret held her dear friend as she cried. Mary was inconsolable, only able to utter the words "how?" and "why?" through gasping breaths. Piero wished he could withhold what he still had to tell Mary but knew she would find out eventually. As his wife cradled Mary, Piero knelt next to them, venturing to take Mary's hand.

"Princess, I fear what I have to say next will cause you more distress, but you need to know," Piero began. "The countess was roused early this morning and told she must prepare to die. She refused to acknowledge the death sentence, saying she had no trial and had not been afforded the opportunity to defend herself. The king sent the Earl of Hertford to oversee the execution, which the earl said was botched."

"God no!" Mary cried out, having gone limp in Margaret's arms. "What happened? What did they do to her? What did they do to a frail sixty-seven-year-old woman?"

"She was afforded a private execution within the walls of the Tower out of respect for her royal rank. Her final thoughts were of you, my lady. She asked that all those in attendance pray for Her Grace, Princess Mary, and for England's future. Reluctantly she laid her head on the block, not wanting to be manhandled by those ready to pounce. But the executioner was an inexperienced youth who made a mess of his job. His first few blows cut into the countess's neck and back. It would take several more before he fully dispatched the lady."

Mary started to tremble. She could not speak for several minutes. When she finally tried to stand up, she couldn't get to her feet, falling backwards against Margaret. Piero scooped Mary up and together, with his wife, brought Mary to her bedchamber. Mary wept when she thought of her loving governess. Her only consolation was the knowledge that the countess was beyond her pain and in the company of Jesus Christ, his Blessed Mother, and Mary's own mother. Thinking of the late queen, Mary wept harder.

Mary spent the next several months grieving for her dear Lady Pole while also attempting to regain and enjoy her quiet country life. Margaret had suggested Mary invite Lady Elizabeth for a visit to cheer her up. Embracing the idea, Mary eagerly greeted her eight-year-old sister when she arrived on a hot June morning. After the child settled and reluctantly attended Mass with Mary, she asked if they could go riding, and Mary was happy to oblige.

In the stables, Elizabeth happily showed off her new green riding habit, which had been the queen's New Year's gift. Mary was struck by how vain her sister could sometimes be—her mother's child, Mary thought.

It wasn't escaping Mary that as Elizabeth grew older, she showed signs of being very much like her mother — a true testament to the strength of pedigree. At such a young age, Elizabeth had Anne Boleyn's youthful grace and charm, even the child's laugh was very much like Anne's. In her grief, Mary was finding that looking at a miniature version of the woman who ruined her life was too much to bear. Old feelings of resentment started to rise to the surface as Mary watched her sister.

"Let's race down to that old broken tree, you know, the one that was struck by lightning, and back again," the excited child exclaimed.

"I don't know that I feel much like racing today, sister."

Mary's formal tone took Elizabeth by surprise.

"Oh, please, Mary, please! Winning a race may make you smile, and afterward we can have a picnic."

Reluctantly Mary capitulated and found that Elizabeth was right. Winning the race against her little sister did make her smile, and Elizabeth was happy with her defeat if it meant Mary wasn't feeling cross anymore. The sisters laid out in the sun, enjoying their picnic and talking about Elizabeth's lessons and her aptitude for music. They decided that after dinner that evening, they would play songs together with Elizabeth on the lute and Mary on the virginals.

"Oh no, Mary, look," Elizabeth said, startling Mary from her daydream. The child got up and ran over to a tree where a bird's nest had fallen from its perch. The frantic chirping of the baby bird had caught Elizabeth's attention. The child carefully lifted the nest off the injured bird.

"Be gentle, Lizzie. We don't want to accidentally hurt the creature further. Here, let me take a look." Mary took the bird from her sister and gave it a quick examination.

"I think this little fellow is going to be just fine. I think he was just scared because he was trapped under the nest. Here, we'll put the nest back in the tree, and soon his mother will return and take care of him."

"I hope she returns home soon. It is a terrible thing when you're afraid and have no mother," Elizabeth said, quickly looking away from Mary. She knew better than to mention her mother, even vaguely, to her sister, but Mary let the comment go. She knew from experience that Elizabeth was right.

Keeping with their jovial mood from the afternoon, the sisters decided they would dress very finely, as if they would be playing music for the court and then dance until they were too tired to move. Mary instructed her cooks to prepare a lavish feast for supper, and after they ate, the sisters and their attendants retreated into a parlor for the evening's entertainment.

Mary was very impressed with how well Elizabeth played. She knew her sister would grow into an accomplished woman; her earlier feelings of resentment and anger had dissipated.

The sisters enjoyed a happy reunion, spending weeks reading, riding, dancing, and playing music. Elizabeth was still unhappy about attending Mass with her sister. She didn't appreciate the religious instruction Mary was forcing on her.

Elizabeth's chaplain was not invited to join the child in Mary's household. Instead, she had her own chaplain tutoring Elizabeth. While Elizabeth wasn't happy about the countless hours throughout the day Mary would spend in prayer, her affections for her sister made it worth it.

After a happy summer that helped to take Mary's mind off Lady Pole somewhat, Elizabeth returned to her home at Hatfield. Mary expected life to move quietly from here on out, and for several more months this was the case. However, the tranquility came to a crashing end in November. Word reached Mary that Queen Katherine had been arrested.

Mary was not surprised when the queen's salaciousness returned to haunt her. There had always been rumors that Katherine Howard was not the chaste flower the king believed her to be when she came to court to serve Anne of Cleves. Now it seemed that a man from her past had returned to court seeking a position within the queen's household, which she foolishly agreed to. All this, while also carrying on an affair with one of the king's grooms.

"My Lord," Margaret said, crossing herself. "How could even she be so foolish? Age is no excuse. She has doomed herself."

"She has indeed," Mary said, shaking her head. "Being a cousin to the great whore, how could the king have expected any other outcome? Chapuys tells me the king has isolated himself and refuses to see anyone. The realm is left virtually with no government."

Mary felt a twinge of guilt as she thought of Katherine Howard languishing in the Tower. Though she never liked the queen, seeing her only as a giddy girl, she felt her actions were more of a spoiled brat who indulged herself in any pleasure she wanted.

She wondered if the king would send her to a nunnery rather than take her life. But knowing the king, this blow to his ego and his imagined youth and virility would not be tolerated. Poor Katherine Howard would lose her life. Mary knew it.

Knowing the impact this news would have on her little sister, Mary called Elizabeth back to Hunsdon, where they would await word of the queen's fate together. Elizabeth's governess had kept the news of the queen's arrest from the child, and Mary thought that best.

Elizabeth liked Katherine, and Mary wanted to break the news to her herself. When word came the queen would be executed on February 13, 1542, Mary decided she would tell Elizabeth during supper the night before. She kept Elizabeth busy most of the day, taking her riding, helping her with her studies, and attending chapel. Mary was not pleased when Elizabeth took the host and made a face. She knew her sister was still being brought up in the ways of heresy and wanted to have a word with the king about the people surrounding his youngest daughter, but she knew now was not the time.

As the sisters dined on roast venison, vegetables, and sugared treats, Mary broached the subject of the queen. "Lizzie, sweetheart, have you heard any news of the court?"

"No, sister, which is strange. The queen has written to me several times but her letters have stopped. I hope I have not displeased her."

Looking down at the innocent expression on nine-year-old Elizabeth's face, Mary dreaded what she was about to do.

"Elizabeth, you have not displeased the queen. In fact, it is the queen who has displeased the king."

The child tensed as she remembered a time, long ago, when she had heard those exact words.

"I know you know what adultery is," Mary said as the child nodded silently, fear gripping her body. "Queen Katherine has committed adultery. She was arrested and taken to the Tower where she will be executed tomorrow morning."

Elizabeth's hand flew to her mouth, and she bolted from the table, running straight to the privy closet where she vomited violently. Mary rubbed her sister's back as the child emptied the last of her dinner from her aching belly. Taking her sister to her bed, Mary tucked her in and laid beside her. The child was crying more silently now but would not let go of her sister's waist, burying her face in her shoulder. Mary thought back to that time when she, too, was so afraid and her mother had held her close all night.

Mary noticed Elizabeth's hand under the pillow, apparently clutching something in her fist.

"Lizzie, what is that?"

"Nothing," the child said, somewhat suspiciously.

"Elizabeth, let me see it." The girl refused to hand it over. "Elizabeth, give it to me now."

Mary couldn't believe her eyes when Elizabeth pulled out a small gold locket with the letters *AB* engraved on it. When she opened the trinket, she was face to face with her enemy from six years ago. She thrust the locket back to her sister and angrily got up from the bed.

"I'm sorry," Elizabeth said in a small, weeping voice. "I just miss her."

"How could you miss such a horrible woman? She poisoned my mother! She wanted me dead, Elizabeth, you know that don't you?"

"That isn't the woman I remember. I have so few memories of her."

"You should count yourself lucky," Mary said, cutting off her sister. "I have many memories of that woman! The stories I could tell you would make you glad the king cut off her head!"

Elizabeth attempted to protest, a torrent of tears threatening again, but Mary put up her hand to silence her. "Go to sleep now, Elizabeth. I suggest you pray hard for your sins and the sins of those lecherous women with whom you share blood."

Mary turned and left the room. She refused to look back at the hysterical child she knew she hurt in response to her pain.

As she returned to her chambers, she caught sight of herself in a mirror. Her face was still red with anger, and it seemed for a moment it was the king staring back at her. Clamping her palms to her cheeks, Mary looked in the mirror and asked, "What is the matter with you?"

CHAPTER 11

1542 - 1544

With Katherine Howard dead and the king seemingly uninterested in taking a wife for the first time in about a decade, Mary acted as the First Lady of the land. The king requested Mary take up permanent residence at court.

Though she missed the quiet tranquility of Hunsdon, she felt somewhat triumphant at the reverence being shown to her by the members of the court. Nobles who once berated her as an ungrateful bastard who refused to accept her place were now creeping up to her in an attempt to get close to the king, who seemed less interested in the government of his realm.

Mary worried about her father. His temper was shorter and his appetite more robust. After Katherine's death, he fell into a depression that only seemed to lift when it was time for a meal. He abandoned all decorum and propriety during a meal. He'd slump over his plate, abandoning his fork, tearing at the meat with his massive, paw-like hands. He'd slurp goblet after goblet of wine or ale, belching loudly, much to the disgust of those sharing the king's table. Of course, nobody dared to say anything to the king about his table manners.

As the king grew larger, his leg troubled him more. He would spend days confined to his bed. He would scream at his doctors, who tried in vain to administer what the king deemed useless remedies to ease his condition. Even Mary was not permitted to see him.

Mary began to notice she was being deferred to more and more. While the council handled government business, she was called upon to perform tasks typically undertaken by a queen consort.

Mary found it all exhilarating. All her new responsibilities kept her busy late into the night. She stood as godmother to several noble children, visited poor houses, endowed convents and dined with ambassadors. But after a few months of this pace, Mary started to feel ill, and by April of that year, she had been confined to her bed with terrible headaches and pains in her stomach. She couldn't eat and slept fitfully. Margaret stayed with her as often as possible, taking little Kate along to try and cheer her, to no avail.

The king began to feel better as Mary grew worse; he sent his own physician to see her but would not visit her himself for fear of contagion. As Mary's illness stretched into weeks, real concern for her for her life grew. The physician told the king he didn't believe Mary was long for this world.

Through her haze, Mary could hear the commotion around her. Doctors came and went, and Margaret held Mary's hand each time they decided bleeding her was the best option. As she lay abed wondering why she was once again so afflicted, Mary thought about Queen Jane.

She wondered how aware the queen had been during her illness, thinking about their conversation regarding what Jane believed was her great sin. If she really was close to death, would she see her mother again or Jane? Her beloved Lady Pole? There had been so much death in her life, so much hurt. Mary wondered if quietly slipping from life to death would be so bad. Perhaps it would bring her the peace she needed.

Her thoughts were the worst of all sins. If she did not fight for her life, she would never see her mother again. Heaven was no place for those who forfeit their own lives. Still, the thought of giving up was appealing.

As her fever raged, Mary heard a familiar voice repeating the Lord's Prayer. It wasn't Margaret. Whose small voice was cutting its way through the noise? To her shock, Mary realized it was Elizabeth.

The child had written to the king relentlessly when she heard how sick her sister was. She begged him to allow her to visit the court and see Mary. Eventually, the king allowed it. Looking over at her little sister, whose face was bright red from tears and fervent prayer, Mary knew there was more she was meant to do on this earth.

Remembering her promise to Queen Jane about Edward, she vowed again to turn the prince's heart to Catholicism. As Elizabeth prayed, Mary remembered how cruel she was to her over the portrait locket. Why should she fault a child for missing her mother? It was a state she was in every moment of every day? Looking at Elizabeth, Mary mustered all her strength. She lifted her hand and stroked her sister's face. The child's eyes were big and pleading, full of an apology she longed to offer but was too afraid to give.

"It's going to be all right, Lizzie," Mary said. "I'm not leaving you. You will always have your big sister to watch over and protect you."

Elizabeth crawled onto the bed next to Mary, cuddling into the crook of her arm. She started to weep until both sisters fell asleep from exhaustion. When she was well enough, the king allowed Mary to leave the court and return to her country home, where she recuperated fully.

She was surprised that the king allowed her brother to visit her towards the end of the summer. That precious jewel was so rarely out of his box. Strict rules were in place for Mary and Edward to follow for that visit, but Mary enjoyed the few days she had with her little brother.

Although, there was one incident Mary found disturbing. At five years old, the prince was already a serious and devout boy. He was being raised as a heretic, and Mary knew heretics frowned on dancing, music, and other things they believed to be frivolous, like lavish clothing. When Mary welcomed the boy, he was in somber black attire, and when she bowed to him, the boy gave Mary a disapproving look. Later the child would chastise Mary for her sumptuous dress, complaining that she ought to be more modest.

Mary could hardly believe what the prince was saying. He was so much older than his five years. It had to be all the isolation. Being surrounded by heretical adults was taking its toll, and Mary saw her opportunity to make good on her promise to Queen Jane.

Mary pulled out Queen Jane's rosary and presented it to Edward at supper.

"Do you know what these are, brother?

"Popish beads," the boy said with a childish lisp.

"They are rosary beads, which once belonged to your mother, Queen Jane."

Mary noticed Edward stiffen at the mention of his mother. She wondered how much he knew of her and if he felt any sorrow at having never known her.

"These were very special to your mother," Mary went on. "She had them with her all the time. She left them to me, but I think it would make her profoundly happy if you were to take them."

"Sister, I cannot take this from you. They represent those who pray in error, and I do not."

Mary was shocked. "No, Edward, these represent the true faith! The faith of our mothers! You are being raised in error, child. You are so young yet, we have time to remedy that. You will understand when you are older."

"I understand now," Edward said coldly. "Excuse me, sister, I am not hungry anymore."

Without another word, the prince left the table, his food scarcely touched and his sister in distress. It would not be easy to keep her promise, but she had to try again.

At Christmas, all three royal children attended the festivities at Hampton Court. The king asked Mary to preside over the court in the absence of a queen; she was happy to oblige. Each guest presented themselves to Mary, who welcomed them graciously to her father's court. Later that night, there would be a lavish feast and dancing to start off the holiday season.

"Dear cousin," Frances Brandon said with a low bow to Mary, "it is so good to see you. You look well."

"Welcome to court, cousin, and Merry Christmas. Who is this shy creature behind your skirts?"

"Come here at once and bow to your cousin princess...err umm, Lady Mary," Frances said to her frightened child. The girl did as she was told and bowed low to her royal cousin.

Mary was annoyed by the way Frances chastised her daughter. She had still not forgiven the child for being born a girl.

"You must be Lady Jane Grey," Mary said in a soothing tone that eased the child somewhat. "I have so looked forward to meeting you, child. I hear you love to read. That is also one of my favorite things to do."

Little Jane Grey smiled from ear to ear before being brushed away by her mother, who made her nurse take the child to their apartments.

"Really, cousin, must you be so hard on her? She is only a child," Mary said to Frances, who looked as though she wanted to ask Mary what she knew about being a mother but thought better of it.

"She is too willful and stubborn, my lady. She must learn her place."

Mary just rolled her eyes. Frances walked away, and Mary greeted more guests.

"Lady Latimer, it is so good to see you," Mary said to a tall, blond-haired woman who was only a few years her senior. Mary and Lady Katherine Latimer had known each other from when they were much younger. Back then, Katherine went by her maiden name, Parr. Katherine's mother was in the service of Mary's mother, and Katherine had spent a few years as a maid in Mary's household before the Great Matter. She left Mary's service after King Henry disbanded her household and went on to marry her first husband, who left her a wealthy widow. Rumors were swirling that her second husband was about to make her an even wealthier widow and free to marry her true love, Thomas Seymour, another brother to the late Queen Jane and uncle to Prince Edward. "You are very welcome to court."

"Thank you, Lady Mary," Lady Latimer bowed low and when she rose kissed Mary on both cheeks.

"It seems a lifetime ago that you served in my household when I was only a little girl. So much has changed since then," Mary said. "I was a princess, and you were simply Mistress Katherine Parr."

The Christmas festivities were full of joy, laughter and peace. The king was in good spirits. He even felt well enough to dance; his leg was hardly troubling him this season. Mary and Katherine Parr were talking by the fire when the king approached and began speaking to them.

"Where is your husband tonight, Lady Latimer?" the King asked.

"I am afraid he is unwell and unable to make the journey, Your Majesty."

"Well, since you are without an escort tonight and I am without a queen, would you do me the honor of dancing with me?"

Off they went. The King seemed very relaxed with Lady Latimer, who Mary knew had to be nervous but showed no outward signs of it.

A few weeks after Christmas, Katherine Parr became a widow for the second time. By July, she was the king's sixth wife.

The wedding was a subtle affair, about two dozen guests filed into the queen's closet at Hampton Court. Mary acted as chief bridesmaid and Elizabeth was in attendance as well. When Archbishop Cranmer asked the king if he would take Katherine to be his lawful wife, he replied with an enthusiastic yes. It seemed the omnipresent specter of Katherine Howard had finally vanished.

During the wedding feast, Mary spied Anne of Cleves sitting among a group of ladies. She had heard that the king had invited the woman he now called his "dearest sister" to attend his wedding and, from the look of it, being divorced was agreeing with Anne.

Mary was pleased to see Anne again. She felt sorry for her one-time stepmother, it could not have been easy to be so humiliated, but Anne seemed to be handling it well. She was aware that the vultures of the court would be making comments behind Anne's back, but Anne held her own, and Mary felt proud.

"Dear Anne," Mary said. "I am so pleased to see you again. You look splendid. Come walk with me." The gaggle of ladies flocking Anne, including Mary's cousin Frances, bowed low and dispersed.

"Lady Mary, thank you, that was getting to be too much," Anne said with a giggle. "All of those ladies asking how I am, feigning compassion when really all they are after is gossip and hoping I am nothing more than a bitter old crone."

"My poor friend. I saw that look in your eye," Mary said. "I could tell you were feeling how I have felt on many occasions at court. Vultures, every one of them."

"Indeed, a fine burden Madam Katherine has taken upon herself," Anne said, though Mary knew she wasn't talking only about a backstabbing court.

Looking at the king as he dined with his new queen, Mary couldn't help but wonder how long this new stepmother would last. Would she end up divorced or make some fatal error that would cost her life? Mary noticed her sister Elizabeth. She was entertaining their cousin Jane Grey while a group of adults hovered nearby. Taking notice of the way Elizabeth was frequently glancing at the queen, she knew her sister was wondering the same.

Elizabeth was more often at court after the wedding, as was their cousin Jane. Katherine took a special interest in both Elizabeth and Jane, providing for their education and taking them under her wing. She wanted Mary, Elizabeth, and Prince Edward at court more often so they could spend time with their father.

The queen's fervent desire was for the rift between the king and his children to be healed. She insisted the king and the royal children dine together as often as possible, which to Mary's surprise were jovial affairs. The king seemed genuinely pleased to have his daughters around. They talked and laughed, and the girls delighted in the king's affections.

One night after supper, Mary and Elizabeth enchanted the king and queen when they played the lute and virginals together.

"No father has ever been so blessed to have such beautiful and talented daughters," the King exclaimed.

Mary and Elizabeth looked at one another in pure ecstasy over the king's comment. Edward's appearance was still rare. The king never ceased to fear over his health and any possible tragedy that could befall him. Katherine and Mary soon became great friends and, being so similar in age, had many common interests.

Mary noticed the queen avoided the subject of religion when they were together. Katherine's household was filled with people who had heretical leanings. The more conservative members of the king's court, like Bishop Gardiner, weren't taking too kindly to the new queen.

Gardiner had come upon Mary while she was walking in the gardens of Hampton Court and warned her to take care about building such a close relationship with one who favors heresy. Gardiner warned Mary to have a care for her soul and noted that her late mother would not want her to continue such a friendship. Mary didn't appreciate the reference to her mother, but thanked the bishop for his concern and walked away quickly.

The conversation with Gardiner left Mary feeling uneasy. What if the new Queen was indeed a heretic? She was already building a relationship with her siblings and cousin. How could she keep her promise to protect those young souls if the queen herself was instilling heretical beliefs in them? Mary slept fitfully that night and decided to keep a closer eye on those around the queen.

Not long after this, the king had three Protestants burned to death in the Great Park at Windsor Castle, where he and the queen had been residing since the wedding. Although Henry had been making reforms to the Church of England, he was not permitting any open show of Protestantism in his realm. Though she abhorred taking any life, Mary was pleased to hear that England was being made safer from heresy. The queen showed no sign of being affected by the burnings. She did not intercede on behalf of the victims, instead busying herself with charitable and domestic affairs.

Academic pursuits were a favorite pastime of the queen; she often invited Mary to study with her, and under the queen's influence, Mary undertook a translation of Erasmus's *Paraphrases on the Four Gospels.*

"Tell me, daughter, do you want this to go forth to the world under your name or as the production of an unknown writer," Katherine asked one day as they were close to completing their work. "You will, in my opinion, do yourself a real injury if you refuse to let it go down to posterity under the auspices of your own name."

"Oh, in all honesty, I hadn't given it much thought," Mary replied. "Perhaps I should keep my name off this? It may not seem proper for a woman to author such an intellectual work."

"Mary," Katherine said disapprovingly, "I do not see why you should repudiate that praise which all men confer on themselves, justly or not."

Katherine convinced Mary to allow the work to be published under her name. The king, the court and intellectuals across Europe lavished praise on the two royal women. The editor of the translation paid tribute to Mary, calling her "the most noble, virtuous, the most witty, and the most studious Lady in Christendom." He added that Mary was a "peerless flower of virginity"—a reminder Mary did not need.

Mary was thriving at court again thanks to the favor of her intelligent and benevolent stepmother. In February 1544, a ball was held during the visit of the Spanish grandee, the Duke of Nájera, and Mary outshone everyone. She danced elegantly and dressed lavishly in a gown of gold cloth under a violet-colored velvet robe with a coronet of large precious stones on her head. The duke was charmed by Mary and was not shy about referring to her as "the princess" to anyone who would listen.

Chapuys was beaming when he saw Mary at the banquet He was thrilled that the duke was so enchanted by her. He was hoping that when Nájera returned to Spain he would be able to convince the emperor to once again approach King Henry about a Spanish marriage.

"Will you not dance, ambassador?" a flushed Mary asked when she spied her most loyal supporter sitting alone.

"Unfortunately, my dancing days are behind me, princess," Chapuys said. "I am suffering from gout."

"Oh, I am terribly sorry to hear that, my dear friend," Mary said. "We must get you the finest doctors available."

"I have seen all the doctors that I can stand, my lady. I did not want to do this tonight, but you must know that I have decided to retire and enjoy what time I have left on this earth back in Savoy."

Mary was stunned, but the shock of Chapuys' departure would soon be replaced by a fantastic event she never saw coming.

A few weeks after the banquet, Mary, Elizabeth and Edward were having another intimate family supper with the queen. The king would be late to the meal as he was busy with a new act of parliament to be passed. They dined on roasted venison, and seven-year-old Edward was regaling the group with the progress of his formal education, which had begun the year before. He loved learning the classics and theology, mathematics was his favorite subject, and Mary thought how strange it was that her little brother seemed to only enjoy life's cold pursuits. When Mary asked how he liked learning music, Edward stiffened.

"I pray you, dear sister, will no longer attend such dances and merriments which do not become a most Christian woman," the child said, lecturing his older sister about the frivolity of such things. The table grew silent.

The king finally arrived to the relief of the stunned ladies, who suddenly felt wary of dining with the child. The king hobbled as he made his way to the head of the table, wincing in pain with each step. His limp had gotten worse, but he'd be damned if he showed any weakness in front of his wife and children. He was in constant pain from his leg wound, which had grown more putrid. When the king sat down, he got right to the point.

"Daughters," the King began, "in a few days, parliament will pass a new and radical act of succession that will restore you both to the line of succession after your brother and his heirs."

The sisters sat in stunned silence.

"I know not if the Almighty will bless my union with the queen with more sons." Henry took Katherine's hand and kissed it. "If it should happen that I depart this life without any more sons and it should happen that Edward leaves behind no heirs, the throne will pass to Mary and her heirs, followed by Elizabeth and her heirs."

Still the sisters were silent, too shocked to speak. Mary never believed this could ever happen. She thought about the likelihood of her ever becoming queen. She thought about her mother and how pleased she would be at this turn of events.

Edward was still so young, and negotiations were already in progress to marry him to Mary Stuart, the child Queen of Scotland. There was no reason they wouldn't have a nursery full of children when the time came.

Mary knew the king was only doing this as a worst-case provision. Still, her restoration to the succession had to mean her father loved and respected her, didn't it? Mary looked at Elizabeth. There must have been a thousand thoughts running through her mind as well.

Mary wondered if it was necessary for the king to give Elizabeth a place in the succession. He must believe she was his child. As soon as her place in the succession was restored, old feelings and suspicions regarding Elizabeth resurfaced. *Don't go down this road again*, Mary thought.

"Of course, should either of you marry without my permission or Edward's after me, you will forfeit your claim to the throne and any other inheritance I may seem fit to bestow," Henry went on.

"Oh, I have no intention of marrying, father," Elizabeth said. She did not appreciate the laughter that erupted from her family following her comment.

"Of course, you will marry Elizabeth," Henry said, still amused. "It is a woman's duty to marry and have sons."

"Perhaps my destiny lies elsewhere, father." Henry laughed again. He would not battle his youngest daughter on this further now.

"Mary, you have been silent through all of this. What are you thinking?" Queen Katherine asked her.

"I am...I am just so grateful," Mary said, choking up. "Does this mean that we are no longer...no longer considered," she was having a hard time getting the words out. "Does this mean we are legitimized?"

Katherine regarded Mary with pity, knowing her stepdaughter wanted her mother's marriage recognized more than having her place in the succession back. Mary's guilt over having signed the submission eight years ago was not a secret to her. Tensing, she braced for the king to explode with rage at the question, but surprisingly Henry was gentle.

"No, daughter, you and Elizabeth can never be regarded as trueborn. My marriages to both of your mothers were unlawful and incestuous, as you both well know. Do you both understand?"

Heartbroken, the sisters looked down at their laps, and in unison, said: "Yes, Your Majesty."

Now that the succession was settled, Henry sought to recapture the glory of his youth. The following year, he and the emperor made a secret treaty for a joint invasion of France, which would begin that summer. While Henry campaigned in France, he left Katherine as regent in his place. The old Catholic faction within the court didn't appreciate the king's decision. While he was away, that faction, led by Stephen Gardiner, worked to gather evidence of heresy against the queen.

Mary could sense there was some uneasiness within the court. She noticed Gardiner and his friends were cozying up to her more, showing her even more deference than before. Though troubled by what Gardiner and the others had to say about the queen being a secret heretic, Mary was nonetheless impressed with how the queen was governing and imposing her authority on her male councilors.

Mary was with the queen in her chamber when Gardiner came in with a stack of death warrants for her to sign. Gardiner listed out the charges against each man and woman, all of whom he claimed to be heretics. If the queen recognized any of the names, she showed no sign of it.

Again, Mary was impressed by how composed the queen appeared. She offered a silent prayer that the queen was simply abiding by the king's religious decrees and was not the perfidious Protestant she was accused of being. Mary and Gardiner watched the queen intently as she examined the charges against the suspected heretics. After a long wait, she finally spoke:

"My lord bishop, I must thank you for your diligent efforts in helping to keep his majesty's kingdom safe from those who seek to destroy it from within. However, I see that some of these charges lack sufficient evidence to proceed with the death sentence."

"Your Majesty, I can assure you that..." The queen held up her hand to stop him from speaking further.

"Bishop, the king has left the care of his people in my hands while he fights in France. What kind of wife and queen would I be if I signed death warrants that I am unsure the evidence supports? No. I will not let it be said the king left his country in the hands of a tyrant. We shall speak with him when he returns, and I am sure the king will come to a just decision. He is, after all, the most just of all princes, wouldn't you agree, bishop?"

"Of course, Your Majesty," Gardiner said through gritted teeth. He offered the queen a shallow bow, turned his back to her, and left in a huff. Despite his blatant disrespect, the queen could not help but smirk at her victory over the bishop.

Mary was equally impressed and disappointed with the queen. On the one hand, she was thrilled the queen was so strong and unafraid to stand up to those around her. It was a quality Mary wished she possessed more of. But the seeds of doubt planted in her mind about Katherine started to grow when she allowed the heretics to live.

As she grew older, Mary became sterner in her belief that God wanted the world to be rid of heretics. Allowing them to live would pose the greatest danger to all good Christians around the world. Looking around her father's court, she saw them everywhere. They were swarming like angry bees, and they were planning to take control of the prince.

Mary was failing in her promise to Queen Jane. She knew it. But she hoped that when the prince eventually assumed the throne, she would be able to use her powerful familial connections to bring the prince into Catholicism. She knew she could convince her cousin, the emperor, to act as a father figure to the boy. Together, they would be able to convince him that the true path to salvation was through the one true faith, and they would help him remove his faction of heretics from power and restore England's obedience to Rome.

Feeling agitated after what just happened between Gardiner and the queen, Mary sought out Margaret and bid her come pray in the chapel. After hours of prayer, Mary asked her old friend to dine with her and explained her troubles.

"I love the queen; I have tremendous respect for her, yet I cannot help but wonder if she is dangerous."

"Madam, I have always been honest with you, and I will not stop now. I think you should be careful when dealing with Bishop Gardiner. He is a fanatical and dangerous man who craves power. Piero does not trust him. The bishop sees heresy in everything. He would turn on you in an instant if he believed it would secure him a more powerful place in this world. Piero says he wants to oust Archbishop Cranmer, not just because of Cranmer's heresy, but so he can take his place."

Margaret's words made sense to Mary. She decided she'd keep an eye on both the queen and Gardiner. But soon, her worries were replaced with joy. On September 14, 1544, the

French town of Boulogne fell to King Henry. Four days later he entered in triumph, riding through the streets at the head of his army. That same day, the French king was forced to sign a peace treaty with the emperor. Thrilled, Mary wrote to her cousin to congratulate him.

Queen Katherine knew how important this victory was to the king. She ordered that a prayer of thanksgiving be offered in every town and village in England. She held a lavish feast at court, raising a cup to her husband. Standing up before the court, Katherine gave a toast:

"I thank God for a prosperous beginning of the king's affairs, and we must all rejoice at the joyful news of his good health!"

On September 30, the King returned to England. Landing at Dover, he hastily made his way to Greenwich to see his family. The queen, his daughters, and the prince were all there waiting when he entered the courtyard.

Katherine made her way to her husband and bowed low. Henry appeared more youthful than when he departed, clasped his wife by the shoulders and raised her up into a passionate kiss. The crowd erupted in applause mixed with some hoots and hollers. Mary and Elizabeth exchanged looks of delight and giggled, while Prince Edward looked on, stone-faced.

Henry's energetic mood would last for the rest of the year. He spent the autumn hunting and touring the country. He continuously invited Mary and Elizabeth to court, dining with them on multiple occasions.

In one instance, he insisted Mary and Elizabeth accompany him on a hunt. Mary was already an accomplished huntress, but Elizabeth still had a lot to learn. But she didn't seem to mind her inadequacies at the sport. Like Mary, Elizabeth was thrilled to have been invited to spend so much time with her father. She beamed when the king complimented her riding skills. Mary prayed this tranquility would last the rest of her days.

CHAPTER 12

1546-1547

It was a sweltering July day, and Mary and Margaret walked along the river Thames trying to catch a breeze to no avail. While making small talk, Mary hoped they would make it down to the Tower in time to see Anne Askew being led from her prison to the stake at Smithfield.

Mary had heard from Gardiner how he knew of Anne's heretical preaching. The worst, in Mary's opinion, being that she had the audacity to claim that no miracle took place when a priest raises the host to the sky and proclaims it the body of Christ. and only a month before, she was arrested and brought to the Tower. It was a surprise to learn the king had consented to her being examined. Everyone knew what that meant, and everyone knew what Gardiner was up to. Rumors swirled that Anne and Queen Katherine were connected in some way. Gardiner must have hoped Anne would implicate the queen in her heresy, but Mary hadn't heard if she had.

Lost in thought, Mary was startled when she heard Margaret gasp. The pair had made their way to Tower Hill. Overlooking the Tower gate, they saw Anne Askew emerge. Her body was so broken from the torture she had to be carried out on a chair. Mary looked over at her friend, who was visibly shaking, tears streaming down her face.

"My God," Margaret cried. "What have those animals done to her? Look around her neck. That is a pouch of gunpowder. At least she will have a quick end. Thank Jesus for small mercies."

Mary was perplexed by her friend's reaction. Margaret was as devout a Catholic as she was, so why should she feel pity for a woman who denied God's truth and sought to tempt others into her way of believing? Mary looked around at the crowd who at first were baying for the heretic's blood but had now gone silent.

She found herself feeling hardly any emotion at all. Though it was difficult to look at Anne, Mary felt the world was being made a better place for having one less heretic in it. She wondered what would possess Anne to deny the true faith and turn her back on her salvation. Mary knew the agony of the flames she was about to feel against her flesh would be nothing compared to the flames of hell. Mary crossed herself when she imagined Anne engulfed in flames, screaming in pain for all eternity.

Why did she insist on damning herself? Mary wondered. *What do these heretics get from their beliefs other than an eternity of torment and pain?* Mary couldn't understand.

Standing stone-faced and staring ahead, Mary realized Margaret's gaze was fixed on her. She wondered what her friend must be thinking, if she was looking at her differently because of her lack of empathy.

Few constants existed in Mary's life. The only thing that remained the same was her absolute certainty that the Roman faith was the only faith. Her mother died knowing the pope's law was God's law, that her marriage to the king was good and true, and that no matter what man's laws may say, Mary knew she was the king's legitimate daughter.

"We should get back," Mary said to Margaret without looking at her. Walking home in silence, the women were frightened by the sound of an explosion. Anne Askew was dead.

As the weeks went by, Mary found herself seeking out Bishop Gardiner more regularly. She was becoming more interested in how his hunt for heresy was progressing. She could see her father growing weaker and knew in her heart he would not be with them much longer.

Her greatest fear was what would happen when Edward became king at such a young age. Surrounded by heretics as the prince was, she knew she would need an ally in the fight for his soul. She was glad to hear the king was happy with the bishop's progress in rooting out heresy. But she swore she would never ask him about the queen. In her heart, she just didn't want to know.

Several weeks after Anne Askew's execution, Mary joined the king and queen in the gardens at Hampton Court. She and the queen played cards while the king sat sour-faced in a chair. His leg was hurting him again and could not take the weight of his massive form very long.

As Mary and the queen laughed during their game, the jovial mood came to a halt when they saw Lord Chancellor Wriothesley, a staunch Catholic and friend of Gardiner, arrive with a garrison of 40 men at his back.

"Your Majesty, we have come to execute the warrant for the queen's arrest and conduct her to the Tower," Wriothesley firmly addressed the king.

Fear gripped Mary. She looked at the queen, who went pale. Mary thought she might scream out in terror, but slowly Katherine rose from her chair and looked at the king, whose face had gone blood red.

"Knave!" the king shouted, "Arrant knave! You are a beast and a fool! Take that false document and leave our sight!" Henry made his way over to his wife who was clutching Mary's hand.

"Sweet Kate, be well," Henry soothed. "That knave would never be allowed to take you from my side. All is well, sweetheart, I promise. You and I are perfect friends."

Mary was stunned by what had just happened. She knew Wriothesley would never have tried to serve a warrant against the queen if the king did not approve it himself.

What kind of game was her father playing, Mary wondered. Not for the first time, Mary was aware of how her father toyed with the people around him.

•   •   •

By Christmas, it was abundantly clear to everyone at court that this would be the last holiday season Henry Tudor would celebrate on this earth. After the plot to remove the queen failed, the staunchly Protestant Seymour faction sought to rid the court of their enemies and solidify their power before Edward became king.

They set out to take down Bishop Gardiner and the powerful Howard family, the highest-ranking Catholics at court. In early December, Thomas Howard, Duke of Norfolk, and his son Henry, Earl of Surrey, were arrested on charges of treason and taken to the Tower. Surrey had been foolishly boasting about his royal Plantagenet blood and declared that when the King died, his father would be the one to rule the prince.

The Seymours took full advantage of Surrey's drunken visit to a tavern, where these claims were made, and it took a jury no time to find him guilty. The prince's maternal family was cleaning house.

The Christmas season was somber that year. The king did not join in the festivities, leaving it up to Mary and the queen to preside over the court. Elizabeth sought Mary out in her private apartments after she arrived to express how worried she was about the king. Elizabeth was distressed at not being allowed to see her father and asked about his health.

"There is nothing to worry about, Elizabeth," Mary tried to comfort her sister, but the truth was Mary hadn't been allowed to see her father either. "The king sometimes has bouts of ill health, as you well know. But he always recovers. There is no reason this time won't be different."

Elizabeth wasn't buying it but knew better than to push her sister when she offered a firm response. Mary could see her 14-year-old sister was not the naive little girl she once knew. Elizabeth wanted answers and to be treated like an adult.

How sad it was, Mary thought, that the Tudor children were forced to grow up so fast. Looking in the mirror, Mary was surprised by how her face was beginning to betray her. She was almost 30 years old. Already her face was becoming lined, and streaks of gray mingled with her bright red hair. Here she stood, second in line to the throne, older than the heir and likely never to marry, have children or become queen.

And there was Elizabeth, about to enter womanhood, her youth and life still in front of her. How she resented her sister even more at that moment.

Mary and her siblings returned to their own homes before the new year; the Christmas celebrations at court were cut short on the king's orders. Before his children left, he wanted to see them each alone for what he felt would be the final time. Edward went first, then Elizabeth. Both emerged from their respective audiences with the king in tears. Elizabeth tried to put on a brave face, hustling quickly back to her rooms, her governess Kat at her heels. Henry asked to see his eldest child last.

Walking into the king's chambers, the smell of putrefying flesh hit her in the face as she entered. She prayed for Jesus to give her the strength to hide her uneasiness and disgust in front of the king. The queen was present to comfort them both, as she had been when each of Mary's siblings had visited. Henry beckoned Mary closer, and she seated herself on a small pallet next to the king's bed. Henry took Mary's hand in his in a rare act of affection.

"Daughter," he said as he gasped for breath. "My sweet, beautiful first born, pearl of my world."

Mary's heart lurched. She had not heard that special way the king referred to her since she was a child. She couldn't fight the tears.

"Life has been cruel to you, my girl," Henry said, failing to grasp that he was the cause of his daughter's suffering. "But you are strong. You have that proud Spanish blood that has always vexed me so. But you too are an English woman, Mary. I see much of my mother in you. How she would have loved you."

Mary looked at Katherine, who seemed to be saying through her eyes to just let him speak. Mary wondered if there would be something of an apology in the king's speech. But what good would those words do now? The damage was done. Her mother was gone, her faith under attack, and any hope of an advantageous marriage was long gone. So, she sat quietly and let the King go on about how proud of her he was and how he wanted her to care for the prince when he is gone.

"Father, I beg you. Don't make me an orphan so soon," Mary pleaded. "There is still much for you to do in this world," she sobbed.

"No, Mary," Henry wheezed. "Sweet, kind, virtuous Mary. It is my time. We cannot fight it when God calls us home."

•　　•　　•

The new year came with little fanfare. Mary held a small celebration at Hunsdon with the closest members of her household. She invited her cousin Frances, wanting to show her cousin some kindness since her father, the Duke of Suffolk, had died the previous summer. Frances came with her husband Henry and two of her three daughters.

The girls were delighted to spend the New Year with their royal cousin.

Little Katherine Grey, the younger of the two girls, was enraptured by the pageantry and merriment at Mary's celebration. She had yet to attend the court, and this gave her a glimpse of what awaited her.

Mary knew her cousin to be an ambitious woman. No doubt she would try to find a place for her daughters at court when Edward married, and a new queen presided. Katherine reminded Mary so much of her late aunt, the French Queen. Frances could see it too. She made sure Katherine knew she was the family beauty, like her late grandmother.

Still, Mary felt pity for Jane. Frances never forgave her eldest child for being born a girl, and with the complications of her last pregnancy, it seemed unlikely Frances would give her husband a son. Jane joined in on some of the festivities, but Mary noticed she liked to spend time alone.

Learning that Queen Katherine was taking an interest in Jane made Mary happy. She had seen her little cousin at court and could see the difference in the girl when her mother wasn't around. While her guests ate, drank, and danced, Mary approached Jane where she sat alone.

"Happy New Year, Lady Jane."

"Happy New Year, Lady Mary," Jane said bowing.

"I am delighted you and your family are here celebrating with me. I remember how shy you were when we first met at court. I think, my dear cousin, you still prefer solitude to mixed company."

Jane blushed.

"Yes, madam. It is true. I do prefer to be alone with my books or in the school room with my tutor. My sister Katherine isn't a good pupil, but I love to learn."

Mary was glad the girl opened to her, and Jane felt at ease in her cousin's presence. "Here, a New Year's gift for you, my cousin." Mary removed a gold ring with ruby from her finger and handed it to Jane. "I can tell by your modest dress that you may think this ring extravagant, but I hope you will wear it in remembrance of me."

Looking at her cousin, Mary could see that Jane was filled with gratitude. It was true that she preferred to dress modestly. Her tutor explained to her how a proper Protestant woman should dress and behave. Even in the gown she had on, Jane felt too lavish, but her mother demanded she wear it. She also ordered Jane not to discuss their faith openly with Mary. Frances told Jane how Mary was still a wrong-headed Catholic, and she would never tolerate an open show of Protestantism in her home. Jane made the mistake of telling her mother this was the wrong approach to take with Mary. The sting of the slap across her face told her all she needed to know about her mother's position on the subject.

"Thank you, Lady Mary. I will treasure this until the end of my days."

Mary smiled and left her cousin to her thoughts, smiling inwardly at how serious her nine-year-old cousin was.

•   •   •

Only a few weeks later, Mary was in her parlor with Margaret and young Kate working on embroidery when another of her maids told her she had a visitor. Without waiting to be called, Edward Seymour, Earl of Hertford, strode in. He had a strange look of triumph on his face. What now, Mary thought.

"Lady Mary, I have come here on the king's orders to tell you of the death of His Majesty King Henry VIII, who departed this life four days ago. His only legitimate child is now King Edward VI. He rode into London yesterday to take possession of his kingdom. I, as lord protector, was of course at his side."

Mary was speechless. She felt the color drain from her face. It actually happened. Her father was dead.

Her chest felt tight, her knees buckled underneath her, but she'd be damned if she showed any emotion in front of the earl. She knew he did not come out of friendship or concern. He was here to show Mary his power. But the earl wasn't the only one whose status had changed upon Henry's death.

"I appreciate the king sending you here to tell me of the death of our dear father," Mary said. "Now you may leave. I must write to my brother, the king. As his sister and heir to the throne, I want to offer him my comfort and allegiance."

Without another word, Mary swept past the earl, Margaret following quickly behind her with Kate in her arms. Telling Kate to go to the chapel with her nurse to pray for the late king, Margaret went straight to Mary's room where her dear friend was sitting on her bed, tears streaming from her face.

Margaret sat beside her and took Mary's hand. Mary's heart did not break at the news of her father's death. Her sadness was mixed with feelings of guilt and relief, as well as concerns for the future. The tears were flowing, but no sound came from Mary except for a few gentle sniffles. Tightly squeezing Margaret's hand, Mary turned to her friend as she finally spoke.

"It is all going to start again. My little brother may be the king, but he is ruled by evil counselors. They will work to destroy the true faith at all costs. We must be ready for what is coming."

Mary sent Piero to London to get as much detail about her father's death as possible. She also demanded he make an attempt to attend the king's funeral. None of Henry's children were permitted to be there. It was one of the late king's final commands. When he returned, Piero had some unbelievable news to share.

"My lady, I don't know where to begin," he said with disbelief in his voice. "Firstly, I heard it said that the king died peacefully in his sleep, succumbing to his many illnesses. But what happened at his majesty's funeral has me aghast."

"What happened?" Mary asked.

"Madam, the king's coffin was being taken to Windsor for burial, but it had been weakened from the motion of the carriage and," he paused uncomfortably, "the great weight it carried. As the coffin was lifted out, the pallbearers lost their grip and dropped it. The coffin burst open upon hitting the ground and liquid matter from the king's body spilled all over the church pavement. Suddenly, a rush of stray dogs emerged as if from nowhere and began to lick it up. They were eventually shooed away by the horrified pallbearers."

"So, the prophecy came true," Mary said, almost in a whisper. "Just as that Friar had predicted all those years ago, when my father was intent on marrying Anne Boleyn."

"I remember," Piero said. "I was still serving my Lord Cromwell at that time. The friar had delivered a sermon to the shock of the congregation, shouting that if the king persisted down his path, he would follow in the footsteps of Ahab, and the dogs would lick his blood."

CHAPTER 13

1547-1549

Mary sat in her pew in Westminster Abbey, her face contorted with rage. Her eyes were wide with shock, her lips tightened, and her hands balled into fists. It was a frigid Saturday in February, but her anger was keeping her warm during her brother's coronation. She was disgusted by the Protestant ceremony that, in her mind, was spitting on a thousand years of tradition.

Mary felt as though her heart were in a vice the entire time. When Edward was proclaimed Supreme Head of the English Church, it took all her strength not to cry out against the title. She wanted to shout that only the pope could rule the English church. But she didn't. Instead, she sat quietly, the events of the day eating away at her.

Elizabeth was there, enjoying the ceremony in ignorance of the fire raging in her sister's soul. When Archbishop Cranmer gave his sermon, Mary wanted to be sick. In his speech, Cranmer explained that the oaths Edward had sworn were "not to be taken in the Bishop of Rome's sense, as the clergy has no right to hold kings to account. Though the king is to be anointed," Cranmer continued, "it is only a ceremony.

"Edward Tudor is king not in respect of the oil which the bishop used, but in consideration of the power which is preordained. The king is yet a perfect monarch," Cranmer shouted from the pulpit. "He is God's anointed as well as if he was inoiled. Our king has come to the throne fully invested and established in the crown imperial of this realm!"

Mary saw the coronation as an opportunity for the heretics surrounding the king to showcase their goals for the new regime. England was to become fully Protestant. The changes made by the late King Henry were to worsen, and Mary knew she'd be powerless to stop it.

During the coronation banquet, Mary and Elizabeth were hurt by what they saw as a snub by the king's uncle, Edward Seymour. They were not granted seats next to the king on the dais. Instead, they were placed at a table below the dais, seated so far back as to have no opportunity to speak with their brother during the meal. Mary and Elizabeth exchanged a telling look. With just their eyes, they could tell each other how they knew things were already changing. It seemed they weren't important anymore. No doubt the King would marry in the next few years and produce a nursery full of heirs. Elizabeth and Mary made small talk for a while, and when her sister excused herself, Mary was joined by the new Spanish Ambassador van der Delft.

"Princess Mary, it is a profound honor to meet you," he said in Spanish with an extravagant bow.

"I am pleased to meet you as well, excellency," Mary responded in fluent Spanish. She was always glad for an occasion to speak her mother's native language as it helped her feel close to her mother.

"I bring word from your cousins Emperor Charles and Mary of Hungary, Regent of the Netherlands. They want you to know that you still have their support, as well as all of Catholic Europe."

Mary looked at him, puzzled.

"Princess, you must know that many, your cousins included, view this boy king as a pretender and that you should be the one wearing the English crown."

"Those are dangerous words, Your Excellency," Mary responded. "I have no intention of challenging my brother's claim to the crown. Like me, he was born of a lawful union. As my father's son, it is natural that he should proceed me in the succession. I wish to avoid saying anything that might prejudice my right to advance to the throne if God should see fit to make it so."

"I understand your grace's position," van der Delft said. "As will your cousins. Know that you can count on me to be a true and loyal friend, as your dear Ambassador Chapuys once was."

•   •   •

As the privy council was seeing to the late king's will, Mary was delighted to learn that as part of her inheritance, her father had left her Beaulieu, one of her former childhood homes. She set out to make it her permanent residence and establish her household, which she vowed would be made up of her most loyal Catholic supporters. She appointed her dear friends Margaret and Piero as managers of her household and gave their daughter Kate a high-ranking position as one of her maids. The couple's young son would also be given an appointment with Mary when he got a little older. Other members of Mary's household would include Catholic men and women loyal to her and the true faith, many of whom had already been in her service for years.

Mary had been spending the months after her father's death with her sister Elizabeth in the household of their stepmother, who was now known as the Dowager Queen of England. Elizabeth was to remain in Katherine's household, and though she was invited to do the same, Mary decided she would establish a new independent household. She did not like the idea of leaving her sister in Katherine Parr's care after the queen remarried in an indecent haste, but Elizabeth insisted that all would be well. She too was not happy about the queen's precipitous marriage to their brother's uncle, Katherine's lost love Thomas Seymour, but Mary knew this was the first time in years Elizabeth felt as though she had a mother. Mary didn't want to upset that. Though she viewed the dowager queen in a new light and believed Thomas Seymour to be an ambitious snake of a man, she left her sister in their home, telling Elizabeth she must alert her if any issues arose or if she felt unsafe in their home for any reason.

"You will always have a home with me, sister," Mary told Elizabeth when they said goodbye.

"I will miss you so much, Mary. You must come visit us again soon."

When she arrived at Beaulieu, Mary summoned her entire household with the intention of setting the rules for how her house would be governed and what would be expected of her servants.

"My most dear and loyal friends and servants," Mary started, "it does my soul good to see you all here, and I welcome you into my home with humility and joy in my heart. I know we all still grieve the heavy loss of my father's death. We must remember to always keep him in our prayers. Pray for his soul, which I know is now in the blessed company of our Lord and Savior, Jesus Christ, and his mother, the Virgin Mary. My younger brother now sits on the throne. We must pray for our new king as well. I will not lie to you. My brother is being led down the path of heresy by evil counselors who will further my father's reforms beyond anything we could have imagined. But I swear to you all here and now that no matter what heresy is forced upon this kingdom, you will never be required to bow to it. Our home is that of the true faith, and I expect all who serve me to adhere to it. Your souls are in my care, and as your mistress, I will not see them endangered! I have had ordinances drawn up providing for religious services. All in my household will observe Matins, Mass, and Evensong. Every gentleman, yeomen, and groom not having reasonable impediment is expected to be at services daily.

In this most Christian household, service and sanctity are inextricably bound together."

The household erupted in applause when Mary finished. They crossed themselves and wiped tears from their eyes. They swore their loyalty to her and vowed to never waver from their faith, which Mary knew to be as strong as her own.

As the year progressed, her brother and his advisers set their reforms in motion. In July, new church injunctions were issued in the king's name, and it was ordered that saintly images be destroyed, processions abolished, and lighting candles on the altar was forbidden. Additionally, Edward declared the use of rosary beads prohibited.

Mary was disgusted and felt a familiar urge to fight against these atrocities. She stood firm, hearing up to four Latin Masses daily in her chapel. She publicly repudiated the king's reforms when she traveled north to inspect her establishments and invited the people who came out in throngs to see her to celebrate Mass with her.

It did not go unnoticed.

When Mary returned to Beaulieu, a messenger from Lord Protector Seymour was waiting. The duke chastised Mary for her actions in the north and accused her of endangering the souls of the king's subjects by inviting them to hear Mass in the outlawed popish fashion.

"You may tell the lord protector that I make no apologies for my actions," Mary told the messenger. "Those loyal subjects I attended Mass with are true Christians, who adhere to the word of God as our Savior Jesus and his apostles meant them to. There can be no path to salvation other than the one cut by the Catholic faith."

The messenger, aware that he was out of his depth, simply bowed and scurried away. Mary had to smile. That they would send such a man to deliver a message meant they were underestimating her, just as Cromwell had done all those years before. Mary came out on top in that situation, and she swore to do the same this time.

"There is something troubling you, my friend," Mary said to Margaret as they dined one evening. Margaret looked at Piero, who shook his head slightly. "Do not silence your dear wife, Piero. If there is something on her mind, I would know what it is."

"Forgive me, my lady," Margaret said. "But I am worried for you. You are right, the king's reforms are going much further than your father's. It seems that you have more enemies at court than you do friends. I worry for your safety if you continue to openly defy the king's laws. Things are not the same as when your father was alive. You don't have the protections you once did."

"Dear Margaret, you have worried over me since we were young girls," Mary said. "You forget, my cousin Charles is the most powerful man in Europe. He will not allow any harm to come to me, especially when I am this country's only hope to return to the true faith."

"Madam, please listen to me," Margaret pleaded. "The king is young. He will marry eventually and produce an heir of his body. In that case, you will be in a more precarious position. Piero, please tell her."

"My dear wife is right, madam," Piero said. Though he'd been in England for years, he never lost his Italian accent, which Mary found charming and made him more attractive. She still envied her friend over her happy marriage. "Your cousin the emperor is a politician above all else. If it is in the best interest of the empire to work with England, he may be slow to support you, even in matters of the true faith."

Their words hit Mary hard. Looking down at the fish on her plate, she suddenly lost her appetite. "Piero, go to court and seek out the Spanish Ambassador van der Delft. Tell him it would be my great pleasure to host him here for dinner. When he arrives, I shall seek to discover the validity of your suspicions."

During the Ambassador's visit, Mary complained bitterly about the fantasy and newfangledness of the Edwardian church. She declared that her father's reforms had been established by parliamentary statute, and it was illegal to defy it.

"My father left this realm in Godly order and quietness, ambassador," Mary said. "The council is now trying to disrupt that tranquility with these heretical innovations."

"I agree with your grace," van der Delft said. "Indeed, there should be no changes made to the Six Articles of Faith your father established until the nine-year-old king comes of age and can make his own decisions about religion. But I fear the council will never allow his majesty an opportunity to be brought back into the fold."

"I fear for my poor brother's soul every day. I worry my prayers will not be enough to save him from the fires of hell."

"You are indeed a virtuous and wise lady, Your Grace," van der Delft said.

"I fear I am in need of further wisdom, Ambassador. I need to know where my cousin the emperor stands on the issue of my resistance to the king's reforms and the free practice of my faith. I worry I will not be permitted to do so without the intercession of His Majesty King Charles."

"I promise you, my lady, that the emperor is determined that you will suffer no pressure to abandon your faith, our faith, the faith of your sainted mother," van der Delft said. "The emperor has already asked that I entreat the protector, the king, and the council to allow you to live in the observance of our ancient religion regardless of any new law or ordinances."

"How have they responded?"

"There has been resistance. The lord protector claims such a request is a danger to this kingdom, but the emperor is determined to guarantee your freedom of worship."

Mary felt she could breathe better after the ambassador's visit. She knew the emperor was on her side. Still, Margaret and

Piero worried as the king's reforms were intensifying and Mary was fighting harder.

On the day the Book of Common Prayer became the only legal form of worship, Mary summoned her household, and they all celebrated a Latin Mass in her chapel. The Mass included incense, candles, the ringing of bells, the elevation of the Host, and the Catholic doctrine of the sacrifice of the Mass—all of which were now illegal.

The Privy Council responded rapidly, sending Mary a letter in which she was advised to conform and be obedient to the law and cease the practice of the Catholic Mass. Mary wouldn't budge. She told the council she would not cease celebrating Mass and would obey the religious laws her father established during his reign. She demanded the council not trouble her again in matters that touched her conscience.

Seymour and the council were growing more impatient. They knew they could not touch Mary without angering the emperor. For the moment, the king would not allow any action to be taken against his sister. But there was nothing stopping them from tormenting Mary through her servants.

The household was awoken early one morning when Seymour and a few members of the council arrived at Beaulieu intent on taking Margaret to the Tower to interrogate her for breaking religious laws.

"I will not turn over my good servant and friend when the charges against her are so outrageous," Mary said. "You are more of a fool than I took you for, Lord Protector. Do you think I don't know what you are doing?"

"Lady Mary, your slander is outrageous," Seymour said. "The king discovered that a member of his dear sister's household has been openly breaking his laws. The king insists that the accused be examined and, if found guilty, immediately removed from your service."

"You will not take her!" Piero yelled, clutching his terrified wife to his chest. Seymour gestured to the guards, who went to the couple and violently pulled them apart.

Margaret screamed and fought as the guards manhandled her into the carriage, ignoring her protests. It took three guards to restrain Piero. They fought him to the ground, one of them placing a knee in his back, pressing his face into the cobblestones as another restrained his arms. Another guard blocked Mary from running to the carriage while she protested. She yelled at Seymour that his actions would not go unanswered. The guards restraining Mary and Piero did not leave until the carriage was out of sight.

Mary and Piero spent weeks agonizing over what was happening to Margaret, letters to the king and the Privy Council went unanswered and van der Delft could provide no insight. Piero did his best to reassure his children. While his son Giovanni was only five years old and young enough not to understand, Kate was 12 and not so easily placated. She witnessed the ugly scene of her mother's arrest from her window. Mary found her afterward crying in the chapel.

"Why did they take my mother away?" she begged to know. "She didn't do anything wrong. She is good. You must tell them, my lady, please!"

"Sshhh, sweet Kate," Mary said, hugging her goddaughter. "You are old enough to understand that there are those in this world who believe in hurting the innocent if it means achieving their goals. That is what has happened here. Come, we will pray for your mother's fast return. God will not abandon her. Nor us, I am sure of it."

But the silence was deafening. Mary sent letter after letter; she had gentlemen of her household visit the court only to return having been denied access.

After almost a month, Margaret was brought back to Beaulieu in the company of the lord chancellor and one of the men whom she hated with a burning passion, Archbishop Cranmer. Mary ran to greet Margaret in the courtyard, holding her friend close, clutching her face, and looking for any signs she was cruelly handled.

"Go," Mary gestured to the house. "Your husband and children cannot wait to see you." Margaret bolted into the house and the loving embrace of her husband and children. Mary turned to face Cranmer, but he cut her off before she could speak.

"Lord Protector Seymour has graciously allowed your servant to return to your service," Cranmer said. "He hopes she and all those in your home have learned a valuable lesson about defying his majesty's laws."

"Tell me, archbishop, who rules this land? The king or my Lord Seymour? For it seems that nothing is done without his approval."

"Nothing happens without the king's knowledge. But the king is still a boy, and until he comes of age, he will be advised by those who will help him make the best decisions for England and its people."

"Even if those decisions are leading his people into the hands of the devil?"

"My lady, you are but a woman, and I do not expect you to fully understand the ways of ruling and government. The weakness of your sex forbids it."

"I am the daughter of a king, the sister of a king, cousin to the most powerful ruler in Europe, and granddaughter to the strongest monarchs who have ever lived. I may be just a woman, Your Grace, but I am a woman you ought not underestimate. Your good friend Cromwell made that mistake once. Where is he now?"

Without a word, Cranmer left, visibly shaken.

Rushing back into the house, Mary found Margaret and her family crying in each others' arms. She had to know what had happened to her and what Seymour and Cranmer wanted to know. Sending the children from the room, Mary asked her friend to tell her and Piero about her ordeal.

"I was taken directly to the Tower and lodged comfortably enough. I was brought my meals, a few books, and some embroidery. But I was denied pen and ink. I wanted to write to you, Piero and the children. I missed you so much and was so afraid I would never hold you all again. After a few days, Edward Seymour arrived. He wanted to know about the goings on in your household, the comings and goings, and who you met with my lady. I told them the truth. That you run a good Christian household, and that you would never disobey the king on matters that did not touch your conscience. Seymour smiled and left. That was the last time I saw him, or anyone, except my jailer. My lodgings may have been comfortable on the surface, but I know I was deliberately placed. Some of my companions in the Tower were not treated as well as I. I could hear their anguished cries all day and night," Margaret said as she wiped tears from her eyes. "Then today Cranmer arrived and I thought he was going to tell me that I was to die, but he brought me home."

Mary was seething. "I knew it. I knew your arrest was a farce. Damn them all. They will try to break us. They will try to break our commitment to the true faith and holy mother church, but we will not let them. I was forced to succumb to the will of an unjust government once. I will not bend again."

For his part, Cranmer was quite disturbed by his encounter with Mary. For a moment, it was as though she were not herself. Indeed, it was as if her father, King Henry, was standing before him. The fire that raged inside her would consume him if unleashed. Cranmer could see those flames engulfing him. The pyre plagued his dreams; he knew it to be his fate if Catholicism was ever allowed to return to England. Nightly he saw himself tied to a stake, screaming in searing agony. In the distance, he saw a cloaked figure holding the torch. For years he wondered who it could be. Now he knew.

The figure who haunted his dreams was Mary. Long ago, his benefactor Anne Boleyn once told him of Mary, "She is my death, and I am hers." Cranmer felt it in his bones. What was true for Queen Anne is now true for him. He left Mary knowing he made an enemy of the heir to the throne.

•   •   •

Not long after Margaret returned home, Mary learned of an outbreak of rebellion at Sampford Courtenay in Devon. The local villagers were angry about the introduction of the Common Prayer Book and had petitioned their parish priest to defy the law and say the Mass in the way in which they were accustomed.

Though she could not publicly condone an act of rebellion among the people, Mary quietly donated funds to that particular church for much needed repairs. Rebellion and discord spread to other areas. The people were demanding their local priests flout the law, calling the Common Prayer Book a Christmas game and demanding the restoration of King Henry's Six Articles of 1539. Mary hoped her brother would heed the wishes of his people and restore the Mass.

However, the people were unhappy with more than just religious reform. Seymour had been implementing a policy of land enclosure, which had crippling economic consequences for the rural poor. The rebellions grew violent in some areas, resulting in the destruction of property and even a few deaths. Because some of these incidents took place near estates Mary owned, suspicion fell on her as their cause, and Cranmer saw an opportunity to pounce.

He sent the lord chancellor to interrogate Mary and her household, threatening again to remove certain members of her service as had been done before. Mary would not budge. She adamantly denied the accusations.

"I do not a little marvel," she told the lord chancellor, "for to my knowledge I have not one chaplain in those parts. None of my household was ever amongst those commoners, nor came into their company."

"Madam, it is you above all others who would benefit from such discord," he responded. "It is better that you admit your involvement now. If you do so, things may go easier for you in the long run."

"Sir, no true and loyal subject of the king, as I am, could ever benefit from the sin of rebellion. These claims are baseless."

The chancellor left, but Mary knew it wasn't over. Her brother was young. He had a long reign in front of him. The battle was going to rage on. Mary considered she may need to leave England, as she had once thought to do in the past. But again, she knew in her heart that she must remain in her native land where she alone stood between the people's ruin and salvation.

CHAPTER 14

1549-1552

"Matters in this realm are restless for change," van der Delft wrote to Mary. "The people are all confused, and with one common voice lament the state of things." The ambassador told Mary how Seymour's handling of the rebellions as well as issues with Scotland and France had resulted in his fall from favor among the nobility and the gentry. Seymour's younger brother Thomas, who had married Dowager Queen Katherine not long after King Henry died, had already met his end on the block for staging a failed coup to overthrow his brother and seize the protectorship.

After Katherine died in childbirth, it was discovered that the younger Seymour had planned to marry Elizabeth and take control of the king. Elizabeth and her household had been investigated, but Mary knew there would be no evidence produced against her sister. She knew Elizabeth could never participate in such a plot. Mary wrote to her sister after it all happened, begging her to come and stay in her house, but Elizabeth wanted to retreat to her own country home with only her household and the remainder of her reputation intact.

It appeared the elder Seymour was about to follow his brother to the block. The Privy Council grew tired of Seymour and believed he saw himself as more of a king than young Edward.

Eventually, the council closed ranks against him and, in a coup d'état led by John Dudley, Earl of Warwick, Seymour was removed from his position as lord protector and sent to the Tower where only days later he lost his head. The government and the king were now entirely in the hands of Dudley.

Edward finally broke his silence and reached out to Mary after his uncle was executed. Mary's heart was breaking for her little brother. How it must have pained him to learn of both Seymour brothers' treachery and to order their deaths. How it must weigh on someone so young to end a life with just the stroke of a quill. She wanted to go to her brother, to hold him close as she did when he was a baby and tell him it would all be okay. In his letter, Edward invited both his sisters to court for Christmas. At first, Mary was pleased and wanted to accept the invitation, but then her instincts kicked in.

"They want me to come to court so that I cannot celebrate a Christmas Mass," she told Margaret. "The king wants me with him so that I may hear their sermons, but I tell you, I would not find myself in such a place for all the world."

Mary wrote a heartfelt letter to her brother expressing her love and devotion as his sister and subject. The only falseness in the letter was her excuse for missing the Christmas festivities. Mary claimed she had been laid low by a familiar affliction of the head and stomach.

She felt a pang of guilt when the king sent back a letter full of worry, in which he begged that she come see him as soon as she was able. Though her guilt would lift after she learned that on Christmas Day the king and his council, under the influence of Dudley, publicly pledged to make further reforms within the church.

Mary was heartsick, but she refused to stop hearing Mass and made sure her household's daily routine was based around the Mass. As a result, another member of her household was taken into custody. Mary's chaplain, Francis Mallet, was arrested after the council learned he had celebrated Mass in Mary's home on an evening when she was visiting her cousin Frances Grey, Duchess of Suffolk.

When Mary returned home, she found her servants in terror and a summons to court waiting for her. Again, she refused. She demanded the council release her chaplain and cease harassing her. Again, she declared her unwavering faith in Catholicism and vowed never to renounce it.

Mary reached out to van der Delft after the council dropped another blow, issuing a decree that forbade chaplains from "saying or officiating Mass in her household in accordance with the ancient religion." She requested that the ambassador remonstrate with the council as soon as he could and declared that she would persist in her desire to live in accordance with her Catholic faith. She also wrote directly to her cousin Charles, begging him for his help.

"We have never been in such great necessity, and I therefore entreat Your Majesty, considering the changes that are taking place in this kingdom, to provide, as your affairs may best permit, that I may continue to live in the ancient faith and in peace with my conscience."

Weeks went by, and Mary's letter had gotten no direct response. All she heard was that van der Delft appealed to the emperor to intercede on her behalf once again. She was starting to wonder if the emperor was just paying her lip service and was more concerned about a working relationship with England than his cousin's rights and the re-establishment of the true faith.

"My cousin disappoints me," Mary told Margaret. "He places politics over what's right. How can he sit by while our entire faith is constantly attacked? Those members of my brother's council whom he seeks to work with will stop at nothing until the whole of Christendom is destroyed."

"Madam, may I suggest something that you might not wish to hear?"

Mary shot her friend with an aggravated look. She knew what she was about to say. She had just been thinking about it.

"Perhaps it would be best to show the king an outward display of conformity. It would save you these frustrations and reassure your household that you have their best interests at heart."

"How dare you suggest such a thing! Do you think I would so easily turn on my faith? My mother was told to conform to a king as well! You should remember that. You have been at my side from the beginning of that ordeal."

"Mary, I don't mean to insult you, and I would never suggest you betray your mother. It's just that you focus so exclusively on what you say is right that you cannot see what it is doing to those around you. Every member of your household lives in terror that they will be dragged off to the Tower at any moment."

Mary slammed her hands on the table. "Enough! I can protect my own household! And anyone in my service who is not willing to suffer for their faith as our Lord Jesus Christ suffered will not be in my service for long! Perhaps you are trying to tell me that you no longer wish to be a part of my service."

"Mary, how could you suggest such a thing? I am telling you this because I am your most loyal servant and friend. I love you like a sister. I think I love you more than my own sister. All I am asking is that you consider..."

"I am the heir to the throne of England," Mary cut Margaret off. "I will not betray my people. I will not betray the good loyal Catholics who wish to see their country returned to the fold. I will not compromise my beliefs and my soul."

"The king is almost 15! He will marry soon and have heirs of his own. How likely is it that you will become queen?" Margaret gasped at her own words. Regretfully, she had gone too far.

Margaret had hurt Mary immeasurably and fundamentally shifted their relationship. The only thing keeping Mary going was the possibility of her becoming queen one day. As queen, Mary could restore the Catholic faith, but deep down, likely there was more to it than that. As Queen of England, Mary would be the most desirable match in Europe, and she could finally have a husband and child of her own. Mary left the room without saying anything, tears welling in her eyes. Margaret's words pierced her heart. She felt wounded and betrayed by the one person she would turn to for comfort. Besides her faith, Margaret's unwavering companionship was the only other constant in her life. Mary retired to her room where she wept silently.

The next morning, when Margaret went to wake Mary and help her dress—as she'd done every day for years—another of Mary's ladies, a higher-ranking woman with noble blood called Eleanor Jerningham had already taken over that duty. Typically, Mary liked a minimal number of ladies with her in the morning. Usually, it was Margaret and one more person, but this morning Mary was presiding over a gaggle of ladies, all clamoring for a chance to help her get ready for the day. When Margaret entered the room, Mary refused to look at her, but Eleanor wasn't shy about letting her know she wasn't needed.

"Oh Margaret, did we oversleep?" Eleanor asked with a conniving smirk. "Perhaps that charming Italian husband of yours kept you up all night. We are all quite aware of his prowess. It makes no difference. My lady is well attended, so you can run along and find some duties more befitting your station. Perhaps there are some chamber pots to be emptied."

If Margaret expected Mary to jump in and defend her, she was mistaken. Still her friend refused to acknowledge she was even in the room. It took all of Mary's strength not to run after Margaret when she exited her chamber. As hurt and betrayed as she felt, Mary just wanted her best friend back. She knew she could never cry in front of the other women in her household. She could never be as vulnerable with them as she could with Margaret. The same thought kept repeating in Mary's head: *How could she say those things to me?* Each time Mary was about to forgive Margaret, she would hear that question in her head, and the anger and hurt would flood through her body again.

Mary spent weeks avoiding Margaret, allowing the other women in her household to perform the more personal duties that had always been left to Margaret. Mary's stubbornness could rival her father's, but Margaret refused to give up. One morning after Mass, Margaret approached her friend to make amends. Mary stood up from the altar, crossed herself and turned around to find Margaret on her knees in front of her. The women flanking Mary tried to cut Margaret off and hurry Mary out of the chapel.

"Please, Mary, please just hear me out. What I said to you was unforgivable, but I am asking you to find it in your heart—your good, loyal, kind heart—to forgive me for what I said. From the moment I came upon you in the chapel when we were just girls, all I have wanted to do was protect you. The kindness you have shown me, raising me from a simple maid servant to running your household, I am so grateful for everything. Being your closest friend and confidant is one of the great joys of my life, second only to my children. There is no greater honor than serving you. I don't say that the way these other vipers do. They want to be close to you because you are a princess and heir to the throne. I see the real you, Mary. The people see it too. They love you. It is true, as they say, they look to you for support and guidance. I only said what I said because I am worried for you. I have spent too many nights in the Tower, madam. It grieves me to think of you languishing there. Please, I..."

Mary took Margaret by the shoulders, raising her up. Listening to her friend she was transported back to that first night they ever spoke, years ago when her father had yelled at her for questioning him over the divorce. She could see that same concern on her friend's face, the same face she wanted to slap only days before.

"You are more of a sister to me than my own blood," Mary said, choking up. "Your words crushed me. I wanted to dismiss you the moment those vile things came out of your mouth, but I couldn't. I need you, Margaret."

"I swear to our Holy Mother that you will never have cause to doubt me again. I would die before I betrayed you."

The two women hugged and cried. Mary dismissed most of the ladies around her, telling them Margaret would take care of whatever she needed. Mary's closest friend was by her side again. But what she really needed was the support of the emperor, who had been growing more distant. Her cousin was trying to placate her with promises and assurance, but very little action.

"Words he sends to me, deeds he keeps for others. My father once said that of my cousin, but I didn't want to believe it," Mary told Margaret.

"Perhaps, madam, you should rely on the supporters you have here rather than those abroad."

•   •   •

By Christmas that year, Mary was out of excuses to avoid going to court. She knew the Christmas season would be difficult, but she decided to take Margaret's advice and see if she had any friends within her brother's court. Mary wanted to make a statement with her arrival.

Mary arrived in London accompanied by 50 knights and gentlemen in expensive velvet coats and chains of gold. More than 200 ladies followed behind her as well, each one of them wearing a black rosary. Mary wanted to show her little brother and those around him that she had more loyal supporters than they realized. She knew a very real possibility existed she would end up in the Tower during this visit when she once again refused to submit to the king's religious laws. With the rest of her retinue heading to her London house at St. John's, Clerkenwell, Mary took a small company of ladies and gentlemen to Hampton Court. She was met by John Dudley, Duke of Northumberland, at the gateway, who led her through the great hall where servants were bustling about getting the court ready for the Christmas festivities. She noticed how the court had changed since her father's time. It seemed poorly run, with very little jocularity in the air.

Since the king was still unwed, no other women beside herself were allowed in his presence, save her sister and some servants. She was offered no deference by the men at court when she arrived, other than a shallow bow from Dudley. They entered the hall and made their way toward the privy chamber where the king was waiting to dine privately with both his sisters. When they reached the door, Mary handed her cloak to one of her maids. She allowed Margaret to remain behind at Beaulieu and spend the holidays with her family, though she wanted her with her desperately, especially after their fight. When she removed her fur-trimmed cloak, Dudley looked at her disapprovingly.

"Is something wrong, Duke?" she asked.

"Lady Mary, the king will not take kindly to such an outward display of extravagance. A godly woman would dress more modestly."

"I believe you mean a Protestant woman, like your daughter-in-law, my cousin Lady Jane Grey, or is it Lady Jane Dudley now? Though I would say she is hardly a woman, she is just 15 years old after all. I was quite distressed when I did not receive an invitation to the wedding, an oversight, I am sure."

"Lady Mary, I have more important things to worry about than wedding guest lists. If you have an issue, you should speak to my wife or Jane's mother, Frances."

"Indeed. Well, we have spent enough time outside this door. Shall we go in?"

"Madam, I must protest again. Your attire is not appropriate. You should first go to your apartments and change."

"Dudley, my brother, the king, is expecting me. Either escort me in or get out of my way."

The duke opened the door and announced Mary. She walked in to find her brother seated at the head of the table and Elizabeth at his right. Elizabeth rose and gave a curtsy while Edward remained seated. Mary bowed to her brother and Elizabeth bounded over to hug her sister.

"It has been too long, Mary! Where have you been hiding yourself?"

"No doubt our sister has been busy breaching the laws of this realm by continuing to adhere to her popish beliefs."

Mary was hoping they could at least make it through the first course before it came to this. She saw how her brother was looking at her, judging her attire. Mary was dressed in a gown of crimson velvet, trimmed with fur and jewels, a pearl-lined French hood on her head, and accented with the broach gifted to her by her late aunt, the French Queen. Each finger bore a gold ring set with large precious stones. Elizabeth was in a simple black damask gown, only a gold cross around her neck. Mary knew it was her sister's attempt to show the king that she is a good Protestant maiden. Mary seated herself next to Edward and prepared for a battle.

"Your Majesty, I am your loyal subject, but you are wrong on this matter of religion. You are so young and have been led down a dangerous path by those who deny God's truth. You should cease these changes to our holy mother church until you have received the wisdom that God grants by the passing of years."

"How dare you, sister!" the young king yelled, looking so much like their father that both Mary and Elizabeth jumped. "How dare you challenge my authority and what I know to be right for my people. Am I not God's chosen king? I was born to continue my father's good work, to reform his church and save my people. It was his dearest wish."

"And what of your mother's dearest wish, little brother," Mary asked. "I knew her well, and I assure you that her heart is breaking over your so-called reforms. I was there with her the night she died. Her love for you knew no bounds. She made me promise to take care of your soul and educate you in the true faith. It is my greatest shame that I have failed her. I pray every night for her forgiveness."

Mary hoped that the mention of his mother would stir some emotion in her brother. Never once had he mentioned Queen Jane, he never asked questions about her, and as far as Mary knew, showed no interest in learning about the gentle soul that died to bring him into this world.

"Like you, Queen Jane was brought up in error," Edward replied. "She too adhered to popish nonsense. Prayers for the dead, veneration of saints, toying with rosary beads, it is ridiculous! She was a foolish woman, and she paid for her folly."

Mary looked down at her palm, trying to understand why it was red and stinging. She looked at her sister, whose hands were clasped to her mouth in shock. Suddenly she understood what had happened.

Edward rose from his chair, his face a deep shade of red, a combination of Mary striking him and the utter rage he was feeling.

"That sister was treason..."

"Sire, I am so..."

"Silence! I should have you dragged to the Tower in chains for this! It would be well within my right to have your head struck from your body. Perhaps I will! They tell me I should, you know, my advisers! They say there would be no Catholic threat to my throne with you gone!"

"Stop it, both of you, please!" Elizabeth shrieked. "This has gone too far! Look at what has happened here. Why must we hate each other over religion? Why can't religion be a private thing? I beg you both, for the love of God, for our poor father's sake, please find a resolution to these matters."

"There can be no resolution, sweet sister," Edward softened for Elizabeth. "Not while our sister openly violates the laws of this realm."

"Sire, I..." Mary tried to speak, but Edward cut her off.

"Lady Mary, I did not realize how unwell you are. I should not have dragged you from the comfort and quiet of your country home. You may return there tomorrow to recover and enjoy the Christmas season. Lady Elizabeth shall remain here with me through the New Year. Good night to you both." Edward left before the sisters had a chance to bow.

"Don't look at me like that, Elizabeth. God knows I am right about these matters. You won't be able to dissemble forever. God knows if a heart is true or not. Sooner or later, you will have to declare your beliefs and choose a side."

"Why must there be sides, Mary? Why is it not enough to know that I believe in and follow the word of God? Jesus Christ is my lord and savior. Why do you and the king need more than that from me, or anyone else?"

"There is only one true religion, Elizabeth. The other is heresy and can only lead to hell."

The rest of the meal passed in awkward silence, until Elizabeth finally excused herself. She walked by her sister and placed a hand on her shoulder and left without a word.

CHAPTER 15

July 1553

Mary sat silently as Margaret ran a brush through her red hair, which was so long now Mary could sit on it, but it bore more gray streaks in it than Mary was comfortable with. Her eyes also betrayed signs of age. thin lines stretching from their corners and around her mouth.

"Who is that old woman looking back at me, Margaret?" Mary asked her friend, who had been on this earth for the same 37 years as herself yet did not seem as old as Mary believed she looked and felt.

"I see no old woman, my lady. I see my dearest friend, who has the kindness of the angels. My mother used to say we are only as old as we feel."

Mary laughed, "Then I am 100 this day, my Margaret."

Both women began to laugh. Mary patted her friend's hand, signaling she could stop combing her hair. Then Margaret's 16-year-old daughter Kate came in.

She was fair, with her mother's youthful beauty and her father's dark Italian features. Mary and Margaret had noticed how Kate and another of Mary's lady's daughters had struck up a close friendship. The two girls reminded them so much of themselves at that age when their friendship had just begun to bud. It was difficult for both women to be mad at the girls when they abandoned their duties on one sweltering day to swim in the pond within Mary's estate. They had been gone for hours and when Mary and Margaret came upon them, they could not help but envy their youth and vitality. The swim ended when the older women noticed the girls were being watched by some stable boys and kitchen help. Still, they longed for those days when they had the gift of beauty and youth.

"Are there any letters this morning?" Mary asked Kate.

"None so far, my lady," the girl responded in her silky voice.

Mary had been writing to the king ever since that awful Christmas at court. She apologized to her brother for her behavior but refused to compromise her religious beliefs. She wrote begging her brother's forgiveness and beseeching him to listen to her on the matter of religion and cease his reforms until he was older. Her hope was that the delay would give her cousin, the emperor, more time to gain influence over the boy and sway him to the true faith. But her letters were going unanswered, save one message that the king was ill and unwilling to deal with his sister while he recovered.

"It is not as hot as it was yesterday," Mary said. "Let's go for a ride and picnic down by the water this afternoon."

As Mary and some members of her household enjoyed their afternoon in the sun, a rider appeared wearing the green and white Tudor livery. Finally, a message from the court had come. Mary eagerly took the letter, but her excitement turned to apprehension when she saw that she was being summoned to court, not on the orders of her brother, but by the authority of John Dudley, Duke of Northumberland. Immediately Mary knew something was wrong.

She gathered Margaret, Piero, and some of her advisers in her privy chamber to discuss her next move. Her heart told her she needed to be at her brother's side, but her head urged caution.

"Is it possible my brother is dying?" she asked Piero. "The last message from court told me the king was too sick to deal with me, and now this latest message comes not from the king but from his puppet master Northumberland."

"I think Your Grace is right to be concerned," Piero responded. "Mary, you are safest in the north where the people long for a return to the true faith and obedience to Rome. I would counsel you to make your way north, feign your own illness as the reason why you cannot attend court. Move ever further north, gathering those most loyal to you and our faith, and wait for word about the king from sources we can trust."

Mary knew Piero's advice was the right thing to do. She decided to take a small number of her household north. The fewer people she traveled with the fewer suspicions would be raised. Piero would use his network of sources to keep tabs on what was happening at court and get her news about her brother.

"If the king, my poor brother, is indeed dying, Northumberland will do all he can to keep me from the throne," Mary said. "Margaret, send a messenger to Northumberland. Let him know that I am grateful for the invitation to court and long for nothing more than to see my brother again. However, tell him I cannot make the journey due to my ill health as I am again plagued by familiar pains in my stomach and head. You may also say that I will visit my brother as soon as I am able."

Margaret left to tend to her task. The rest of Mary's household prepared for her journey north. She took only a handful of guards, ladies, and attendants. She instructed the rest of her household to continue as if nothing were amiss. That night she and her party fled Hunsdon and rode through the night to Sawston Hall in Cambridgeshire, to the home of Sir John Huddleston, a loyal Catholic gentleman.

When the small riding party arrived at the gate at dawn, Huddleston greeted his unannounced guests with hostility— unaware that the heir to the throne had just arrived at his home. "What is the meaning of this?" Huddleston, a middle-aged man with soft blonde hair and a battle-hardened face, thundered when he came to see who was at his gate. "Take your begging elsewhere!"

"Please, sir, wait," Piero cried after Huddleston as he walked away, refusing them entry. "We seek refuge. There is a very great lady in our company. She requires loyal men like you to rally to her cause, the cause of all true Catholic subjects."

Huddleston turned around in stunned silence, wondering just who was at his gate. Mary brought her horse forward and removed the hood that was hiding her face. Instantly Huddleston knew who had come to his home.

"Your Majesty, please forgive me," Huddleston begged as he fell to his knees, his eyes fixed on the ground. "Of all people who could have arrived here today, I would have thought it more likely that the Holy Mother herself would pay me the honor of a visit than Your Majesty."

"Why do you call me majesty, Sir John? My brother, the king is...."

"Forgive me, Your Grace," Huddleston interrupted, feeling anxious and flushed, his words coming more quickly than he intended. "We have heard it said the king has died and that you left Hunsdon for London, where you would assume the throne. The people here rejoiced at the news that you had become Queen of England, as we have all prayed that it would be so."

Hearing that her little brother may be dead made Mary's heart lurch. She turned her face so that none would see the tears threatening, but there was no time for emotions. Mary had to think and act pragmatically. One misstep could cost her everything; she had not come this far to lose it all now.

"Sir John, we must know for sure if our dear brother has indeed been called to God," she said. "Until we know for sure, I will hear no more talk of the death of the king, as you are well aware such talk is treason and must not be uttered by any true and loyal subject."

Huddleston caught the meaning in Mary's words.

"Sir John, we are making our way north, to visit some dear friends," Mary continued. "Would you be so kind as to allow us to rest here in your home for a while before we move on? My attendants are tired and hungry, as are our horses."

"My lady, it would be my great honor to host you here for as long as you may need."

"I am grateful to you, Sir John. I would also impose upon you to make use of your chapel. There is much I need to pray on."

Sir John had his wife escort Mary to the chapel where she asked to be left alone. Nobody was to disturb her until she emerged from the chapel. While Mary prayed for guidance, Piero and Sir John got to work compiling a list of loyal Catholic men with enough soldiers at their disposal to build an army for Mary.

Piero and Margaret knew Mary would not like the idea of a fight to take the throne; she was counting on her brother's counselor to consider the justness of her cause and acknowledge her right to the throne. But Piero and Sir John knew that when it came to power and politics, men did not care much for what was right, only what was right for them.

Mary exited the chapel after several hours of solemn prayer. During supper, Sir John assured her of his loyalty and pledged that the men at his disposal would gladly fight for her when the time came. Sir John also gave Mary the names of several other loyal Catholics in the north, men whose homes she should visit as she continued to gather support and soldiers.

"I don't like the thought that innocents may die in pursuit of what rightfully belongs to me, in the event the rumors about my brother prove to be true," Mary said.

"Your Grace has a kind heart. The care you have for the people of England is known by all. Unfortunately, there are those who would see that kind heart as a woman's weakness and use it as another reason to keep you from the throne. As abhorrent as the idea may be to you, Your Grace, you must reconcile that before this is all over, the blood of the innocent will be spilled."

Mary crossed herself, but she knew Sir John was right. Mary decided they would not spend the night at his castle; she knew they had to keep moving. Northumberland was not going to stop until he had her in his grasp. She couldn't figure out if he meant to keep her from the throne, who would he place upon it? Her sister Elizabeth would not be a viable option. Forgetting the fact of her questionable birth, Mary knew Elizabeth would not betray her. Plus, Mary was sure Northumberland would not be able to bend Elizabeth to his will. Perhaps Northumberland meant to kill both Mary and Elizabeth and simply take the throne for himself? She pondered this as they rode the 28 miles, almost non-stop, from Sawston to Hengrave Hall, the seat of the Earl of Bath. This time there would be no confusion upon arrival. Word had gotten out that Mary was on the move.

While Mary was moving north, another young woman was greeting the dawn in an enormous four-post bed at Syon House. She was grateful for the extra room, wanting as much space between herself and her husband as possible. Lady Jane Grey had not wanted to marry Guilford Dudley, son of the Duke of Northumberland. It was a marriage forced upon her, much like the way Guilford forced himself upon her almost every night since the wedding. She had not been able to sleep since they arrived at Syon, where she was told that as his death drew near, King Edward declared she should succeed him on the throne. She had been replaying the moment over in her mind.

She recalled vividly how Northumberland gathered her family and the men who had served Edward to proclaim that the king had died. With a throng of people gathered, Northumberland told how the late king made the decision to exclude his "wicked sisters Mary and Elizabeth from the succession."

"The Ladies Mary and Elizabeth are unfit to rule," Northumberland bellowed. "Though the daughters of his late Majesty King Henry, they are of bastard stock. Lady Mary is of the most unnatural ancient religion, and Lady Elizabeth had the misfortune of being born the daughter of a great and infamous whore! Being so unfit, King Edward has declared his sisters ineligible to inherit and thus passes the crown to Lady Jane Dudley, a most virtuous and Protestant lady."

Jane stood in stunned silence. She was stupefied by what she had just heard. For a moment she wondered if she misheard what her father-in-law just said. She stood in front of all those gathered to hear her proclaimed queen, eyes wide with shock. Suddenly, Jane felt as though she would collapse. She scanned the crowd frantically for her younger sisters, but they were out of reach, relegated to the back of the room where they were clinging to each other in fear. Still feeling unwell from a recent illness, she was struggling to understand what just happened. Finally, she gave into her anguish and fell to the floor with a heavy thud, her head smacking the ground in a painful, jerking motion. She could not stop the tears or the tormented cries from fleeing her weakened body. Those around her stared in uncomfortable silence at the reaction of their new queen. They seemed unable or unwilling to help the teenage girl to her feet.

Realizing she could not continue in this way, Jane pushed herself up. Refusing to look at those around her, she stared above their heads at the large crucifix on the back wall of the chamber. Looking at the agony on Christ's face, she knew she was being judged, not just by those in the room, but by a divine presence none could see.

Filled with a sense of strength she didn't expect to feel, Jane finally addressed the group. "The crown is not my right. It does not please me to receive it," she said. "Lady Mary is the rightful heir."

"Your Grace does a great injustice to yourself and your house," a mortified Northumberland responded. He expected Jane to readily submit. "The late king chose you to succeed him, which means you are also God's choice! How will this kingdom continue on the path of the true faith if we are subjected to the rule of a woman who would make us bow before the Bishop of Rome?"

Jane's mother, Frances, stepped forward and drew her daughter to her in a loving embrace. Jane didn't think she could grow more shocked, but her mother's sudden affectionate gesture puzzled her. This was the first time in sixteen years that Jane's mother showed her any kind of love and tenderness. When Frances pulled away, she looked down at her daughter and spoke softly so that Jane was the only one to hear.

"You will do this, daughter. It is your responsibility to advance our family, to raise us up, and see God's will done. You will do this."

Jane swallowed, her eyes filled with tears and rage. She gave her mother an almost imperceptible nod. Frances stepped back, and Jane was again facing Northumberland and his supporters. She knew what she had to do.

"I greatly bewailed myself over the death of such a noble prince, and, at the same time, turned myself to God. I humbly pray and beseech Him that if the crown is rightfully and lawfully mine, His divine majesty would grant me such grace and spirit that I might govern it to His glory and to the advantage of this realm."

Pleased with her response, Northumberland led the congregation in a deep bow and in unison, they all exclaimed, "God save Queen Jane."

• • •

When Mary arrived at Hengrave Hall, throngs of people eagerly awaited the chance to see her up close. As the earl welcomed her, the people cheered her name, yelling "God save, Your Grace!" Children tossed flowers towards her as she rode by. Women curtsied and smiled from ear to ear, while men bowed, shouting their vows to fight for her until the end.

Mary was uplifted by this show of support. She knew at that moment that if Northumberland and the council meant to keep her from the throne, then it would be the people themselves who would place her upon it.

The earl greeted Mary before she could dismount. He walked over, fell to his knees and kissed her skirts.

"Your Majesty, we have received word from London. King Edward died on the sixth of July, just two days past. God have mercy on his soul."

Mary stared at the stranger on his knees, looking up at her with tears in his eyes.

Overwhelmed with emotion, Mary could not form the words to thank God for raising her to such a position, nor could she express any prayers for her dead brother. Thoughts of Edward consumed her. She remembered the first time she held her baby brother, recalling the memory so vividly it was as if she were reliving it in that moment. She could remember every feature on his cherubic face, the sparkle in his eyes, and the innocence. She was glad that her stepmother, Queen Jane, did not live to see her only son so cruelly snatched from this world so young. Her heart ached again when she remembered how she failed in her promise to see the prince raised in the true faith. Mary snapped back into reality, thinking that her brother died a heretic. She needed to pray for his soul in the hopes of saving him from the fires of hell. She would pray with all her strength and hope that mother and son would be reunited in heaven.

Dismounting her horse, Mary finally spoke to those gathered in the courtyard of the earl's residence.

"Good Christian people, it has pleased God to call my brother the king home to him. Our hearts break at the thought of losing such a noble king and so dear a brother, but it is not for us to question the wisdom of God. He has seen fit to place us upon the throne, and we will work tirelessly to right the many wrongs done to this kingdom and to the one true faith."

Those gathered around her cheered and bowed as Mary spoke. But her victory wasn't complete.

"Your Majesty, we must continue to gather soldiers and weapons before we can make our way south and march on London," the earl said. "We will have to take the city by force and remove the usurper that now sits upon your throne."

Mary was stunned. "Who, who sits upon my throne? Who could possibly think they have a claim greater than mine?"

"Northumberland has placed his daughter-in-law, your cousin Lady Jane, upon the throne. He convinced the late king to alter the line of succession in his will, removing you and Lady Elizabeth, due to your...forgive me, but because you were declared a bastard."

"That scum," Mary hollered. "He seeks to place a child and her husband, his son, upon the throne and rule through them. We will not allow this."

"Your Majesty should know that when Jane was proclaimed queen in London, nobody showed any sign of rejoicing, nor were there any cries of 'God, save the queen.' In fact, when a young man, no older than 16, cried out that you are our rightful queen he was arrested, pilloried, and his ears were cut off."

"I doubt very much that it was my cousin, Jane, who ordered such brutality. She has always been such a gentle soul. This all reeks of Northumberland. We will deal with him appropriately. And when we reach London, we must provide care for that poor boy and his family. True and loyal subjects will not be butchered while I am queen!"

Mary could not deny she was in a precarious situation. Jane had possession of the Tower, the Great Seal, the armory, and the treasury. Letters to her cousin the emperor had been going unanswered, but Mary just assumed because she had been moving around so much, they simply weren't reaching her. She had no idea the emperor doubted her chance at taking the throne. He was waiting to see how it all played out.

That evening after supper, Margaret found Mary sitting alone in the chapel, she had her mother's rosary in her hands.

"Do you remember the first time we spoke in a chapel?" Mary asked.

"Of course, Your Majesty, it was during your father, King Henry's Great Matter."

"Yes, his Great Matter. He had just yelled at me for questioning his motives. We were just girls then. Children with no idea of how cruel life could be," Mary was looking down at her mother's rosary. "That night, my mother came to me to tell me how brave she thought I was. I cried in her arms all night, she just held me close, and despite everything that was happening, I felt so safe."

"Queen Katherine loved you more than anything, Your Majesty. She knew this day would come. She fought and died for it."

"If I cannot win, she fought and died for nothing."

"You will win, Your Majesty. God did not put you through all your troubles so it could end with another on your throne."

The next day Mary received a letter, a reply from Jane's council to her demand they renounce their loyalty to her cousin and declare for her. The letter addressed her simply as The Lady Mary. It demanded she cease to call herself queen, asserting that by King Edward's will and the endorsement of the nobility of the realm, Jane was undoubtedly Queen of England. Attached to the letter was a circular drafted by Northumberland which he had sent to the justices of the peace ordering them to assist in Jane's rightful possession of the realm and to resist the "feigned and untrue claim of the Lady Mary, bastard."

Mary was warned by the Earl of Bath that Jane's father, the Duke of Suffolk, was leading an army to capture her. Northumberland ordered that when apprehended, she should be brought to London in chains in an open cart for all those who opposed him to see.

"He wants to make a spectacle of me, humiliate me, and show the world that he truly rules England, not my cousin. He will not have the chance. We will be victorious, and I will have the crown, or I will die here, with those most loyal to me and to the true faith. That heretic will not get the chance to parade his prize before all of England."

Mary spent the next several days gathering as many loyal supporters as possible. Her small forces were enhanced by the arrival of Sir Henry Bedingfield, Sir John Shelton, Sir Richard Southwell, and Henry Radcliffe, Earl of Sussex. Each brought with them soldiers, money, and arms.

With her army reinforced and the morale of her troops high, Mary decided it was time to move south. She would make her stand at Framlingham Castle, a fortress that could withstand a siege. As they had done so before, the people came out to see Mary. When she arrived, they called out "God save the queen." They cheered when her standard was unfurled and displayed over the gate tower.

As the people gathered outside the castle walls, Mary decided it was time to address her people for the first time as queen. She planned to look every inch the part. She stood along the castle walls wearing a gown of green and white velvet with an assortment of large, precious jewels around her neck and on her fingers. There would be no mistaking who their queen was.

Raising her hand to silence the growing crowd, Mary spoke to her people.

"My most true and loving subjects," Mary's voice rang out. "I am here to take back that which is mine by right. It is through God's great wisdom that I stand here today and did not fall prey to the trap of those evil nobles who would strip us of what is ours and place a usurper upon our throne. We do signify unto you that according to our said right and title, we do take upon us the just and lawful possession of this realm, doubting not that all our true and faithful subjects will so accept us, take us, and obey us as their natural and liege sovereign lady and queen! I say unto you, on the word of a prince, that no subjects have ever had a sovereign who loved them better. I do hereby pledge my life to you, my good people. I shall die in service to you!"

The crowd erupted in cheers once more, shouting, "Long live our good Queen Mary" and "death to the traitors." Mary's soldiers fell to their knees, vowing to give their lives for their queen.

The tide was turning in Mary's favor as more cities, towns, and villages declared for her. Even members of Northumberland's own faction were abandoning him for Mary. Northumberland left the Tower to deal with Mary himself, but the longer he was away, the weaker the resolve of those who had pledged themselves to Jane became.

The final blow to Northumberland's plans came when the sailors on the seven ships he had sent to guard Yarmouth harbor, in an effort to trap Mary in case she decided to flee abroad, mutinied against their captains and declared for Mary. By the next day, Mary's camp had grown by 2,000 sailors and the 100 cannon from the warships anchored in the harbor. The actions of the sailors scared Jane's council into defection. The treasurer of the mint had escaped the Tower, where Jane and her councilors had been told to remain to await the outcome of the battle. Taking all the money in the privy purse, the treasurer made his way to Mary's camp. The rest of the counselors declared Northumberland a traitor and offered an award for his arrest.

After the councilors informed the Lord Mayor of London and the Imperial Ambassador of their plan, the men went out into the public square and proclaimed Mary Queen of England. The people celebrated in a mad display of joy. The bells rang out, the wine flowed freely, and bonfires were lit through the night.

Two former members of Jane's council, Lord Paget and the Earl of Arundel, were making their way to tell Mary that she was in fact Queen of England. Meanwhile, it was left to the Duke of Suffolk to tell his daughter Jane that she was no longer queen.

•   •   •

Sitting at the head of the dining table, under a canopy of estate, young Jane was picking at her roasted venison, her appetite had been failing her since the crown first landed on her head. When her father entered the chamber, she knew the situation was dire. He looked pale, angry, and defeated. Without saying a word, Suffolk lunged at his daughter, forcing her to leap from her chair in terror. Her father grabbed hold of her canopy of royalty and tore at it feverishly.

Throwing the cloth down onto the floor, he proclaimed loudly, "God save Queen Mary!" Then he turned and left the room. Stunned, Jane chased after him.

"Father, wait, what has happened?"

"It is over, daughter. Mary is our Queen, and you are a traitor. You must beg forgiveness for what you have done and pray for the queen's mercy."

"Forgiveness for what I have done? It was you and Northumberland who placed the crown upon my head. I told you it was not mine by right but belonged only to Mary, our dear cousin. I never wanted it, and I am glad to be rid of it. I just want to go home."

"You may not leave the Tower, Jane," her father said, with no emotion in his voice. "Your mother and I may return to our estates, but you must stay here to await the queen's pleasure."

Without saying another word, Suffolk left his daughter in the Tower. Her fortress was now her prison.

•   •   •

Mary kept Lord Paget and the Earl of Arundel waiting for an audience for hours. When she finally allowed them into her presence, they were not permitted to stand, but had to remain on their knees.

"My lords," Mary said, standing over the two men, taking notice of their anxiety and unease. "It pleases us to see you as you bring us glad tidings and tales of rejoicing at our accession to the throne. Yet, only days ago, you had pledged yourself to another who claimed to have a right to my throne."

"Your Majesty," Arundel ventured, "the crown belongs rightfully to you by direct succession as the lawful and natural daughter of our late King Henry VIII. We let ourselves be corrupted by Northumberland. Having sinned so egregiously, we can do nothing but beg for Your Majesty's mercy."

"It would appear there are many who must beg for my mercy, but one to whom I would grant it unwaveringly is my poor cousin Jane. I know it was not her desire to take the throne. I would not punish the innocent for the sins of scheming, ambitious men.

Arundel, I have a task for you, a way for you to prove your loyalty."

"I will do anything, Your Majesty."

"Northumberland is hiding out in Cambridge. You will go there tonight and arrest him in my name and bring him to London where he will be brought to trial for treason."

CHAPTER 16

October 1553

Mary's jubilant and triumphant entrance into London in August could only be rivaled by the magnificence of her coronation. She lay awake restlessly on the evening before her crowning with excitement and apprehension. She thought back to that day in August when she claimed her capital city.

Accompanied by her army, her knights, trumpeters and heralds, Mary entered London to the cheers of an elated populus who were thrilled at the sight of their new queen. They shouted "Jesus save our queen!" and "The voice of the people is the voice of God." The people were well aware it was their support that put Mary on the throne and Mary knew it too.

The people were in awe of Mary as she rode by on a palfrey richly adorned with cloth of gold. She wore a gown of purple velvet, the sleeves trimmed with gold. Her kirtle was made of purple satin set with large pearls, and the headdress she wore shone brightly in the summer sun. She was determined to appear every inch a queen. Reunited with her sister Elizabeth, the epitome of youth and grace, Mary rode through the city gates and made her way to the Tower.

There she was greeted by the constable and lieutenant who were waiting to present some of the fortress's prisoners to their new queen. Mary was stunned to see an old ally from her father's court, Bishop Gardiner, who had been sent to the Tower by her younger brother for refusing to betray his Catholic faith. Gardiner spoke on behalf of the prisoners, congratulating Mary on ascending the throne.

"You are my prisoners," Mary said. "It is our desire that you be granted liberty." Mary then walked over to each prisoner, raised them up, and placed a kiss upon both their cheeks. Even her old enemy, the Duke of Norfolk, who had been imprisoned in the last years of her father's reign, was granted freedom and forgiveness. But there was another prisoner Mary needed to see. She would visit that particular guest of the Tower later.

That evening Mary wanted to dine with only a few close members of her entourage—Margaret and Piero, her sister Elizabeth, her former stepmother Anne of Cleves, some other noble ladies, and finally Simon Renard, the latest Imperial Ambassador at the English court. Renard was the essence of charm and deference to Mary. His hope was the queen would forget her cousin's lack of assistance in putting her on the throne. Though Mary could see through his gesture, she didn't mind letting the ambassador fawn over her, plying her with compliments about her bravery in seizing the throne, comparing her to her grandmother Queen Isabella of Spain.

Mary's smile was genuine at that compliment. It reminded her of the last person to make that comparison. She thought back to that night when she was still called princess, and the awful scene between she and King henry in the chapel, the first of many. Mary could still see her mother bathed in candlelight and could feel the warmth of her hands around her face. Mary remembered hear the sound of Katherine's heart beating as she laid her head against her mother's chest and wept uncontrollably that night.

Her mother always knew Mary would sit on the throne one day. Queen Katherine died fighting for her, never wavering in her absolute belief that her marriage to Henry was valid and true.

Her joy at the memory of her mother was clouded by the familiar sting of guilt. Signing the paper that acknowledged her illegitimacy was the greatest regret of Mary's life. No matter how long she reigned or how much good she knew she would do for the people of England, Mary believed she could never atone for her greatest sin.

Following a delicious supper with music, wine and dancing, Mary dismissed her guests and servants for the evening. She asked that Elizabeth remain behind. She wanted to catch up with her little sister whom she missed dearly.

"More wine, Elizabeth?"

"I have had too much already tonight, Your Majesty."

"I can see that; you are grinning like a fool."

"It is not the wine that is making me smile. I am so proud of you, Mary. What you have accomplished here is truly remarkable. I believe even our father is impressed by what you were able to do."

Mary wondered how true that was. Could her father be looking down upon her from heaven with pride?

He had torn the country in half to sire a male heir and keep her from inheriting the throne. Their father found women useful as partners in the marriage bed, as pretty ornaments to sit at his side, but he believed with all his soul that women could not rule men. He believed such a thing unnatural, as did many of the men currently acting as Mary's counsel.

"I still have much to prove and a lot of work to do returning England from heresy and back into the fold of the true faith," Mary said, noticing Elizabeth's reaction. "You don't approve, sister?"

"I would never presume to tell my queen her duty," Elizabeth said. "I would caution her about making too radical a change too soon. We both know there could be serious consequences in that course of action."

"You have always been wise beyond your years, Elizabeth. How else would you counsel the Queen of England?"

"Were it my place, Your Majesty, I would advise mercy for the innocent, those poor pawns who were caught up in a game they never wanted to play."

"You're talking about Jane."

Elizabeth nodded. "She can't take back what happened, but I know she would if she could. Jane and I lived together in Queen Katherine's household after our father died. She was so happy there. She told me how harsh her mother and father were to her, and how freeing it was to be with Katherine. All she ever wanted was a quiet life in the country."

"I know. In the few encounters she and I had, that became very clear quickly. I know she is innocent in all of this. Still, I cannot be seen to be too merciful. She must stand trial, and she will be found guilty. But I have no intention of taking our cousin's life. She will have to spend a while in the Tower, and when things have settled down, she will be banished to the country to live that quiet life she is so eager for."

Tears filled Elizabeth's eyes. "Your Majesty is truly merciful. Thank you for seeing the truth. I know there must be those around you calling for her blood. Will you speak to her at all?"

"Tonight," Mary replied.

Accompanied by Elizabeth and a Tower guard, Mary paused for a moment to gather her thoughts and calm her nerves about seeing her young cousin again. She wondered how Jane had been faring through all this. The girl must have heard the cannon firing in celebration and the people cheering for Mary, something she herself never experienced. Mary wondered if Jane was grateful to be relieved of the burden of the crown, and if Jane feared for her life. Did she expect Mary to order her execution?

The door opened, and the queen was announced. Mary asked Elizabeth to wait outside, and a shocked Jane jumped up from her seat by the window. The book she was reading crashed to the ground as she fell into a deep curtsy. Jane was thinner than the last time Mary saw her. She looked like she had aged about ten years, but an innocence still shown in her eyes. Jane had a difficult time looking at Mary, even when the queen bid her do so.

"Jane, are they treating you well?"

"Better than I deserve, Your Majesty."

"I know you did not want to take the throne. Were it up to you, you would be living quietly in the country right now, surrounded by your books. It is all you have wanted since you were a girl."

"Yes, that is true, cous...Your Majesty. But my parents had other plans for me." Jane was choking up now, her words coming in a rush. "When they brought the crown to me, I almost fainted. I couldn't believe what was happening. I didn't want it, but I was told the late king decreed that I have it so that I could...could..."

"So, you could continue my brother's heretical policies. I am not ignorant of what they tried to do, the reason my brother chose to try and leave the throne to you. As hard as this is to say, my brother was a heretic, and so are you." Mary looked back at the door where Elizabeth was waiting on the other side. "As are some others, I am afraid to say."

"Your Majesty, I am no such thing," Jane's tone grew more defiant. "I have been brought up in the true religion, one that does not adhere to idolatry or superstition. One that is beholden only to our Lord and Savior, Jesus Christ, and not to a corrupt old man in Rome."

Mary could see the passion in Jane's eyes. She was as fervent a Protestant as Mary was a Catholic. Still, Mary would not be persuaded to see her side of the religious argument.

"Child, you are in error! Were you anyone else, I would see you burn for those words! I could not save my brother from heresy, but I will save you. You were led into treachery and heresy by those around you. I will not fault you for their sins."

Jane went to speak again, but Mary raised her hand to silence her. "You and your husband are going to be put on trial for treason. It is likely that you will be found guilty. I am, however, determined to save your life and your soul."

Mary left Jane in her chamber shaking with fear. The impression she left in her wake was clear—the subject of religion was closed and, more personally, despite Mary's words, it was likely Jane would never leave the Tower alive.

The next day, Mary rose early, filled with child-like excitement at the thought of attending her first Catholic Mass as queen. She instructed the priest to remove all the English Bibles from the chapel; the Mass was to be conducted in Latin, and the congregation was to pray for the soul of the late king.

The evening before, after her visit to Jane, Mary told Elizabeth she wanted her seated on her right when they attended Mass in the morning. Elizabeth boasted of the great honor, but Mary could see conflict in her sister's face. When she failed to appear at breakfast, Mary knew there was a problem and went to her sister's rooms.

"I have chills and terrible pains in my head and stomach, Your Majesty," a visibly shaken Elizabeth claimed. "Please, I beg your indulgence. Excuse my absence from Mass today."

Looking at her sister, Mary was plagued by old thoughts which she hadn't had in years. She hardly recognized the young woman in front of her. She could see her mother, the great whore, staring out through her dark eyes, yet there was hardly anything of the king in Elizabeth's face, or so Mary had convinced herself.

"I expect to see you at Mass tomorrow," Mary scolded. "You don't seem to need much more than a day's rest."

Things were never easy where Elizabeth was concerned. Trying to force her worries out of her mind, Mary had spent a restless night in preparation for her coronation. But as she watched the sunrise, she was filled with a renewed sense of victory. Suddenly she could see herself as a young girl again, the girl who went from princess to bastard with the stroke of a pen, the girl who was forced to deny her mother's marriage and was made to wait upon a child who had stolen her father's affection. She could see that young girl wracked with fear, terrified that at any moment her father could give the order to end her life. She never expected to be standing here. Everything that girl had been through brought her to this moment.

On the morning of the coronation, the streets of London were strewn with flowers, and the first of the 500 nobles, gentlemen and officials who would lead the queen to Westminster came out of the Tower and began their journey to Westminster Abbey, where Mary would be crowned and anointed with the full authority of a sovereign.

As the procession made its way to the church, Mary rode in an open carriage upholstered in white cloth. The six horses pulling her coach were draped in white trappings woven with gold that shimmered and shone in the breeze. Mary sat up straight, happily waving to the people as they cheered her along her journey. She, too, was dressed in white cloth woven with strands of gold. Her kirtle was furred with a miniver and her mantle with powdered ermine. Her hair was bound up in a net of cloth of tinsel, which sparkled with precious stones, over which she wore a round circlet of gold set with jewels of extraordinary value.

As the open carriage drove by, people cried out, "God save the queen," and children tossed flowers to Mary, which she happily picked up and held close to her heart. She was basking in the people's love, filled with gratitude and the hope that she would never disappoint them. As they continued on their way, Mary offered up a silent prayer and vowed to God that she would carry out the task he had given her.

Finally, they arrived at the abbey. Mary was greeted by Bishop Gardiner and 10 other bishops and members of the clergy. They sprinkled the queen with holy water and draped her in Parliament robes of red velvet.

It was time. Norfolk and Arundel walked ahead of Mary, carrying her crown, orb, and scepter, while the Barons of the Cinque Ports held the canopy of estate over her head on four silver staves that were hung with silver bells. When Mary was escorted to the throne, Gardiner called out in a loud voice:

"Sirs, here present is Mary, rightful and undoubted Queen of England! By the laws of God and man does she inherit the crown and royal dignity of this realm! Understand that this day she is appointed by all the peers of this land for the consecration and coronation of the said most excellent Princess Mary; will you serve at this time, and give your wills and assent to the same consecration and coronation?"

In response, the people joyfully shouted, "Yea, yea, God save Queen Mary!"

Mary then made her oaths upon the sacrament and was anointed with holy oil and chrism. Then Gardiner at last placed the crown on her head. Tears of joy streamed down her cheeks as she scanned the crowd for familiar faces. She spotted those she loved most — Elizabeth, Margaret, Piero, and more — beaming with excitement, joy, adulation, and pride. For a brief moment, as she took it all in, the abbey fell quiet. Mary heard a familiar voice in her ear. Her mother was there with her. She could feel her love as surely as she could feel the holy oils on her skin.

"You have done it, my daughter," Mary heard her mother say. "You have fulfilled God's great plan for you, and your reign will be a golden age for England."

As the voice faded, Mary breathed in deeply, sure in the knowledge that her mother was right.

AUTHOR'S NOTE

The novel you just read is a work of historical fiction and should not be taken as historical fact. Though I did my best to stay true to the real events of Mary Tudor's life, this book is meant to entertain, and I have therefore taken some license. The timeline of several events has been changed, condensed or removed altogether for the sake of story flow and narrative. I have also invented several characters and events, including Mary's loyal friend Margaret and her husband Piero.

If you would like to read more about the very real and extraordinary life of England's first Queen Regnant, I highly recommend some of the books I used to research this novel, including: The Six Wives of Henry VIII, by Alison Weir; Bloody Mary: The Life of Mary Tudor, by Carolly Erickson; and Mary Tudor: England's First Queen, by Anna Whitelock.

When learning about Mary, we are taught that her reign was a failure and that she was a tyrant, but when you judge someone based on only five years of their life, you are of course going to get a blurry picture of who they really were. The tragic events of Mary's reign cannot be excused, much in the same way the atrocities of her father, Henry VIII's reign cannot be excused. Yet for some reason (and we all know what that reason is) Mary is held to a different standard, she is given the title "Bloody" and portrayed in the media as elderly and unattractive, while some of Hollywood's most desirable men have played the king most famous for his six marriages and the beheading of the woman he was said to have loved beyond all reason.

The decision to write a novel about the early life of Queen Mary came from a desire to read one. Not many novels about Mary exist, especially when compared to the number of books (fiction and nonfiction) about her sister, Elizabeth. It has been my view that Mary's story is often treated as something to "get through" in order to focus on the glory of Elizabeth I. But the argument can be made that a lot of Elizabeth's success wouldn't have been possible without Mary. But I will leave it up to more expert historians to take you on that journey.

I want to express my gratitude to Black Rose Writing for taking a chance on this novel. Telling Mary's story in the most well-rounded way has been a passion project of mine for years. Thank you for giving me the chance to do so.

Thank you also to my amazing group of friends and fellow writers, your edits, suggestions, and most importantly your support has made this novel what it is. I could not have done it without you. Susmita Baral, thank you for being one of the first people to read a draft of this novel. And I cannot thank you enough for designing the cover. It came out better than I could have imagined. Natalie Walters, Andrew Meola, thank you for being my first test audience! To my sister-in-law, Lynn Wiegelman, thank you for doing the initial edit for this. Steven Paulino, thank you for your contributions to the cover art! To my brother, Michael, thank you for all your support and help while I was promoting this book.

William Cannon, my best friend, my person, my soulmate, I felt your hand on my shoulder throughout the final stages of this project. I wouldn't be the person I am without your friendship. I miss you every day.

There aren't enough words to thank my mother for all she has done for me. So, I will just say I love you, mom, and this is because of you.

ABOUT THE AUTHOR

Amanda Schiavo is a NYC-based journalist who holds a B.A. in History from Pace University. Currently, she is an editor for a healthcare magazine, and spends her free time riding her horse Della and playing with her dog, Spencer. She is also an avid reader and is always planning her next international trip.

NOTE FROM THE AUTHOR

Word-of-mouth is crucial for any author to succeed. If you enjoyed *In Her Own Right*, please leave a review online—anywhere you are able. Even if it's just a sentence or two. It would make all the difference and would be very much appreciated.

Thanks!
Amanda Schiavo

We hope you enjoyed reading this title from:

www.blackrosewriting.com

Subscribe to our mailing list – *The Rosevine* – and receive **FREE** books, daily deals, and stay current with news about upcoming releases and our hottest authors.
Scan the QR code below to sign up.

Already a subscriber? Please accept a sincere thank you for being a fan of Black Rose Writing authors.

View other Black Rose Writing titles at
www.blackrosewriting.com/books and use promo code
PRINT to receive a **20% discount** when purchasing.

CPSIA information can be obtained
at www.ICGtesting.com
Printed in the USA
JSHW081732170523
41779JS00001B/68